THE LIEUTENANT

NICK ADAMS

Elliptical
Publishing

PROLOGUE

Tallamainian-registered freighter Chrysos II,
Unknown location

THE FIRST THING Malic Dess sensed was a low pinging noise. She also noticed it was in time with a dull flashing redness, pulsing through her closed eyelids. As the fog of sedation slowly began to recede it allowed her to remember where she was and the operation she'd had to reset a badly broken arm. She became aware of the arm in question, her left arm. It ached and the pain seemed to pulse in time with her heart beat.

She lay there grimacing, waiting for the medical officer to answer the alarm and thought back to what an idiot she'd been to climb onto the ore canister without a safety harness. She knew full well she'd be up for a disciplinary and wasn't looking forward to explaining to the captain and the other five crew why she'd ended the ship's one hundred percent safety record on her first voyage because of a collapsing ladder.

After a few minutes, when no one appeared, she opened her eyes and squinted as the pulsing red light assaulted her retinas. Other than that, she saw nothing. Then she remembered more. Doctor Grosser had placed her in one of the healing cells before sedating her, to allow the bones to meld overnight. The cover was still in place, cocooning her inside.

'Open please,' she croaked, recalling the instructions Grosser had said about the machine being voice-activated.

A clunk to her right made her jump and a bolt of pain ripped through her arm. She snatched her right hand up over her eyes as the cover hissed open, flooding the cell with bright white light from the medical suite.

She sat up and took a deep breath as her arm disagreed fiercely with the sudden movement. The smell of disinfectant, mixed with the odour of last night's dinners in the mess room next door, assaulted her nostrils. Her stomach rumbled and, thinking back, she realised she'd had nothing to eat since breakfast yesterday.

With gritted teeth, she slowly climbed out of the cell and stood shivering in her underwear. Her ship suit was still on the table where the doctor had put it after cutting it off her. She realised wearing that was not an option and looked around for something else to cover herself. Puzzled at why no one had entered to answer the alarm, she asked the ship's computer to inform Doctor Grosser she was awake and waiting for him.

'*Doctor Grosser is not on board the vessel at this time,*' said the synthesised and emotionless voice of the computer.

'What?' she said, staring up at the ceiling.

'*Doctor Grosser is not on board—*'

'Yes, yes, I got that the first time,' she said, impatiently. 'Where is he then?'

'*Doctor Grosser's current location is unknown.*'

'Is the ship docked?'

'*Negative, the vessel is not docked.*'

'Can you inform the first officer then?' she asked, thinking it was a bit weird the computer didn't know the whereabouts of the doctor.

'*The first officer is not on board the vessel at this time.*'

Malic stared at the ceiling for a moment, wondering if the computer had contracted a virus or something.

'What about the captain?' she asked.

'*The captain is not on board the vessel at this time.*'

'Well, where in the name of the ancients is he?'

'*The captain's current location is unknown.*'

'Oh, for fuck's sake,' she shouted, throwing her right arm up in disgust, which sent a stab of pain up her left. She held onto the side of the healing cell, grimacing until the agony subsided. Taking a deep breath, she looked up again.

'Computer, who is aboard the vessel at this time?' she asked, with a slightly sarcastic tone.

'*Assistant Engineer Malic Dess is the only member of the crew aboard the vessel at this time.*'

'What?'

'*Assistant Engin—*'

'Yes, yes, shut up…oh shit…oh shit. I'm the only one aboard.'

'*Affirmative. Assistant Engineer—*'

'Shut up, that was a statement, not a bloody question,' she snapped.

Walking to the door, she opened it and peered up and down the corridor. Knowing the mess hall was next door, she shouted out in that direction.

'Hello, is there anyone there?' She hoped the computer was having a little glitch and someone would answer.

Apart from the regular background humming of the ship's systems and the wheezing of the environmental vents, the ship was totally silent.

'Hello, anybody?' she called again, thinking someone might be in the mess, there often was because of the different shifts.

Again, no reply.

She turned back into the medical suite and looked up at the ceiling and asked a question, already guessing what the answer would be.

'Computer, where's the rest of the crew?'

'*The rest of the crew's location is currently unknown.*'

'Bloody hell,' she mumbled to herself, before opening her eyes wide as she realised she was the only one in control of the ship.

'Where are we?' she asked, nervously.

'*The vessel is currently stationary in the Dresse system.*'

She exhaled a sigh of relief at that, not realising she'd been holding her breath. At least the ship wasn't heading straight at a star or anything serious.

'I don't remember the Dresse system being on our route, why are we there?'

'*We answered a distress call from another Tallamainian-registered freighter.*'

'Is that vessel nearby?'

'*Negative, the vessel jumped away five hours ago.*'

'To where?'

'*The jump was embedded, present location unknown.*'

'Are there any other vessels in the vicinity?'

'*Negative,* Chrysos II *is the only detected vessel in the Dresse system.*'

'You said "detected", for what reason did you say that?' she asked, knowing that word wasn't a generally recognised computer response.

'*A second unclassified vessel of unknown origin uncloaked nearby when we arrived.*'

'What happened then?'

'*The* Chrysos II *was disabled, held by a tractor beam and boarded.*'

'Boarded by whom?'

'*A humanoid race of unknown origin.*'

She turned to the wall screen and pointed at it.

'Show me the camera footage on here.'

'*The cameras were disabled at that time.*'

'Shit.'

She stood and thought for a moment.

'Do you know which ship the crew were taken to?'

'Negative, I was disabled at that time too.'

'Oh, joy,' she grumbled and, starting to feel a little chilly in just her underwear, she turned to glance around for something to wear. The doctor's coat was hung on a peg in the corner of the room. She grabbed it, slipped it on, wincing as she pulled the sleeve over her left arm and left the medical suite en route for the bridge.

When she arrived, the holomap high in the centre of the room showed a small system of six planets orbiting the largest star in a binary pair. The ship was indeed stationary and after touching a few icons on the navigator's console, it showed the ship was around one hundred million kilometres from the star. A planet, Dresse, the third out from the star, shone brightly around one hundred thousand kilometres away.

'Computer, is the ship in any immediate danger?'

'Negative. The gravitational pull of the

planet Dresse will prove a danger to the ship in approximately seventeen days and fourteen hours. Can I remind you that Dresse is PV-designated and classified katapato red.'

'Oh, right,' she said, desperately trying to remember her recruit training course on what all the designations meant.

'I can't remember what those mean. Can you remind me?'

'PV is primitive and violent. Katapato red designates it's illegal to encroach.'

'Yeah, okay, can we move the vessel out to five hundred thousand kilometres and hold there, so we don't get spotted by the population?'

'Unable to comply.'

'Why?'

'A senior officer has to provide the authorisation to move the vessel.'

'But there isn't one aboard, is there? There must be an emergency protocol.'

'If the vessel is in imminent danger, I am permitted to intervene.'

'Well, do it then.'

'The vessel isn't in imminent danger.'

'It will be in seventeen days.'

'*That doesn't quantify as imminent.*'

'Oh for ancients' sake,' she snapped.

Noticing the load master's empty seat in the corner of the bridge, it gave her an idea for another question.

'Is the cargo still aboard?'

'*One ore canister is missing from cargo hold six.*'

'Just one?' she asked, bemused. 'Why would they only take one? The cargo's probably worth billions.'

'*Unknown at this time.*'

'What was in it?'

'*The cargo manifest lists it as containing duradium ore.*'

'What do the other canisters contain in hold six?'

'*The canisters in cargo hold six all contain duradium ore.*'

'That stuff's rare and expensive,' she mumbled to herself. 'Why only take one?'

'*Unknown at this time.*'

Malic slumped into the pilot officer's seat,

staring bamboozled at all the dozens of icons, mini screens and the hand-sized control yolks extending from the seat arms in front of her. She knew how to fix a lot of the ship's systems, but had absolutely no idea how to fly one.

'Shit,' she shouted. 'Why didn't I do just a basic flying module as a recruit?'

'*Unknown at this time.*'

'Oh, shut up you,' she snapped, glaring at the ceiling and then thinking of something, she turned towards the senior engineer's seat. 'Are you able to launch a jump-capable distress buoy?'

'*Affirmative.*'

1

Katadromiko 2, *orbiting Dasos, Prasinos system*

CAPTAIN GASTION WHIPPER stood with his arms crossed and scowled at the vast holomap hanging above the bridge officers on his vessel, the *Katadromiko 2*, a fourteen-kilometre battle cruiser of the GDA Naval Command. They had only that morning returned from a seven-month-long hearts and minds deployment out on the New Outer Arm of the Milky Way. The forty-seven thousand officers and crew were looking forward to a break, visiting the huge Stathmos Vasi space station just off their port side, and Dasos, the home of the GDA, slowly turning majestically below them.

A few moments ago, Naval Command had sent them a recording of a distress call, received only minutes ago via a jump drone coming in from somewhere in the Perseus arm. Hence the frown on the captain's face.

'Are you absolutely sure we're the only vessel available?' Whipper questioned, the irritation evident in his voice.

'Affirmative, Captain,' came the immediate and curt reply. 'All other vessels are currently on deployment.'

From experience, Whipper knew not to press the point. Upsetting Naval Command had never proved a successful technique for career advancement and the newly promoted admiral of the fleet was a cantankerous pain in the arse.

'Understood, will comply, *K2* out,' he replied, rolling his eyes at his newly promoted first officer, Hegg Falenthraite who also frowned and shrugged in return.

'I'll give the crew the good news, Captain,' said Falenthraite, sighing and glancing apologetically at the communications officer.

'Thanks, Hegg,' said Whipper, turning and approaching the navigators. 'Can you put the origin of the signal up there please,' he said, pointing to the holomap.

The three-dimensional display expanded out into the Perseus arm of the Milky Way and a small system began flashing in red.

'Distance?' Whipper asked.

'Two hundred and twenty-three thousand light years, Captain, give or take,' the senior navigator said.

'ETA?'

'There's a super massive black hole on the direct route, Captain, so we'll have to circumnavigate that. My estimate is approximately seven and a half days.'

'The message states the ship will drop into a red katapato planet in just over seventeen days,' said Whipper. 'How long did that drone take to get here?'

'Ten days, Captain.'

'Oh, crap,' he mumbled. 'Get underway now, jump as soon as you're ready and do your best to shave some time off the journey without going too close to that black monster.'

'Yes, Captain,' said the navigator, nodding at the pilot to take them out of orbit.

A young lieutenant had entered the bridge a few minutes earlier, had listened to the distress call and witnessed the captain's consternation at the journey time.

'May I make a suggestion, Captain?' he asked.

'Go ahead, Lieutenant Loftt,' said Whipper.

Bache Loftt approached and stopped at the base of the captain's raised dais and glanced up at the holomap.

'If I took one of the marine fast attack gunships, I might be able to save half a day and tractor that freighter away from the planet before it hits the atmosphere.'

The captain took a deep breath, exhaled and pondered the lieutenant's idea for a few moments, eyeing Loftt as he did so.

'Could the tractor on just a small gunship have enough clout to do the job?' he asked.

'The freighter isn't moving quickly and so long as I have a couple of hours with it still in space, I should be able to slow it down enough and manoeuvre it into orbit.'

Whipper rubbed his chin in thought.

'The two ships could be seen in orbit, any amateur astronomer with a half-decent telescope could photograph them and then we'd really be in the mire with the council.'

'Better than a ten million tonne UFO dropping on one of their cities.'

The captain grimaced and looked up at the holomap.

'Don't take any unnecessary risks,' he said, coming to a decision. 'Getting the girl off is a no-brainer, but don't endanger yourself or that ship. If you can't stop it going down, just get well away and hope it drops in a deep and remote ocean somewhere.'

'Thank you, Captain,' said Bache, turning to leave.

'And take Mye with you too,' the captain called before he was out of earshot.

Bache immediately called Lieutenant Zaphir Mye, told her of the plan and to meet him in hangar 41 in twenty minutes with her emergency grab bag.

After quickly visiting his cabin and retrieving what he thought he would need, Bache went straight to the hangar. Two technical support crewmen were already there and had prepped one of the latest and fastest gunships on the *K2*'s inventory. It sat with its rear door down and all four antigrav motors spinning at idle, the low grumble of the powerful engines echoing around the hangar.

He nodded at one of the crewmen as the man secured an auto trundle piled high with emergency survival equipment. It was one of Bache's own designs and had been an early project for him when first promoted to lieutenant three years ago.

'Send Lieutenant Mye up to the cockpit as soon as she arrives,' he said, making his way through the payload bay and towards the narrow stairway at the front.

'Yes, sir,' the crewman said, standing stiffly and giving him a quick salute.

Ascending the narrow winding stairs to the cockpit, Bache relieved the crewman prepping the ship and jumped into the pilot's seat, quickly downloading the route to the Dresse system. He was halfway through a complete systems check when a sudden voice from behind made him smile.

'Taking me somewhere romantic, darling?' said Zaphir, dumping her bag behind the co-pilot's seat with a clunk.

Bache stole a glance at the oversize bag and raised his eyebrows.

'Is that the kitchen sink that's clunking around in there?' he asked, po-faced.

'You know very well I'm not a travel light kinda girl—where're we going anyway?'

'Dresse system.'

'Never heard of it.'

'Nor had I until a few minutes ago,' Bache admitted. 'It's a distress signal before you ask. We need to get going, so can you secure the ship downstairs and I'll tell you what we know once we're on the way.'

Zaphir pursed her lips and glared for a second.

'Aye, aye, skipper,' she voiced, with just a hint of dissent and disappeared back the way she'd come.

2

*GDA marine gunship, entering the Dresse
system*

IT HAD TAKEN six days and twenty-three hours to
reach the Dresse system. Zaphir initiated the last
jump, putting the gunship in behind one of
Dresse's three moons to avoid any eagle-eyed
astronomers on the planet. They'd taken it in
turns piloting and discreetly pushing the jump
boundaries a little more than standard regulations, which is how they made up the time that

the *Katadromiko 2* was prohibited from doing for safety regulations.

'Wake up, Loftty—we're here!' she called, reaching over to shake the co-pilot's seat.

'Very pretty,' blurted Bache, sitting bolt upright and turning to stare at Zaphir with eyes like saucers. 'Oh!—right,' he exclaimed, gathering himself and glancing up at the holomap.

'Who's very pretty?' she asked, raising her eyebrows and feigning jealousy in her tone.

'Was I dreaming again?' he said, wiping the sleep from his eyes as he motored the seat back up into an upright position.

The conversation was cut short by an audible warning from the ship.

'Katapato red alert,' said Bache, as Dresse hove into view from behind the moon. He reached across and cloaked the vessel, just as another tone sounded indicating the freighter close to the planet.

'Crap, it's getting near,' said Zaphir, accelerating the gunship straight towards it.

'Let's hope it hasn't been spotted from the surface,' said Bache.

'Do we know how advanced this civilisation is?' Zaphir asked.

'No one's been anywhere near here for decades,' replied Bache. 'It's just too remote and there's nothing here to interest anyone.'

'I'm sure the population down there would disagree. To them it's everything.'

'I'll give the planet a scan and see what we're dealing with,' said Bache, caressing several icons on the touch screen in front of him.

Leaning forward, he read the information as it appeared.

'Approximately zero point four million population, with—'

'That's odd!' said Zaphir.

'Why?' he asked, looking over from the screen.

'That's less than ten percent of the estimate from two hundred years ago,' she said, pointing at a second screen where she'd brought up the previous planetary statistics.

'I'm getting derelict overgrown cities with very few life signs, just hundreds of small agricultural communities in more remote areas. They don't even seem to have steam power.'

'They did have two centuries ago,' she said. 'Perhaps they had a war that knocked themselves back into the stone age.'

'Perhaps,' he said. 'We'd better contact Malic and let her know help has arrived.'

Zaphir sent a narrow beam message, aimed at the freighter to avoid too much overspill reaching the planet's surface—although it seemed very unlikely there would be anything down there capable of receiving any frequency of signal anyway.

Three minutes later the reply came.

'GDA vessel, this is *Chrysos II*. Thank the ancients. I was beginning to think I'd be sitting in this thing until I ran out of food.'

'We need to stop your vessel dropping into the planet's atmosphere,' replied Bache.

'When the situation becomes critical the computer will move the ship away from danger, or so it tells me.'

'You do realise that's a katapato red-designated planet below?'

'It informed me of that days ago.'

'Does it not consider the situation as critical right now?'

'Apparently not without an officer's authorisation or until the ship is on the verge of de-orbiting.'

'Can your computer hear what I'm saying?'

'You're on speaker, so it can now.'

'*Chrysos II*, this is Lieutenant Loftt of GDA Naval Command—I'm ordering you to reposition your vessel two hundred thousand kilometres distant from the planet Dresse immediately. Will you comply?'

'Repositioning,' replied the dispassionate voice.

Bache noticed Zaphir flinch and sit up straight suddenly.

'What is it?' he asked.

'We've just been scanned,' she said, looking over at him with a concerned expression.

'It's probably the ship making sure it doesn't collide with us when it initiates the move.'

'No, Bache—the scan came from the planet's surface.'

'What? how can that be?'

'It was a wide beam covering the whole region we were in.'

'That can only be—move the ship, NOW,' he yelled.

The massive bolt of energy from a large planetary-based laser cannon ripped up through the atmosphere in the blink of an eye, ricocheting off the gunship's upper shields before zipping away into space at light speed.

'Hell, that was close,' said Bache, picking himself up off the cockpit floor where the jolt from the glancing blow had thrown him.

'I'll keep moving randomly,' said Zaphir. 'If that bolt had been twenty metres lower,' she added, her face white with the realisation of what nearly came about.

GDA gunship shields are good, but no match for a land-based cannon of that magnitude.

'Where in the name of the ancients did it come from?' Bache asked. 'I thought this planet was back in the stone age?'

'There was nothing on the scans that showed any technology at all,' said Zaphir, as she repeatedly changed course, gradually nearing the freighter. 'It must be hidden below the surface. Thank the ancients we were cloaked.'

'This puts a whole new prospective on things,' said Bache, rubbing his chin in thought. 'We can't transmit anything to the freighter again,' he added. 'They were using those for the initial ranging.'

'Why haven't they fired on the freighter? That's in plain sight,' asked Zaphir.

'Because it's going to drop into the atmosphere and be destroyed anyway. They're hiding again now. They gambled on one shot taking us out and now they have a dilemma. They, whoever they are, can't let us leave now.'

'D'you think they kidnapped the crew of the freighter?'

'If they did, we need to be very wary— there's most likely another cloaked ship around here somewhere.'

A sudden brightness on the holomap caught their attention.

'It's the freighter!' exclaimed Bache, watching as parts of the ship's main drive expanded outwards, causing the large vessel to begin a slow roll end over end.

'I didn't see the cannon shot,' said Zaphir.

'There wasn't one,' said Bache. 'It was an internal explosion.'

'Sabotage?'

'Most likely set to detonate if the drive was initiated.'

'That's just what the computer was going to do,' she said.

The gunship was nearing the freighter now. Zaphir brought the nose of the ship around so they could see the Tallamainian vessel through the front screen. They squinted as the brightness of the planet silhouetted the slowly turning freighter.

'Oh shit—look at the state of that,' said Zaphir. 'Now it's got no chance of staying up.'

'There's been no call from Malic either,' said Bache. 'Either she's unconscious or the explosion took out the array too.'

Zaphir gave Bache a worried glance.

'What do we do?' she asked. 'We can't just

watch her die, and let's face it, the katapato red designation is all in the wind now surely?'

'Hmm,' grunted Bache, bumping his chin with his fist. 'Think, Loftt, think.'

'You're the engineer,' she said. 'Is there enough time to get her out of there?'

'No, but there might be another way.'

3

GDA marine gunship, orbiting Dresse, Dresse system

'ARE YOU MAD?' said Zaphir. 'What, ride down on the back of the freighter? Surely we'll burn up too?'

'Not if we stabilise the freighter and present its shielded underbelly at the correct angle.'

'But it'll still hit the surface at several times the speed of sound.'

'We'll be locked onto the back of it with the tractor and use the antigravs to slow the descent.'

'Will it be enough?'

'Probably not—so we need to aim for an ocean.'

'All this assuming that the laser cannon and a cloaked warship of some kind hasn't vaporised us in the meantime?'

'And that the freighter doesn't break up on impact with said ocean—something like that, yes. I'm also hoping they only have one cannon because it'll be over the horizon in a few minutes.'

Zaphir puffed out her cheeks, exhaled noisily and shrugged.

'Right, okay,' she said. 'But I reserve the decision to release the freighter if I still think we're going in too fast, Malic will have to take her chances.'

'Agreed.'

.   .   .

It took Zaphir around six minutes to creep up and match the freighter's roll. She locked on to the bigger ship with the tractor, lowered the struts and with a tooth-jarring bang, the gunship slammed itself onto a flat section of the upper hull.

'Ouch,' she said, pulling a face. 'Never landed a ship using the tractor before.'

'Don't sweat it,' said Bache, reaching over to squeeze her shoulder. 'I couldn't have done any better—you did well.'

'What now?'

'Prepare the shields to encompass us and the freighter just in case the other cloaked ship is out there and decides to intervene when we re-position for the de-orbit.'

Zaphir pointed out the front screen as the planet rolled past.

'There's a sizeable ocean coming up underneath us shortly, d'you want me to encourage the drop?'

'I think it's a big landmass after that, so probably a wise move,' said Bache, pulling the lever under his seat to release the crash harness.

'Strap yourself in,' he said. 'It could get a bit rough lower down.'

She did as he said and began nudging the bigger ship, partly downwards and partly to slowly eliminate the spin.

'What's the ideal de-orbit angle for a Tallamainian freighter?' she asked, keeping her eyes firmly on the screens in front of her.

'Hang on—I imagine it'll be forty degrees, but I'll check,' said Bache, tapping away and delving into the ship's data bank. 'Most vessels are designed to have the same angle of attack so pilots don't make a mistake—yeah, there it is, I was right, forty degrees is good.'

Zaphir nodded and continued to gradually encourage the big ship to adopt a more sensible attitude to the rapidly approaching atmosphere.

'I'll spin up the antigravs so I'm ready to give them the bad news,' said Bache, caressing the touch screen in front of him and sliding on a POK helmet. 'It'll be the hardest they've ever worked.'

'Just don't overload them—we'd be in serious trouble too if we lost 'em,' said Zaphir, rolling her eyes and pulling a face.

A sudden shudder ran through the ship causing anything not bolted down to rattle.

'Here we go,' said Bache, checking his belts were tight. 'What's the angle?'

'Thirty-nine point two,' she said, swiping the ship's attitude display across to his screen with a wave of her hand. 'It's all yours now.'

Bache ramped the antigravs up to ninety-five percent, the engine noise surged up to a rasping howl as the powerful motors bit into the gravity well and struggled with the massive added weight. Zaphir peered out the front screen and could see the black smoke trail and sparks flowing off the freighter's leading edges. Slowly and with the increasing atmospheric density the immense speed of both the freighter and the gunship began reducing.

'We need more,' she said, watching the rapidly reducing figures of both speed and altitude.

Bache took the motors up to one hundred and five percent. She could feel the vibration change through her seat as the now overloaded engines bellowed their disapproval.

'Mach five,' she said, her fingers white as she gripped her seat arms.

Bache was in deep concentration and just grunted. He began turning the freighter and bringing the nose up slightly to enable the big ship's winglets to bite into the ever-increasing atmospheric density.

'Mach four, twenty kilometres,' she shouted above the deafening racket.

They were in a giant spiral over one of Dresse's biggest oceans, and odd glimpses of the water could be seen through the occasional gaps in the clouds kilometres below.

Bache again brought the nose up slightly and Zaphir winced as he rammed the antigravs to one hundred and ten percent, their maximum possible setting. Only recommended for extremely short bursts in matters of life or death, Zaphir remembered her flight instructor drilling into them. This was certainly that, but she knew it was going to be anything but a short burst.

A red light began flashing in front of her, and she cursed as she realised what it was.

'The tractor's overloading, Bache,' she called.

'Understood,' he replied, without taking his eyes off his screens.

Then a tell-tale rattling developed on the starboard side. She stretched over as far as her belts would allow and peered out the side window to witness a thin trail of smoke emanating from the starboard front antigrav nacelle.

'We're losing a motor,' she called, pointing out the side window.

'Understood,' he said again, pulling the ship up into an even steeper nose-up attitude.

'Woah, Bache,' she shouted, spreading her hands out in front of her. 'We'll stall at this angle.'

'Not at Mach two and being pulled by that thing we won't,' he said, calmly.

She pushed herself back in her seat with a discernibly worried expression and re-tightened her harness, more out of muscle memory than the fact it would make any difference if things did go wrong.

The steeper angle produced a considerable amount of vibration, as the freighter's hull became one massive air brake. Zaphir had difficulty focussing on her screens as the gunship shook alarmingly and the intermittent tractor beam alarm randomly squawked as it struggled to retain a firm grasp on the larger ship.

Zaphir lifted her head and peered nervously through the front window. She saw thin streams of vapour vortices streaming upwards as the thickening atmosphere began trailing off the freighter's leading edges.

'We're getting low,' she whispered, more to herself than to her partner.

'I know,' Bache replied. 'It's going to be a bit of a splash, but if I use the bulk of the freighter as a shield and come in at an acute angle, we should be okay.'

'Should be?' she repeated as a question, giving Bache a sideways glance, before turning back to eye the tractor release icon glowing enticingly just in front of her.

'Don't,' said Bache, as he sluggishly turned the two ships in another lazy turn to port. 'Trust me.'

They both turned to stare out the port side window as the ocean below swung into view. Rows of neat white wave crests could be seen stretching away to the horizon and by the direction of the wave tops, they could see the direction of the wind.

'Two thousand metres and still point five Mach,' she said, squinting to read the figures off the vibrating screen.

Bache lowered the nose of the freighter, did another turn to bring the two totally un-aerodynamic spacecraft into the wind and pulled a rueful expression.

'That should about do it,' he said, sitting back. 'Are your belts tight?'

'Any tighter and I won't be able to breathe.'

'Breathe out and tighten them again,' he said, grunting, as he did exactly that to his own harness.

Zaphir couldn't see anything but sky in

front, so she looked down and counted off the altitude.

'One thousand—eight hundred—five hundred—three hundred—one hundred—'

'Chin on your chest,' shouted Bache, as he mashed the engines off icon.

Barely a second later, Zaphir's world went dark.

4

GDA marine gunship, ocean floor, Dresse,
Dresse system

'ZAFFIE GIRL, CAN YOU HEAR ME?' Bache called, rubbing his neck and slackening his belts so he could breathe more easily.

'Huh,' she grunted, opening one eye, before sitting bolt upright and staring around. 'Are we down?' she asked, raising her voice above the cacophony of alarms wailing in the cockpit.

'Seems so,' said Bache, leaning forward to cancel the racket.

'How deep are we?'

'Not sure—one of those alarms was for the array. It might've got damaged in the ditching.'

'Two of the antigravs as well,' she said, surveying her screen and the warning lights.

Bache released his belts and stood, stretching forward to peer upwards through the front screen.

'It is slightly brighter above,' he said. 'We must've made the undersea shelf I was heading towards.'

'How deep was it?'

'Anything from two hundred to five hundred metres.'

'Hmm,' grunted Zaphir, finally disengaging the tractor and grimacing as she initiated a flight worthiness evaluation.

'Do you have a pressure reading on the hull?' Bache asked.

'Ah—hang on, I don't know if it's still—oh, it is. Three zero six four KPa.'

Bache nodded and tapped away on his tablet for a moment.

'Just under three hundred metres,' he said, as Zaphir got the result of the flight worthiness evaluation. He glanced over as she swore under her breath.

'How bad is it?' he asked, not looking forward to the answer.

'We have two motors operational,' she said, shaking her head.

'Not so bad,' he said. 'I told you we'd be all right.'

'Yeah, but one of them is the one spitting sparks and smoke. We might be able to get out of the water, but achieving orbit is a non-starter.'

'Can we get around to one of the freighter's airlocks?'

'Probably, I'll just use the one good motor and give the wonky one a rest.'

Luckily, the freighter had sunk and settled on the flat seabed in the upright position, so Zaphir was able to manoeuvre the gunship off the top of the larger ship using the one operational antigrav and a mixture of the attitude jets. They weren't designed for underwater operations, but seemed to handle the more delicate adjustments just fine.

'The next problem is, will the docking tunnel work down here?' said Bache.

'In a word, no,' said Zaphir, hitting the deploy icon repeatedly to no avail.

'Bugger,' said Bache. 'Now what?'

'You're the engineer,' she said. 'Engineer something.'

'Erm,' was all that Bache could offer as he sat back down and rubbed his chin.

'What about the suits?' she said, raising her eyebrows.

'Yeah, I thought of those.'

'Is there any reason a space suit wouldn't work out there?'

'No,' he said. 'It's just me and spacesuits have a bit of a thing going.'

'Like what?'

'Every time I wear one, everything seems to turn to shit.'

'Oh—get over it and go find that girl,' said Zaphir. 'Nothing's going to happen down here.'

Bache rolled his eyes and made his way

down the stairs to the main deck where the EVA suits were stored in a small underfloor storage unit. It was next to a similar hatch that led down to the armoury. Bache opened the hatch and clambered down the steep steps. Four of the suits were on hangers and ready to go and six more were in carry packs slotted into a rack against the far wall.

He took his time donning one of the hanging suits, knowing that the pressure at this depth would certainly test the suit's seals. They were more designed to keep pressure in than extreme pressure out, but he remembered the requirement specifications of this model because his father had been on the engineering team that designed these newer suits.

Once he was kitted up, he dragged one of the carry packs up onto the main deck and hung it over his shoulder. It was a bit cumbersome, but he reckoned he'd only have to go a few metres over to the bigger ship's airlock before he could dump it, remove his own helmet and traverse the freighter looking for the girl.

'Can you hear me, Zaffie?' Bache asked.

'I've told you before, don't call me that over the air.'

'No one's going to hear me down here.'

'She might and the *K2* might if they've arrived.'

Bache smiled as he activated his life support systems and waddled to the side airlock adjacent to the freighter. Entering, he closed the inner door and did a final suit pressure test. Once satisfied the suit wasn't going to fill with water as soon as he opened the outer door, he stood to one side, with his back against the wall and pressed the outer door open switch.

Water hissed through the tiny gap as soon as it cracked open, hitting the inner door with tremendous force. The hiss became a torrent within a couple of seconds, thundering in through the ever-widening gap.

He found he had to hold onto the side rail for grim death as he was buffeted from all angles as the airlock quickly flooded. Hesitating for a few seconds to allow the water to clear of all the bubbles, he checked his suit wasn't compromised by its recent battering. On finding everything was in the green, he waded a couple of steps across to the threshold and turned his suit lights on to full brightness.

He discovered Zaphir had done well, the light beams illuminated the freighter's hull and airlock across the void. It was about twenty metres away and roughly fifteen metres up from the ocean floor.

He added a bit of pressure to achieve neutral buoyancy and swam off the edge. He was about as sleek as a brick, so it took considerable effort to drag himself and the spare suit across to the airlock only the short distance away. Once there, he grabbed a hand hold, activated the outer door and hung on tight as, similar to before, the water thundered inside and would have sucked him in dangerously quickly had he not done so.

When the water had settled he paddled his way inside, closed the outer door and after checking the girl wasn't loitering on the other side, he activated the inner door.

The water gushed away quickly along the internal corridor inside the freighter and once he'd checked the atmosphere was safe, he removed his helmet and sniffed the air. It smelt stale and slightly metallic, although he knew that wasn't unusual as all ore freighters smelt that way.

'I'm in,' he transmitted to Zaphir.

'Okay,' she replied. 'Go right down the corridor and up three levels to get to the cockpit.'

'Understood,' he said, gladly dumping the spare suit and his helmet just outside the airlock and turning right as instructed towards the stairwell door at the far end of the passage.

The water sloshed around his feet for a while but by the time he reached the stairs, he was walking on dry floor.

'Did you say up three floors?' he asked.

'Yeah,' she replied. 'The only rooms up on that level are the bridge and the mess hall, she's got to be in one of those.'

He clumped his way up the stairs and although he was no stranger to a gym on the *K2*, he was still puffing hard when he reached the top.

'Aren't you there yet?' Zaphir asked, in a slightly irreverent tone.

'Space suit—one point three gees—staircase,' he replied, panting.

'Too may beers in that Krix'irian bar on the *K2* more like,' she said.

'You may piss off,' he retorted with a wry grin.

Lumbering his way up the short corridor, he popped his head into the mess hall as he passed and on finding it empty, continued towards the bulkhead door at the end. It was unlocked and as soon as he entered, he felt something cold and hard pressed against his left ear.

'Don't even fucking breathe,' said a girl's voice.

'I'd rather die quickly from a laser shot than slowly of asphyxia,' Bache replied.

'Who are you?' the voice continued.

'Lieutenant Loftt of the GDA cruiser *Katadromiko 2*. The lieutenant who's just saved your life—you're welcome.'

'Just saved my life?' she said, incredulously. 'You do realise my ship just crash-landed on an alien planet and is presently at the bottom of a fucking ocean.'

'If it hadn't been for my small gunship stabilising your ship from its spin and angling it correctly for the planetary insertion and slowing it sufficiently with our antigravs to land in one piece, you'd presently be a speck of ash blowing around in the upper atmosphere.'

'It wasn't an automated insertion by this ship then?'

'This ship's systems are all offline and I'm here to rescue you.'

'You said that before and then you fired on my ship,' she snapped.

'We didn't fire on anyone,' he said. 'Your engines had been sabotaged and we were fired upon from the planet's surface. Whoever kidnapped your crew, placed an explosive charge in the main engine to ensure the evidence was destroyed. Can you remove the pistol from my neck, please—I'm a bit worried you might sneeze or something.'

Bache felt the pressure being removed from his neck and a short, slightly dumpy girl with close-cropped black hair and wearing a pair of grubby coveralls, stepped around in front of him. The pistol, however remained pointing at his chest.

'You're an engineer,' he said, adopting a friendly grin.

'How would you know that?' she asked.

'I am too and I wear identical coveralls,' he said. 'Although I have to admit, mine are a lot grubbier.'

'I don't know if that's a compliment or not,' she said, raising her eyebrows.

'It was meant to be.'

'Have you found her?' Zaphir called.'

'She's here,' he replied.

'Who are you talking too?' Malic asked.

'My partner, Zaphir. She's piloting the gunship just outside your starboard airlock.'

'Your ship's down here too?'

'We were still attached when we hit the surface.'

'Fuck me, you were brave, we came in hard.'

'It was the only way I could save your life.'

'Didn't your ship get—'

The ship suddenly heaved violently, causing them both to fall over.

'Bache, get back here—I think we've got company,' called Zaphir.

5

*Tallamainian freighter, ocean floor, Dresse,
Dresse system*

BACHE ALMOST TRIPPED and fell twice as he and Malic descended the stairwell on the way back to the airlock.

'What the hell caused that?' Bache called, as they approached the bottom of the stairs.

'A large explosion on the seabed somewhere behind us,' replied Zaphir. 'The shockwave moved the freighter about five metres.'

'I assume it wasn't an undersea vent or anything?' he asked.

'Unlikely, seeing it was so localised and powerful. I think someone up top is trying to finish the job.'

'The bloody suit curse strikes again,' Bache grouched to himself, as he pulled the second suit out of its container and began helping Malic climb painfully into it.

'I've never worn one of these before,' she said, grimacing as her bad arm complained bitterly.

They both staggered as the ship lurched again, only this time it was slightly less violent.

'Whoever it is, doesn't know exactly where we are,' said Bache. 'Their scans don't penetrate this deep in an ocean. We need to get a wriggle on before they get lucky.'

Activating her suit, he made sure it was showing greens across the board before securing her helmet, and then his own.

'Follow me and do exactly what I do,' he said, leading her into the airlock and closing the inner door. He pushed her against the side wall and pointed to the rail. 'Hang onto that as tight as you can.'

The water gushed in as violently as before and he heard Malic cry out as she was engulfed in a maelstrom of cloudy water this time. He turned on his suit lights, only unlike before, he couldn't see a hand in front of his face.

'Shit,' he said. 'The explosions have disturbed the seabed. Are you where you were before?' he asked Zaphir.

'I have no idea,' she replied. 'I can't see shit either.'

'Turn all the exterior lamps on, see if that helps,' he said.

'They already are,' she replied.

'Ah, crap—oh, wait, hang on. Transmit again and keep the signal on even if you're not saying anything.'

'Transmitting now,' she said.

Bache flipped through the suit's operations menu until he found what he was looking for and activated it.

'Swim with me,' he said to Malic. 'Do not lose me.'

The transmission locator winked on his visor display, showing the gunship to be about fifty metres away, slightly higher and off to the left.

'Can you see me and do you need me to move?' said Zaphir. 'I'm just going to stop transmitting for a moment to let you answer.'

The locator vanished.

'Come to port and down a bit,' he said.

'Moving now,' she replied.

Bache kept swimming and checking Malic was still with him, until suddenly he realised the locator icon was moving further away.

Shit, the gunship's the wrong way round, he thought.

He had to wait until she stopped again.

'Is that better?' she asked, stopping the transmission again.

'Wrong way, Zaffie,' he said. 'Turn the ship through one eighty to bring the airlock round to the right side and then go to port for twice as long as before.'

'Oh, understood,' she said, the disappointment evident in her voice.

The third explosion couldn't have come at a

worse time and was closer too. Bache found himself thrust violently sideways and tumbling randomly. He waved his arms around trying to find Malic, to no avail. Just as he thought it couldn't get any worse, an alarm started pinging in his ears.

'Ah, crap, no,' he said to himself. 'Fucking suit's leaking now.'

'Bache, Bache, can you hear me?' called a rather stressed Zaphir.

'I can,' he said. 'My suit's leaking and I've lost Malic. Transmit for ten seconds and move forward slowly so I can locate you and your direction.'

'Okay, okay, I'm moving forward now, let me know how far I am away and what direction you want me to go.'

'I need you to turn ninety degrees to starboard and come forward twice as fast as you're going now for about twenty seconds. Look out for Malic on your way,' he said.

'Coming now,' she said.

Bache could feel one of his feet and legs were getting damp, but the signal was getting closer this time, so he began swimming in that direction. Suddenly and without warning something hit him hard in the chest.

'Oof,' he grunted, as all the wind was knocked out of him. Looking down, he found he was being pushed along by what looked like the leading edge of one of the gunship's winglets.

Finally, after a few seconds the ship stopped.

'Are you close now?' asked Zaphir and stopped transmitting.

'Stay right where you are,' he said, paddling and feeling his way around the ship to the airlock. 'Malic, Malic, can you hear me?' he called, as he hauled himself into the still-open outer door. No answer came.

Shit, he thought. *All this effort and now I've lost her*.

'Bache, where are you?' called Zaphir.

'In the airlock, I'm about to come inside.'

'Stay there—I've found Malic.'

'Where is she? I'll go get her.'

'She's right in front of the cockpit window.'

'Wave to her to come round this side and I'll be waiting to pull her in.'

'She doesn't seem to be conscious.'

'Crap,' he said, eyeing his suit display as more red warning lights began flashing. 'My suit's compromised, I won't be able to get round there and back.'

'No, stay there,' she said again. 'I have an idea. Be ready to catch her.'

'Why, what're you plan—'

Before he could finish, the gunship began moving slowly forward and to starboard. Bache realised what Zaphir was attempting and hanging onto the outer door with one hand he leant out and grabbed around with the other. He knew she was an excellent pilot, but this was going to take a lot of delicacy, to run the unconscious Malic around the hull and bring the airlock to her.

Bache strained his eyes and thrashed his arm around like a mad man.

'Come on, Malic,' he shouted. 'Where are—'

Something clipped the tip of his finger.

'Zaffie, stop now,' he called and plunged outwards.

For a moment there was nothing there and he wondered if he had imagined it, or it was just a bit of seabed churned up by the explosion. Then something hard hit him on the helmet. He grabbed out at it. It was a boot.

'Oh, thank fuck for that,' he said, hauling her down and back into the airlock. It took a lot of effort and his suit was dying quickly now. Shutting the outer door he quickly swam across to the inner door and hit the open toggle just as he could feel water sloshing around his neck.

They were both washed inside the gunship as the inner door powered open and distributed them in a pile of arms and legs. Bache quickly unfastened his helmet as he got a mouth full of salty water. He reached over and did the same to Malic. She immediately came to as her helmet was wrenched off and cried out as the pain from her injured arm overwhelmed her.

He ran to the stairway and shouted up to the cockpit as his suit comms had died.

'Go, Zaffie,' he called. 'Get us away from the freighter.'

He heard her reply but couldn't make out what she said.

He had to grab hold of an auto trundle as another nearby detonation caused the gunship to lurch sideways. Malic cried out in pain again and swore profusely as she rolled sideways, her bad arm banging up against the inner airlock door.

The small ship groaned and creaked as the water pressure subjected the hull to stresses it wasn't designed for and the unusual dampened thrum from the one good antigrav motor echoed around the loading bay.

Bache stripped off his waterlogged suit before helping Malic out of hers. They were both shivering with cold, so he dug out some blankets from one of the many lockers to wrap around themselves.

'You look like homeless refugees,' said Zaphir, as they arrived in the cockpit. 'Hi, I'm Zaphir,' she added, giving Malic a quick glance as she concentrated on keeping the gunship in a straight line.

'Hello,' Malic replied, staring out the front

screen as the ocean floor rushed by. 'I understand I owe you my life.'

'Ah—we're not out of the woods yet,' she said. 'We've got to avoid whoever it is up there for a while.'

'Can't we just get back into space and jump away?' Malic asked.

Zaphir shook her head.

'Engine trouble,' said Bache. 'We need to hide for a few hours until—'

The sound of hissing behind them and an alarm siren cut him off mid-sentence.

'Ah, shit—it's a hull breach,' said Zaphir. 'We're letting in water below.'

'Crap,' iterated Bache. 'We need to go up where there's less pressure quickly. Do we have cloaking?'

'Wadda you think?' said Zaphir, turning to roll her eyes at him.

'How far away from the freighter are we?'

'A few kilometres now.'

'Let's have a quick peek up above and see who's around,' said Bache, sliding into the co-pilot's seat and pointing Malic towards one of the bulkhead seats.

'Who are they?' asked Malic.

'We were kinda hoping you'd be able to tell us,' said Zaphir, as she steered the ship upwards towards the surface.

It didn't take long to get there and Zaphir turned them one hundred and eighty degrees before popping the cockpit above the surface to see if whatever had been attacking them was still visible behind.

As the water cleared away from the screen, they all peered out and scanned the horizon.

'Nothing,' said Zaphir.

'Perhaps they've given up,' said Malic.

'Why are we in shadow?' asked Bache, noticing the cloudless sky. 'Spin the ship around quickly.'

The gunship turned ponderously in its half-submerged state.

'Oh, shit,' said Zaphir, as a large dark purple and black vessel swung into view, hanging stationary about a hundred metres above. It loomed in over them as multiple weapons pods motored out menacingly from its six large winglets.

'They were following us all along,' said Bache.

'What do we do?' asked Malic.

6

______

GDA marine gunship, Dresse, Dresse system

BACHE STOOD on tiptoe and peered down at the ocean underneath the alien warship. He rubbed his chin in thought.

'Interesting,' he said, before turning to Zaphir. 'Zaffie, can you lift us out of the water slowly, bring on the other smoky motor and hang badly to one side. Make it look as if the ship's as good as dead.'

She did as requested, which soon got a

response.

A voice, speaking in Ellinika, the accepted galactic language of the GDA, boomed out of the cockpit speakers, as did a solid tone on the control console.

'GDA vessel, we have total weapons lock. You have no array, no shields, virtually no propulsion and your weapons are offline. You will surrender your vessel and be brought inside one of our hangars. Failure to comply will result in your complete destruction.'

The gunship shuddered as a tractor beam locked onto it.

Zaphir held her hands away from the console and shrugged.

'I no longer have control,' she said. 'Do I shut everything down?'

'Wait just one second,' said Bache, sitting quickly back in his seat, his hands hovering over the weapons console.

'We have no array,' said Zaphir. 'You can't target anything and anyway, their shields will just brush a laser cannon off.'

'They would if they had any activated,' said Bache.'

'They don't?' said Zaphir. 'How d'you know?'

'There's no displacement in the water below them.'

Zaphir stood on tiptoe too and stared down at the ocean below the larger vessel.

'You're right,' she said. 'There's no indentation in the water at all.'

'Be ready to move up over the top of them as quickly as you can,' said Bache. 'I need to time this just right.'

As Bache had hoped, the tractor beam operator dragged them closer, then around to the side of the bigger ship. Their large array was situated amidships and hung down from the belly of the vessel. Knowing the gunship's cannons' default fire position was straight ahead, he waited until the tractor began pulling them up to the hangar door.

When the huge array appeared before them Bache wasted no time, activating and firing the four heavy laser cannons on automatic. The whole underside of the alien vessel lit up as the array exploded, taking one of the weapon pods with it.

'GO, GO, ZAFFIE,' he shouted.

She suddenly found she had control again and heaved the injured gunship up over the top of the bigger ship.

'Point me at their engines,' he said, lowering his voice again.

Bache could hear the big ship's pair of massive antigravs spooling up as the pilot tried to get them away from danger. It was too late as Zaphir slewed the gunship to starboard and pointed it straight at their port-side motor.

The laser cannon spoke again.

They all ducked as the engine spat out huge chunks of hot metal including its immense spooler that disintegrated as it clouted another of the weapons pods. The gunship's front screen cracked as the shrapnel rattled over the gunship's hull.

The big ship sank down on that side, the

pilot desperately attempting to keep it on an even keel.

'The other one,' said Bache, pointing.

Zaphir again turned the gunship, this time aiming the bow at the alien vessel's starboard engine, but from side on this time. She backed away as the deep bass overture of the cannons thudded for a third time.

It wasn't quite as spectacular as before, but achieved the same result. The massive motor emitted a cloud of black smoke, causing the huge vessel to lose its fight against gravity. It dropped into the ocean with an immense splash, throwing a plume of water at least a hundred metres high. It disappeared for a moment before its buoyancy pulled it back to the surface where it sat heaving in the swell with water cascading off its hull. Smoke and steam began billowing from the remains of the engine and weapons nacelles.

'Arrogant prick got what he deserved,' said Zaphir, smirking at Bache.

'Did we just shoot down that huge warship with this little thing?' said Malic, leaning over their shoulders, her eyes wide as she peered below at the stricken starship.

It was now beginning to list to starboard as water filled the voids where the antigrav motor and missing weapon pod used to be on that side.

'Bit more than just a little thing,' said Bache. 'He's certainly not the first to underestimate the usefulness and firepower of one of these, and most likely not the last.'

'Will it sink?' asked Zaphir.

'No,' said Bache. 'Too big and buoyant.' He looked at the compass on the console. 'We need to get to some land before another of those beasts turn up. That last motor could dump us down with them at any time—and we would sink.' He looked up. 'That way I believe,' he said, pointing west and turning for the stairs. 'I'll go and let some of the water out.'

Zaphir took one last look at the huge vessel bobbing around below them, shook her head and turned the gunship in the direction Bache had pointed, accelerating west towards one of the planet's moons hanging low in the hazy blue sky.

'Land,' said Malic, pointing enthusiastically at a dark line on the horizon half an hour later.

'Just as bloody well,' said Zaphir, squinting out the front screen and jagging her thumb towards the screaming antigrav. 'This motor's been getting way too hot for a while now.'

The dark line gradually grew into an inky black cliff face. The ominous vertical rock wall held back the churning ocean and appeared to create an impenetrable land fortress.

'Ancients alive, I'm glad we're not coming in by boat,' said Zaphir, raising the gunship up away from the waves in order to clear the three hundred-metre stockade looming towards them.

'There's a flat area over there,' Malic said, pointing.

'Too exposed,' said Bache, appearing behind them. 'We need to find somewhere to hide the ship. I'm sure whoever owned that bigger ship is going to be severely pissed. Let's not make it easy for them to find us.'

'Had you ever come across a ship of that design before?' asked Zaphir, quickly glancing over at the other two.

'No,' said Bache. 'It's not in the GDA database, so we don't even know if they're humanoid.'

'We definitely know they're unfriendly bastards,' groaned Zaphir.

Malic's expression saddened.

'I hope my crew are okay,' she said, slumping back in her seat. 'They didn't treat me with much respect, but then again, I was the most junior member of the crew and always the butt of a few jokes.'

'We've all been there,' said Zaphir, rolling her eyes.

'Ah-ha,' grunted Bache, suddenly and pointing out the port side window.

The two girls stretched up to peer in that direction. They saw a crevice that initially looked small, but quickly opened up into something bigger as Zaphir turned the ship in that direction. It zig-zagged inland from the ocean, gradually narrowing as it went. Although it only offered the familiar sheer rock cliffs to begin with, the further up Zaphir took them, the shallower the sides became and the sparse vegetation became thicker and more dense until around a kilometre inland it became an almost jungle-like valley.

'Find somewhere here below the ridge line,' said Bache. 'The rock will hide the ship's signature from all directions except directly above.'

Zaphir headed towards not exactly a clearing, but an area of less dense and shorter vegetation.

'Shit,' she said, as only three of the four strut-deployed indicators lit up.

'Three's fine,' said Bache. 'The ground slopes anyway. Just set us down with the missing strut on the high side.'

Malic and Bache hung onto their seats as she did as instructed. The gunship dropped, turned and thudded into the hillside. With the starboard front strut not deployed, it leant alarmingly nose-down on that side for a moment before the hull crunched into the vegetation. They all flinched as a dislodged branch from a tree crashed down on the front screen and a flock of annoyed black, leathery-winged birds flapped and screeched their way skywards.

'We've pissed off the locals already,' said Zaphir, shutting the drive systems down and glancing at a screen to her right. 'Atmosphere and radiation levels are both within safe tolerances. Saying that, I've noticed oxygen levels are high so beware that naked flames might be a bit more enthusiastic than we're used to.'

Bache nodded.

'Gravity?' he asked.

'Point six Dasos,' she answered, raising her eyebrows.

'Point six,' he repeated, glancing at Malic. 'You might want to be careful outside the ship,' he said to her. 'That's less than half what you were running on the freighter. We're all going to be bouncy on this world, but you especially.'

Malic nodded back, then she suddenly turned and pointed out the cracked front screen.

'Movement,' she said. 'Amongst the trees.'

No sooner had she said it, a crack above them on the outside of the hull made them all duck. It was closely followed by another and then three more.

'What the hell?' said Zaphir, as a rock hit the front screen and rattled away back down to the ground. 'Someone's throwing rocks at us.'

7

GDA marine gunship, Dresse, Dresse system

THE CLUNKS and rattles of rocks striking the hull continued as Bache, Zaphir and Malic descended the narrow stairs down to the loading bay.

'Open up some of the ration packs in there,' said Ed, pointing to a row of overhead lockers.

'I'm not that hungry,' said Malic, wrinkling her nose.

'It's not for us,' said Bache. 'I'm going to give it to them out there.'

'Better wear one of those suits then,' said Zaphir, nodding her head towards the individual storage bays at the back of the room where the row of four ugly powered battle suits stood like sentinels. Their sightless black visors staring out ominously.

Bache shook his head and shivered. He hated the things and couldn't remember any occasion where their use hadn't escalated the situation.

'No, I want them to see me unprotected, unarmed and bearing gifts,' he said. 'We need to find out what the hell has gone on here so we can provide a decent report for Mr Whippy when he gets here.'

'Who?' said Malic.

'That's Captain Whipper,' said Zaphir. 'The captain of our Katadromiko.'

'You're from a Katadromiko?' Malic blurted in astonishment. 'What, one of those huge planet-killing battleships?'

'We prefer humanitarian cruiser,' replied Zaphir, cringing slightly and giving Bache a knowing look.

'Yes, well, that is a false impression we're

trying to shrug off,' mumbled Bache as he hooked a universal translator to the front of his ship suit and picked up an armful of the more palatable ration pack items before stepping over to the rear door. 'You two get a couple of rifles, set them to a light stun and keep them well hidden. Only to be used if I get into serious bother. Is that understood? We'll only get one chance at showing them we're friendly.'

Zaphir and Malic both nodded.

When they were all prepared, Bache removed the safeties from the rear door ramp and took a deep breath before beginning to power the ramp down manually and slowly.

There was an audible hiss as the huge seals released and a crack of daylight peeked through the steadily widening gap. Bache immediately noticed the sweet smell of the local vegetation pervading the cabin. It reminded him of camping trips he did with his father on Deelatayne as a boy. Another thing he noticed was the cessation of the rocks raining down on the ship, as it suddenly went eerily quiet.

'Well that's something positive, I suppose,' he heard Zaphir whisper to Malic.

As the ramp dropped low enough to see over, he scanned the tree line some twenty metres away and saw nothing.

He stopped the ramp when it was about two feet off the ground, tentatively stepped out and peered around. It was still unnaturally quiet, even the trees stood as if frozen in time and the noisy leathery-winged birds they could hear from inside the ship had hushed too. Shrugging, he jumped down carefully so as not to drop any of the food, walked out about five metres to the trunk of a fallen tree and carefully placed down all the food items.

Staring out and pointing around the tree line and then down at the food, he nodded, turned around once, deliberately demonstrating he was unarmed and returned to the ship. He sat on the edge of the ramp, his legs dangling below and waited.

It took a few minutes until finally he spotted shadowy movement and the sound of faint murmuring coming from the trees on his left-hand side. He turned in that direction, smiled and pointed to the food again.

A face appeared amongst the underbrush, human, dark-skinned and bearded with characterful craggy features. Bache could see the fear and suspicion in the man's eyes as he stared unblinking back at him, with just the occasional glance over at the food offerings. He could only guess at the man's age; his lined features said sixties, but even at this distance the alertness in his eyes made him seem younger.

The man jerked back nervously as Bache waved, smiled again, brought his hand to his mouth in an eating gesture and nodded at the food. He set his translator to repeat what he said in several of the more common GDA world's languages.

'We're not here to harm you, you're quite safe,' he called, in Ellinika and waited and watched to see if there was any reaction. It was on the seventh translation the man straightened and spoke back over his shoulder. The words were spoken too quietly for the translator to pick them up, but Bache caught a couple of words he thought might be Guasse. It had been a long time since he was at junior school and taught basic phrases in outer planet languages. But he was confident enough in what he'd heard to change the translator to Guasse and try again.

This certainly got a reaction. The man stepped out and stood fifteen metres away from Bache and stared. Some of the fear seemed to have receded, but his eyes remained vigilant.

He spoke and a split second later the translator did its job.

'You not purrers?' he said.

Bache realised from the intonation, it was a question.

'What is purrer?' he asked back.

The man seemed puzzled by this as his brow furrowed and his eyes flicked around randomly as he appeared to be trying to formulate a reply.

'The plaguers,' he eventually said, pointing south.

'Interesting translation,' said Zaphir, stepping out from the ship's interior.

The man immediately took a step back, his eyes wide with more astonishment than fear.

'Feeme,' the man stuttered, gazing upwards nervously. 'Swathe, swathe,' he added, pushing his palms forward and up over his mouth in a gesture inferring she should retreat back on the ship and cover her face.

'Why should she move back under cover?' Bache asked.

'Purrers—sky ship, plague gas,' he replied.

Bache looked over his shoulder at Zaphir.

'Go back under cover,' he said. 'It seems to make him very nervous you're out in the open, and what did you mean by interesting translation?'

Zaphir put her hands up in a placating manner and backed up under cover of the ship.

'Use of the word plague,' she said. 'It might have some meaning to why the population here has plummeted.'

'Hmm,' grunted Bache, turning back to his new friend. 'Did the purrers or plaguers bring a sickness to your world?'

The man's eyes widened at the question.

'Your people not suffer too?' he asked.

Bache realised from the man's reply that he

thought they were from another region of this planet.

'We are not from this planet, we are from far away,' said Bache, pointing straight up.

The man took a step back, and a look of fear washed across his face.

'The purrers come from there—bring death,' he said. 'You come from there—bring death too.'

Bache shook his head.

'No, that won't happen because—'

The sudden scream of antigravs above made them jump and had them both staring skyward. The small ship passed overhead at speed and Bache heard the tone of the motors change as it vanished behind the trees.

'We've been spotted,' he shouted, as the indigenous man dived back out of sight. 'Grab one of those backpacks each—we need to get away from the ship.'

He jumped up, retrieved a weapon and pack for himself, waited until Zaphir and Malic were off the vessel then entered a code into a hidden keypad on the outside of the ship. While the ramp powered closed, the three of them sprinted into the trees.

Moments later the alien ship screamed back overhead, only this time it was travelling much slower and circled around twice before flaring and dropping down to land.

Now about a hundred metres away, Bache, Zaphir and Malic ducked down and concealed themselves. Bache turned and peered back through the foliage, watching closely as the unfamiliar vessel, about the same size as theirs, touched down between them and their ship, but left the antigravs spinning.

For a few moments nothing happened.

'What are they waiting for?' Malic whispered.

'To see if there's any reaction,' Bache whispered back. 'After what happened out on the ocean, they're understandably being cautious.' He had a quick scan around; the locals had vanished but were most likely watching both them and the newcomers.

He turned back to the alien ship as he heard the spoolers dial down to a murmur. A door must have opened on the far side of the ship, as several pairs of legs appeared underneath descending steps. From this distance Bache couldn't see much, but he knew they'd reached the gunship as a loud crack and a flash lit up the clearing between the ships.

'What the ancients was that?' whispered Malic.

'You set the anti-tamper didn't you?' said Zaphir in Bache's ear.

He nodded.

'Don't like my stuff being touched,' he whispered back with a wry grin.

Bache could see the legs returning to the alien ship, and judging by the way they were moving they were carrying something or someone.

'You didn't kill him did you?' Malic asked.

Bache shook his head.

'Heavy stun.'

Once they'd loaded whatever or whoever it was aboard the small ship, three pairs of legs split up and started circling the clearing. Bache and Zaphir both brought their weapon optics up to their eyes and zoomed in, waiting for the first alien to show his face. The one furthest right came around the rear of their ship. At first he had his face in shadow, but he stopped and scanned around the tree line, his features suddenly coming into direct sight.

'Well, fuck the ancients,' exclaimed Zaphir. 'They're the last race I expected it to be.'

8

Woodland area, Dresse, Dresse system

'GATAS!' exclaimed Bache, shaking his head. 'That explains where the name purrers comes from.'

'What are they?' asked Malic, squinting through her rifle optic. 'He's got fur on his face!'

'Yes,' said Bache. 'Human-feline hybrid originally from a planet called Lynkas. They have many clans now and populate several worlds on the fringes of GDA space.'

'Very unusual to find them off their own worlds too,' said Zaphir. 'It's very remote and they're normally extremely shy and don't involve themselves in anyone's business except their own.'

'I've seen a few of them on mining planets like Krix'ir,' said Bache. 'But I've never seen them with weapons before.'

'Or gunships,' said Zaphir.

'No wonder the locals are good at hiding and being quiet,' said Bache, glancing up at the tree-tops. 'Gatas have vastly superior senses, so I'm glad we're downwind from them, otherwise they'd probably hear or smell us.'

Watching closely through his optic as another of the creatures came into view, Bache realised something unusual about these Gatas that he hadn't seen before.

'They have very dark fur,' he said.

'You're right,' said Zaphir. 'I thought it was the shadow of the trees, but they're a dark grey colour aren't they?'

'Is that strange?' asked Malic.

'Yeah,' replied Zaphir, quietly pulling out her tablet and tapping away with a thoughtful expression.

Malic nodded and pulled her optic up to her eye again.

'They're not doing much,' she said.

'I imagine they've called for backup,' said Bache. 'They're down one man and they don't know how many of us there are.'

As they watched, the three remaining Gatas gathered together on the near side of the clearing and stared into the trees almost straight at them.

'How do they know we're in this direction?' whispered Malic.

'Their hunting skills are extremely acute,' said Bache. 'That, and the fact we've left plenty of signs in our haste to get away from the ship.'

'Wow!' said Zaphir, staring at her tablet screen.

'What is it?' asked Malic.

'I was going through the GDA's data files on the Gatas.'

'What have you found?' asked Bache, dropping his optic and looking across.

'Dark grey Gatas are a mythical clan from their folklore called the Nkris. Aggressive, meddling, violent and a Gata society-wide catchword for anything that goes wrong.'

Bache raised his eyebrows.

'Seems their folklore was correct then, looking as to what these grey ones have been up to,' he said.

They all ducked out of instinct as another two ships roared overhead, the sound of their antigravs changing pitch as they scrubbed off speed and turned to land.

'We need to get out of here,' said Zaphir. 'There could be dozens of them roaming through here in a few minutes.'

Bache watched as the original three Gatas looked up and turned away as their backup arrived.

'Come on,' said Bache. 'Let's go while they're preoccupied with the arrivals.'

Staying crouched, Bache led then off to the

right and circled around for about fifty metres, before straightening up and heading away from the clearing again, this time in a completely different direction. The lighter gravity was enabling them to move extremely swiftly.

He could hear the crashing of trees being flattened as the two ships didn't waste any time and clearly sounding as if they were taking no prisoners getting on the ground to disgorge their personnel.

'We need to hustle,' hissed Zaphir. 'They're not messing about.'

'I know,' replied Bache. 'Just stay amongst the trees, If I remember rightly, it should be a bit more rocky in this direction and maybe…'

The local man they'd been conversing with moments ago suddenly appeared on their right-hand side. He beckoned them to follow him and as quickly as he had materialised he vanished amongst the shadows of the undergrowth again.

'How the ancients did he get here so quick?' Zaphir panted as the three of them turned and plunged in after him.

Bache slowed as it took a few moments for his eyes to adjust to the gloom. The smell of rotting flesh assaulted him in this dark, narrow passageway of vegetation.

'What the fuck is that stink?' he heard Zaphir hiss behind him.

They quickly found out, as they had to step over the decomposing corpse of some indigenous four-legged animal. The local man was stooped by a small opening in the base of a rock escarpment that stretched steeply upwards and disappeared through the tree tops.

He had a small branch in one hand and ushered them down and into the opening with the other. Once inside, Bache turned and watched as the man scurried back over the dead animal and disappeared for a few seconds before returning, walking quickly backwards and dusting the trail with the branch.

'Covering our spoor,' he whispered, noticing Malic's puzzled expression.

Joining them in the cave, the man threw the branch to one side as two other similarly bearded locals, who'd up to this point been completely hidden in the darkness, moved in to help the man roll a sizeable boulder across the entrance.

Once done, the man beckoned them on again. Bache noticed him get worried glances from the other two locals. Nodding at Bache, Zaphir and Malic, the man uttered a couple of words that neither he nor the translator picked up. Whatever he said seemed to placate his colleagues somewhat as he got small nods in return, before they quietly fell in behind and the group of six made their way off into the gloomy darkness.

As they rounded a corner, the low ceiling disappeared and the passageway became much higher enabling them all to stand fully upright. Bache realised where the dull glow had come from, as the local man grabbed a hand lamp out of an alcove. It emitted a low yellow glimmer, just enough, as your eyes adjusted, to see your way along the narrow rock-strewn corridor.

The ground became a little more uneven shortly after and began winding gently uphill and pebbles replaced the gravel floor. Bache realised water must have formed this cave system many millennia ago.

'How bloody long is this thing?' griped Malic, after about fifteen minutes of zig-zagging upwards.

'Long enough to get you away from the purrers,' said the local man in front. 'Or you'd be dead by now.'

The adaptive translator was getting much more accurate with the local's particular dialect of Guasse.

'Why would they want us dead?' asked Zaphir.

The man stopped and turned to face them.

'If you're really off-worlders like them, then you could tell others. They won't allow you to do that.'

'They might have taken them to work at the Ballenhyght caverns,' said one of the other locals.

They all turned to face him.

'Where's that?' asked Bache.

The locals looked at him as though he was insane.

'You're right, Kolde,' said the second local a moment later, after they'd all exchanged raised eyebrows. 'They're definitely not from this world.'

'They had a flyer unlike anything I've seen before too,' said the third local.

Bache turned to the first local seemingly known as Kolde.

'Kolde,' he said, pointing at the man. 'Bache, Zaphir and Malic,' he continued, pointing at himself and the other two in turn.

Kolde pointed at the other two locals.

'Geerten and Weltronicas, although we know him as Welt.'

'Thank you for taking the risk with us,' said Bache. 'We fully understand you could've left us out there, with what would've been a pretty futile chance of escape.'

The three locals nodded and Kolde pointed up the passageway.

'We continue,' he said 'Not much further.'

'When did you leave the cities?' Zaphir asked.

Bache noticed the locals glance at each other again.

'You know about those?' Geerten asked.

'We scanned your planet before we came down here,' said Bache. 'So we know your society was a lot more advanced at one time.'

Geerten nodded as he walked.

'It was when we were children, about twenty years ago,' he said. 'I was too young to remember it, so I'm going on what my parents told me. They said the purrers crash-landed in a spaceship that badly needed repairs.'

'And they're still fixing it?' Malic said cynically.

This time Geerten shook his head.

'At first they were friendly,' he said, pensively. 'Our ancestors helped them dismantle the ship and transfer it into a large cavern in the Ballenhyght Mountains region. It had to be under cover for some reason.'

Bache and Zaphir exchanged a glance.

'I think we know the reason for that,' said Zaphir. 'But go on.'

Geerten shrugged and continued.

'From what I was told, it was shortly after this was done their attitude suddenly changed and they started forming forced labour squads to mine a rock that they seemed very excited about.'

'What was it?' Zaphir asked.

'No idea,' said Kolde. 'We just call it the rock of the dead.'

'There was an uprising and several purrers were killed, which was quickly put down quite brutally,' said Welt. 'They have these powerful death ray weapons, hundreds died and then the females began getting sick.'

'Just the females?' Bache asked.

The three locals nodded, their expressions hardening. Kolde swallowed hard before continuing.

'The purrers found out it was the wives and mothers of the forced labourers that organised the revolt. Over two million females died within a week.'

'Oh, no,' exclaimed Zaphir, slapping her hand over her mouth in shock. 'That's horrendous.'

Bache's expression hardened.

'A crime of that magnitude cannot go unpunished,' he muttered through gritted teeth.

9

*Underground cave system, Dresse, Dresse
system*

BACHE WITNESSED the look of horror on Zaphir
and Malic's faces, knowing his would be the
same, as the true extent of what Kolde had said
sank in.

'You definitely think it was the purrers?' Zaphir asked.

'We don't think anything, we know it was
them,' growled Kolde.

'Records from that time clearly state the purrers had all their smaller flyers up spraying something into the air above the cities only the day before the plague began,' said Welt.

'What was the illness?' Malic asked.

'Nobody knows,' said Geerten. 'Within a couple of days, society collapsed. Even more died in the rioting, looting and total lawlessness that followed.'

'It didn't kill all of them then, some females survived,' said Zaphir.

'Remote farming communities mostly, as were we,' Welt said.

'There are still lawless gangs roaming even now,' said Geerten. 'We still have to remain vigilant and hidden, as you will see.'

He nodded forward as they emerged out of the narrow passage into a much bigger cavern. Light streamed in from above through a natural hole that looked like it was formed millions of rotations ago.

Bache saw trees and large shrubs growing around the edge, miraculously clinging on to the near vertical sides and looking like they could fall in at any moment. It was the architecture below that really surprised him and he noticed the awe on the girls' faces too as they took in the scene.

An underground wooden city filled the base of the cavern. It must have been at least a kilometre across and in places reached up five of six storeys high. Walkways and decks snaked randomly in all directions, with perfectly carved spiral stairways connecting the levels. He could smell food cooking and heard the distant laughter of children coming from deep within the sprawling structure.

'I'm impressed,' he said to Kolde, as they were led across a narrow retractable bridge and onto one of the wooden walkways. Bache looked down as they crossed. A purposely dug trench, thirty feet deep with vertical sides dropped away beneath him.

'Formidable barrier, Kolde,' he said.

Kolde nodded as he led them, his expression unchanged. Bache noticed they were beginning to attract attention now, men stopped as they passed, faces of amazement staring at the girls as if they had two heads. Everyone they met outside were males, but he could see the occasional female staring from within the wooden dwellings, their mouths and noses covered.

He tapped Welt on the shoulder and nodded at the homes they were passing.

'We tested the atmosphere when we arrived and it's perfectly safe now,' he said. 'Your females don't need to hide and cover up anymore.'

Welt stopped suddenly, turned and glared, his nostrils flaring.

'It is our culture now,' he snapped.

'Ah, right—I understand—very sorry,' said Bache, holding his hands up in a placatory manner.

Welt continued to stare at Bache for a moment before glancing over at Geerten and Kolde.

'They weren't to know, Welt,' said Geerten. 'They're from another world where everything would probably be very different.'

Welt did one of his now familiar nods, turned and carried on marching through the buildings. They had to almost run to keep up.

Turning suddenly right into an open double

doorway, Welt led them into a large lobby, stopped in front of an inner door, turned and held up a hand.

'You will wait here,' he said, before disappearing through the door.

Bache caught a glimpse of a larger chamber within but little else as the heavy wooden door closed with a thud.

'Don't think he's very happy with what you said,' said Malic, grimacing as she rubbed her bad arm.

'He's been a grumpy bastard recently,' a voice said through the translator.

Bache turned to find Geerten staring at him.

'He wasn't always like that,' he continued.

'It's since his family left,' said Kolde.

'Left?' Zaphir asked.

'Gone to visit relatives—so he says,' said Geerten, giving Kolde a look and a shrug.

'You don't think that's true?' Bache asked.

'Well, they have been gone a long time,' admitted Geerten, staring at the floor thoughtfully.

The big door opened again, ending the conversation.

Kolde and Geerten ushered them into a hexagonal room about twenty-five metres across. It reminded Bache of a small town court room, although there wasn't one judge sitting higher than anyone else. There were ten, all sitting on the top tier of three around the outside of the room. All men, all seemingly elders of the town, with greying beards and scowling deep-lined faces.

Bache noticed the murmuring within the room increased dramatically as soon as Zaphir and Malic appeared. Welt waved them over to a standing area in the centre of the lower level, clearly designed to make you feel inferior.

'Welt has informed us that you're alleging to be from a more advanced human society somewhere out in space,' one of the elders said, his deep voice echoing around the chamber.

Bache stepped forward and addressed the room, turning slowly as he spoke to ensure he got eye contact with all ten.

'That is correct, gentlemen,' he said. 'Our starship will be here within hours to rid your world of the purrers as you call them. We know them as Gatas and they should not be here.'

Bache heard the door open and close behind him as Welt left the chamber.

'How do you intend to persuade them to leave?' another asked. 'They're the rulers of our galaxy and their technology is extremely advanced.'

'Did they tell you that?' exclaimed Zaphir.

The circle of elders sat back in astonishment.

'Females are forbidden to speak in the chamber,' the elder boomed. 'We also find it insulting you have neglected to cover your faces too,' he added, scowling down at them.

'Different rules where we come from,' said Bache, quickly raising his hand to take the attention off Zaphir. 'Females have equal standing in our culture, she and we meant no disrespect.'

'So, you're saying the purrers are not the galactic rulers they claim to be?' the first elder asked.

'Far from it,' said Bache. 'They're guilty of a galactic crime just by being here, let alone what they've done to your society. Believe me, they will pay for what they've done here.'

'You say your starship will arrive shortly,' another of the ten said. 'That's only one ship—the purrers have built fourteen large warships in the mountains of the Ballenhyght. I don't know about you, but normally here, if you're outnumbered fourteen to one, it wouldn't end well.'

'You're just going to have to trust us on that one,' said Bache. 'We do have a few tricks up our sleeve.'

Judging by the perplexed expressions they didn't really understand the last thing Bache had just said.

'Trust?' one of them said, questioningly. 'You see, we trusted an alien race once before. Then two thirds of our civilisation were dead not long after. So, forgive us if we don't jump up and down with glee.'

'I understand,' said Bache. 'But we really don't need you to do anything—except perhaps provide us with some form of transport and directions to get to this Ballenhyght region.'

There was a sharp intake of breath from just about everyone in the chamber.

'You want to go there?' said the first elder, his eyes wide with astonishment. 'Are you completely mad?'

'No one comes back from there alive,' said another.

'Legend has it, they have a weapon there that can level whole cities,' the first elder added, shaking his head.

'Let me worry about that,' said Bache.

'That must be the ground-based laser cannon,' whispered Zaphir. 'Which means where we need to get to must be located on the other side of the planet.'

Bache considered this for a moment.

'How long does it take to get there?' he asked.

'The only way is by flyer,' Kolde said, behind him. 'You would have to cross that ocean first,' he added, pointing back towards the coast.

'Hmm,' grunted Bache, sucking on his bottom lip and looking at a mark on the floor. 'Do the purrers have a base on this continent?'

he asked, looking up and staring straight at Kolde.

'They do,' he said. 'That's how they got here so quickly after you landed.'

'How far?'

'Four hours by calloppe—seven on foot.'

'What's a calloppe?'

'Take them and show them,' said the first elder. 'Give them three if you have to—just get them away from here so we can't be punished.'

10

Underground cave system, Dresse, Dresse system

WELT ARRIVED BACK in the lobby just as they exited the council chamber. His face was flushed and he seemed a bit out of breath.

'Where did you have to go in such a hurry?' Geerten asked him.

'Must've eaten something,' he said, pulling an awkward face and rubbing his stomach. 'What's been decided?'

'Get them on some calloppes and away from here,' said Geerten.

'Point them in the direction of Daamt Rise,' added Kolde.

'Daamt Rise!' exclaimed Welt. 'They can't go there. The perimeter weapons will cut them to pieces.'

'The council want them gone,' said Kolde.

'Guilder won't be very happy losing three calloppes,' said Welt.

'Four counting mine,' said Kolde.

'Five,' said Geerten, pointing at himself.

'You two can't go,' said Welt, his eyes wide. 'It's suicide.'

'Someone has to show them the way,' said Kolde. 'Doesn't mean I'm going to try and enter Daamt too. They're quite welcome to that.'

Kolde and Geerten both stared at Welt, their eyebrows raised.

'No—no way,' said Welt. 'My family need to know where I am.'

'Your family aren't here,' said Kolde.

Welt glowered at him.

'They could come home at any time,' he hissed through gritted teeth.

Kolde shrugged.

'Suit yourself,' he said, turning to Bache and beckoning him to follow. 'Come on, let's go while there's still enough daylight to get there.'

Kolde and Geerten led them through to the far side of the town and across another retractable bridge. An arched doorway in the rock wall beckoned.

'Hey, Guilder,' shouted Kolde. 'Seat up five smellies.'

Bache saw Zaphir give him a sideways glance.

'I fucking hate big animals,' she said.

Bache remembered her falling off a Garlander on holiday once and promising to never get on the back of an animal ever again.

'I'm sure they're not that big,' he said, as he followed her through the archway.

She stopped dead in her tracks, causing Bache to bump into her.

'Ah, crap,' she said, staring at a large corral

full of what looked like giant sabre-toothed polecats.

'Don't worry,' said Geerten. 'They rarely bite.'

'I would've preferred never bite,' mumbled Malic, from behind.

'Even Garlanders would've been better than those monsters,' moaned Zaphir.

Guilder, a short stumpy man with a short-trimmed beard, lurched out of a hut on the right-hand side and leered at the girls.

'Why aren't they under cover?' he grouched, jutting his chin at Zaphir and Malic.

'Because we don't subscribe to your sexist bullshit,' Zaphir spat back, eyeing the man with complete disdain.

His eyes widened at the rebuke and stepping forward towards Zaphir he swept up his hand. Kolde snatched hold of the raised arm and shook his head slowly at Guilder.

'They're from a different world,' he said, calmly. 'They have different rules to us.'

Guilder pulled his arm back forcibly and sneered at Kolde.

'They should have respect for our customs, they haven't even covered their faces,' he hissed.

Kolde looked apologetically at Bache, who shrugged and as he turned, noticed something of interest inside Guilder's hut.

'What's that?' he asked, pointing, walking over and stepping inside.

'Hey,' exclaimed Guilder. 'You can't go in there.'

At that exact moment, five purrers entered the cavern from the opposite direction in military-style uniforms and helmets with weapons up.

'Nobody move,' one of them shouted in Guasse, as they fanned out and covered the five of them standing outside the hut.

Bache ducked down inside, turned his translator off and swung his laser rifle off his shoulder. It appeared they didn't know he was there. He heard Kolde mumble something, but without the translator, he didn't know what.

'Where's the rest of them?' the same purrer demanded.

Zaphir and Malic looked at Kolde for a translation, but didn't get one.

'This is all of them,' he stammered, trying not to glance at the hut.

'That's a lie,' said the purrer. 'They came in a GDA marine-issue gunship. There will be at least six of them and not just two females.'

Before Guilder, Kolde or Geerten could reply, a voice boomed out of the hut in Ellinika.

'You are surrounded—drop your weapons or you will be engaged,' Bache shouted in the biggest voice he could muster, his words echoing around the cavern that made it difficult for the purrers to place.

'There are many more of us on the way,' the lead purrer announced. 'You will be—'

A laser bolt flashed across the cavern from the hut, hitting the lead purrer in the centre of his chest. The other four froze as their leader crashed to the floor.

'I said drop your weapons,' Bache bellowed.

The four eyed each other nervously, before one of them crouched down slowly and placed his hand weapon gently on the ground. The other three following along in a similar fashion shortly after. All of them staring incredulously at their leader's crumpled body.

'Now, step away two paces and lie on the ground face down,' Bache continued, as Zaphir covered them with her rifle and Malic moved forward to collect their weapons.

Guilder, Kolde and Geerten stared on in disbelief.

'We are in so much shit now,' said Geerten.

'You'll be fine,' said Bache, emerging from the hut with the translator turned back on and a tablet in his fist. 'Where did you get this?' he asked Guilder.

'Found it in the woods,' he stammered. 'One of them must've dropped it,' he added, nodding at the purrers.

Bache nodded, rummaged around in his backpack and gave Malic and Zaphir some plastic ties. 'Secure them with these and we'll lock them in the hut.'

'I don't want those smelly things in my hut,' said Guilder, nervously eyeing the body of the leader lying a few metres away. 'Especially not a dead one, because I'll get the blame.'

'He's not dead,' said Bache, holding up his rifle. 'I had it set on a high stun setting.'

'You mean it's just knocked him unconscious?' Kolde asked.

'Yeah,' said Zaphir. 'He'll have a scorch mark and a headache for a while, but otherwise he'll live.'

'Oh shit,' said Geerten, exchanging a glance with Kolde. 'He's a priden too.'

'A what?' Zaphir asked, grabbing hold of the unconscious man's collar and dragging him towards the hut.

'Those silver rings on his arm indicate he's a priden. A senior leader within their organisation.'

'Well, bully for him,' she said, dumping him unceremoniously on the wooden floor.

'Strip his uniform,' said Bache, poking his head in the door. 'I have an idea.'

Zaphir looked at the unconscious body and then back at Bache.

'If you're thinking of wearing the uniform, I

think there might be a bit of a problem with your face. It'll be obvious from metres away you're not a Gata,' she said.

'Not with the helmet's dark visor down,' he replied, with a smirk. 'They're similar to the GDA marine-issue ones and completely cover the whole of your face. They've most likely left a sixth member of the team and pilot watching over the flyer.'

'Hmm,' grunted Zaphir. 'You really are an ideas man aren't you?'

'Saved my life more than once,' he said, moving out the way as Malic pushed the first of the other four blindfolded and cuffed purrers inside. The other three soon followed and were all secured to a central post holding the ceiling up.

'Shall we go and misappropriate a flying vehicle?' said Bache, when they were done and the hut door had been sealed.

'Always had a soft spot for a smartly dressed man,' said Malic, admiring Bache in the priden uniform.

'Oi, behave,' Zaphir snapped, the touch of jealousy in her tone not going unnoticed.

Kolde, Geerten and Guilder stood leaning on the animal corral, their faces a sea of worry.

'What do we do now?' Geerten asked.

Bache gave each of them a purrer weapon.

'Any trouble, shoot them,' he said.

Guilder looked at the laser pistol in his hand as if it might bite him.

'But theirs don't have a stun setting,' he said.

'Make sure you bury the bodies deep then,' said Zaphir without a hint of sarcasm. 'Remember what they did to your females not so long ago.'

'They'll have a flyer somewhere outside,' Bache said to Zaphir before turning to Kolde. 'We'll take it from here, while you deal with them.'

This did nothing to allay the locals fear as they stood staring at Guilder's hut while Bache led Zaphir and Malic away.

'Thanks for your help and good luck, guys,' said Bache over his shoulder, as they made their way towards the arched door the purrers had entered through.

Kolde came rushing up to them as they exited the cavern and followed a passageway downwards.

'It's just occurred to me, how did they know you were here?' he asked, a real look of concern on his face.

'Well, we didn't tell 'em,' Bache answered, leaving a perplexed and even more worried Kolde standing in the passage.

'Stay safe,' Bache heard him call, just before the translator was out of range.

11

Underground cave system, Dresse, Dresse system

THE PASSAGEWAY WAS LESS than a hundred metres in length and turned sharp left at the end, terminating in a narrow gap that Bache realised was just wide enough for those animals to squeeze through.

He put his finger to his lips and signalled for Zaphir and Malic to wait, as he crouched down and peeked through and into the brightness beyond.

It took a few moments for his eyes to adjust before he saw a flyer parked twenty metres away. A purrer sat in the doorway cradling a weapon and swinging his legs nonchalantly.

Bache watched him for a while, remaining hidden in the gloom of the cave entrance. The purrer seemed relaxed and didn't have his finger on the trigger of his weapon.

Turning, Bache whispered instructions to the girls before all three moved out, the girls with hands on their heads and Bache with the helmet's visor down. The uniform didn't fit him perfectly, but he hoped it was good enough to get him within easy range of the pilot before he realised all was not as it seemed.

In the time it had taken them to prepare and emerge, the pilot had pulled out a tablet which worked in their favour. His attention was elsewhere and they managed to approach to within ten metres before he detected the movement in his peripheral vision. Jumping up and uttering something in Guasse, probably an apology to his superior officer regarding his lapse in attention, he jumped down to provide an open door for the prisoners to board the flyer. It was obvious his attention was on the prisoners, as Bache got within three metres of him before giving him the good news square in the chest.

The pilot slumped back against the fuselage, his pistol dropping from his hand. Malic leapt over and grabbed the weapon as the pilot slid down the flyer, sitting hard on his haunches, with a shocked expression on his face.

Bache had given him the lowest stun setting the rifle had, as they might need him to operate the flyer. He was still having involuntary spasms as Zaphir and Bache picked him up and bundled him up into the aircraft.

Turning his translator back on, Bache spoke to the pilot for the first time.

'You will fly us back to Daamt Rise, or I'll be turning the settings up on this,' he said, prodding the purrer in the chest with the rifle.

'I—I can't,' he spluttered, his eyes never

leaving the rifle. 'My priden will have me executed.'

'Well, that just makes you surplus to requirements doesn't it? So we might as well get rid of you anyway,' said Zaphir, ensuring he saw her clicking her rifle up to its maximum setting.

'And your priden isn't feeling very well at the moment,' said Bache, brushing the sleeves of his uniform poignantly.

The purrer's feline eyes opened wide at the realisation.

'That's his uniform isn't it?' he said.

Bache smiled.

'Care to get this thing in the air now?' he said.

The pilot stared at the uniform for a moment, then at Zaphir who casually clicked the safety switch on her weapon to the off position and returned his look with a steadfast glare.

Reluctantly and with difficulty he clambered off the floor and into the pilot's seat. Zaphir watched closely as he prepped the flyer for take-off, the low grumble of the antigravs on startup soon becoming a more businesslike howl.

'You do realise Daamt Rise is a remote citadel?' the purrer said, his hands hovering over the controls. 'With a contingent of fifty five. You can't take that on with just three of you.'

'Fly it now,' Zaphir snarled from the co-pilot's seat and reached across to poke the pilot in the ear with the muzzle of her weapon.

He emitted a low growl before lifting the aircraft, and turned inland away from the ocean towards a range of distant snow-capped mountains.

It was only an eight-minute journey which explained how the purrers had got to the underground town so quickly. The pilot pointed towards a low cavern underneath an overhanging ridge of solid rock.

'Daamt Rise,' he said. 'Do you want me to fly straight in?'

'Is that what you would normally do?' Bache asked.

'Yeah,' said the pilot, nodding.

Zaphir gave him a prod with her weapon again and raised her eyebrows questioningly.

'Yes, yes it is,' he said nervously. 'It'd be

considered very odd if I landed out here or something.'

'In you go then,' said Bache, waving towards the opening. 'Do anything weird or out of the ordinary to warn them…' he nodded at Zaphir '…then I'll let her decide your fate.'

The pilot glanced at Zaphir who raised her top lip and growled. He grimaced and let the aircraft descend and slowly slip under the overhang and into the gloom of the cavern.

Bright floodlights on the front of the flyer came on automatically, illuminating marked landing areas big enough for six aircraft. All of them were empty.

'That's strange,' mumbled the pilot.

'What is?' asked Zaphir, giving the purrer a jab in the ribs with her weapon.

'No one's called to indicate which pad I'm supposed to land on.'

'And they normally do?' Bache questioned.

'Always.'

The pilot swept the powerful lights around from left to right, illuminating all corners of the cavern.

'There's no one here,' he said, sounding genuinely bewildered.

'You better not have warned them,' growled Zaphir. 'Or I'm going to stick those furry ears of yours up your arse.'

Malic gave Bache a questioning glance.

'Yeah,' he whispered in reply. 'She would too.'

'No, genuinely,' the pilot replied, wincing at Zaphir's statement. 'There's always ground crew waiting and all the flyers aren't allowed out at the same time in case of an emergency evac.'

'Land in that corner facing out,' said Bache, pointing to the right-hand side.

The flyer turned and clunked down on the hardstanding, its motors gradually spinning down to an idle, until finally they went silent. They sat, watched and waited for a few moments. Nothing moved. The only sound was the antigravs ticking behind them as they cooled.

'Looks like a trap to me,' said Malic. 'As soon as we step out the door.'

They all turned to stare at the pilot, who

raised his hands in front of him and shook his head vigorously.

'If it is, it didn't come from me,' he said. 'There's something odd going on here. The defensive perimeter weapons didn't demand our disarm code either, which has never happened before.'

A sudden chime from the control console made them all jump. A screen lit up with a message written in Guasse.

'Well?' said Zaphir to the pilot. 'What is it?'

The purrer leant over and read the screen.

'A message for the priden,' he said. 'Demanding his location. Oh, and why he hasn't acknowledged the previous message.'

'What's the previous message?' Bache asked.

The pilot tapped away on the screen for a moment, his feline ears dropping flat against his head as he read what appeared on the screen.

'Well?' grumbled Zaphir.

'Erm,' the pilot grunted, looking up nervously. 'It's a shutdown order and full personnel recall back to Ballenhyght.'

'Does this happen often?' Bache asked.

'Never,' the purrer replied. 'It's never happened before.'

'Wadda we do?' Malic questioned. 'We can't go there, there'll be thousands of them.'

'Acknowledge both messages,' said Bache, thinking fast. 'Tell them we're on our way.'

'Are you insane?' said the purrer, his large eyes wide with astonishment. 'It'd be suicide.'

'Just send the messages,' said Zaphir. 'I read Guasse, so don't try and warn them either,' she added, lying.

The pilot, shrugged and turned back to the screen.

'Impersonating a priden,' he mumbled. 'That's another death sentence to add to my list.'

The transmissions were sent, closely followed by a reply. The pilot sat back in his seat after reading it. Bache noticed he seemed surprised, almost shocked by the wording.

'What is it?' he asked.

The pilot sat and stared at the screen for a few moments before he replied.

'They've ordered me to land inside a hangar

on one of the battleships ready for immediate launch,' he said slowly, almost as if he didn't believe it.

'I take it these big ships don't get launched very often?' Bache asked.

The purrer turned to look at him. Bache thought he looked scared, which wasn't a trait often attributed to a Gata.

'What is it?' Bache asked, pushing the pilot for an answer.

'Err, we were always told the big ships would only be launched when they were going to be used,' he said.

'For what?' Zaphir asked.

'We were never told,' he replied. 'Only the pridens had that information. Or so we thought. It was always compartmentalised. Perhaps they're not told either, I don't know.'

'What do we do?' Zaphir asked, glancing at Bache.

Bache stared out the front screen at the empty garrison and sighed.

'Well, it's pointless sitting around here,' he said. 'Everything seems to be happening on the other side of the planet.' He turned to the pilot. 'Better do as your superiors say then and go find your battleship.'

'Okay,' the pilot said, spinning up the anti-gravs again. 'It's your funeral.'

12

Purrer flyer, approaching Ballenhyght, Dresse,
Dresse system

'HOLY CRAP, BACHE,' exclaimed Zaphir. 'Are you sure you want to go inside one of those things?'

Bache's eyes widened as he looked out over the mountain top and surveyed the valley beyond.

'I did warn you,' the pilot said, as his autopilot locked on to the approach path to cavern 12. The bow of a huge battleship could be seen lurking within.

The deep valley was almost filled with five more hulking black starships. They really were on a scale unknown outside of the GDA. They hung as if weightless a few hundred metres above the surface. Each at least five kilometres in length and bristling with huge weapon nacelles. So much so, that hardly a flat or smooth section of hull existed over their entire outer surface.

Bache couldn't remember ever seeing starships more geared up for war than these ugly black monstrosities.

'Oh shit,' was all he could think to say.

'The *K2* doesn't want to stumble into this lot without some warning,' said Zaphir.

'It doesn't want to stumble into them at all,' Bache added. 'This is not good.'

'There's only six here,' said the pilot. 'Eight must be up in orbit already.'

'There's eight more of them?' Bache asked,

staring at the purrer. 'Ancients save us, we need the whole bloody fleet here. When we were told you were building fourteen ships here, I didn't consider they would be on this scale.'

'What are they for?' Malic asked. 'Or more importantly, who are they for?' aiming the question at the pilot.

'Again, we've never been told, only the pridens have that information,' he said, sitting back as the autopilot did all the work. 'But whoever they're for, they're not going to be very happy.'

'Or alive for long,' said Zaphir. 'Something this big is an invasion fleet.'

As she spoke, one of the warships disappeared, reappearing seconds later.

'Cloaking test,' said Zaphir. 'It's what the GDA ships do before a deployment.'

'Do we really want to continue on inside one of those monsters?' Malic asked.

Bache and Zaphir exchanged a look, but before either of them could say anything, the pilot spoke.

'Doesn't matter what you decide,' he said.

'They're in command of this flyer now, I couldn't divert even if I wanted to.'

'We'd better hide,' said Malic.

'That won't work either,' said the purrer. 'The priden informed them he would be bringing in the GDA spies before he went into the cave. I imagine there'll be a security cadre waiting to board and arrest you.'

'Oh joy of joys,' said Zaphir. 'And you were going to tell us this when exactly?'

The pilot shrugged and sank back into his seat with a wry smile and crossed his arms.

'You're my enemy, why would I?' he said smugly.

Zaphir snarled and shot him from point blank range. A look of shock replaced the smile as the purrer slumped backwards, unconscious on the cabin floor.

'Condescending bastard,' she said, as Malic took a step back and looked at Zaphir with a mixture of disbelief and apprehension.

'Zaffie, get his uniform on quickly,' said Bache, pointing. 'His helmet's over there.'

Malic quickly helped her as the small flyer neared the port side of their designated warship. It went suddenly very gloomy in the cockpit as the flyer entered the cavern. Zaphir just managed to get the helmet on as the automated systems took them along the hull of the battleship and inside one of many hangars. It clunked the flyer down next to a row of spacefaring shuttles.

The pilot had been correct, as four armed Gatas ripped open the flyer's side door and piled on board, the bright white hangar lights reflecting off their gleaming black body armour. One of them, Bache presumed, was the senior officer as he had gold triangular motifs pierced with a lightning bolt on his arms, and he stared at everyone in turn before speaking.

'Only one?' he said, abruptly, his face hidden behind his dark visor. 'I was informed there were three of them.'

Bache winced as he realised he'd forgotten to turn his translator off and the Gata's words were being translated into Ellinika. The officer who'd spoken jerked back and fumbled for his weapon.

It made no difference to the outcome however, as Bache and Zaphir both had laser weapons activated and ready to go, unlike the newcomers who had their safeties on and weapons pointing at the floor.

Three seconds later, all four were unconscious on the deck. Bache stepped over the bodies, checked outside and, finding the hangar otherwise deserted, pushed the door closed again.

'I don't imagine we have long before they'll be missed,' he said. 'These uniforms look more senior and are from this region. So we're more likely to be ignored wearing them,' he added, as he bent down and pulled the helmet off one of the unconscious Gatas.

They all gasped as the face beneath wasn't feline and fur-covered, but clean-shaven and human.

'What the actual fuck?' said Zaphir. 'Is he one of the indigenous locals?'

'No,' said Bache. 'They're all tall and lean because of the low gravity. This man's from a heavier gravity world, like us.'

Zaphir stepped over and pulled the man's sleeve up.

'Oh shit,' she said, turning his wrist upwards so Bache could see the small scar in the middle of his forearm.

'What's that?' Malic asked, peering over Bache's shoulder.

'Something I'm hoping it's not,' said Bache, rummaging in his backpack and extracting his tablet. He surfed through its menu until he found what he was looking for and waved the tablet over the small scar. A double beep sounded. He exhaled loudly and his shoulders slumped as he read the screen.

'Who is it?' Zaphir asked, leaning over to read the data. 'Detective Captain Deelaine Hakk,' she read, her eyes lifting to meet Bache's. 'He's a bloody GDA Skirmat.'

'Mother of crap,' said Bache, crossing over to one of the others. 'I hate these guys.'

'They're not going to be very happy with you either,' said Malic, eyeing the unconscious policeman nervously.

Bache scanned the wrists of the other three and grimaced at the screen.

'All of them?' Zaphir asked.

'All of them, what?' said Bache.

'Skirmat,' she snapped, abruptly.

'No, only him,' he said, pointing at the first one. 'These are all ex-marines.'

'What—GDA marines?' she said, yanking off one of their helmets. Another unconscious human face stared back at her. 'He looks too young to have retired,' she added.

'That's quite correct,' said Bache. 'All three of these are dishonourably discharged marines and should all be serving life sentences for murder.'

'You're kidding,' said Malic. 'What the hell is going on here?'

'D'you think we've stumbled into some sort of GDA black op?' asked Zaphir.

Bache shook his head.

'I don't think so,' he said, rubbing his chin in thought. 'If it was a legitimate GDA operation, then the *K2* wouldn't have been authorised to come here.'

'You believe this is unsanctioned then?' Malic asked.

'Wouldn't be the first corrupt Skirmat we've come across,' said Zaphir, giving Bache a knowing glance.

Bache shivered at the thought of the situation he'd found himself in just before he enlisted a few years ago.

'Was that the Salft scandal?' Malic asked. 'Was that you two?' she exclaimed, a second later, staring at Bache and then at Zaphir.

Bache flinched before nodding slowly.

'Well, save the ancients,' said Malic. 'I read about that fiasco recently. They still let you enlist after that then?'

'Let him enlist!' exclaimed Zaphir. 'He's the president's blue-eyed boy. It was his image they used on all the navy recruitment posters.'

Malic looked at Bache with new-found respect.

'Can we stop with all the over-inflated bullshit,' Bache said. 'We need to make a decision on what we do now.'

'Warn the *K2*,' said Zaphir. 'They're going

to be in the shit if they meet this lot unexpectantly.'

'Quite right,' said Bache, putting his hands
on his hips and staring at the floor in thought.
'We need a plan and we need it quick.'

13

The bridge, Katadromiko 2, *approaching Dresse, Dresse system*

CAPTAIN GASTION WHIPPER watched as the holomap above him reset following their final jump into the Dresse system.

With the planet Dresse having a katapato red designation, regulations dictated they were required to jump in behind one of the system's stars, cloak and only then approach the planet.

He glanced over at the semicircle of array

officers poring over the data coming in as they emerged from behind the star.

'Any sign of the freighter and our gunship?' he asked.

'No, Captain,' wasn't the reply he wanted. Grunting and sitting back in his raised seat, he gazed up at the blue planet growing ever larger above. 'Where the hell are Loftt and Mye?' he said more to himself than any of his bridge crew around him.

'I have a small amount of debris, sir,' said one of the array officers glancing up at him questioningly.

'Ship debris?' he asked.

'Yes, sir. Judging by its speed and distance from the planet, I would estimate whatever happened occurred around eight hours ago if the event happened near the planet.'

Whipper grunted again.

'Can we tell if it's freighter or gunship?' he questioned.

'The composition dictates a ninety percent certainty it's freighter, sir.'

Whipper nodded and pointed at the planet

growing quickly now as they approached and skirted around one of Dresse's three moons.

'Anything on the surface?'

'No, sir—oh, hold that report, sir,' said the array officer. 'I have a marginal reading from a poor aspect. Just waiting for us to navigate around the planet a little more to get a firm reading.'

The bridge went quiet as the officer tapped away on his console for a few moments.

'It's the gunship, sir,' he said, looking up at the captain and nodding.

'What the hell's Loftt doing on the surface?' he mumbled.

'It's quite badly damaged too, Captain.'

'Ah, that's just wonderful,' Whipper grumbled. 'Any indigenous population anywhere near?'

'No, sir.'

'Well, thank the ancients for that,' he said. 'What about Loftt or Mye, or the freighter for that matter?'

'Nothing, sir.'

'Is the gunship in a condition to re-orbit?'

'Negative, sir.'

'What has he been up to?' Whipper groaned. 'Get a recovery ship down there quickly and quietly before it freaks the locals out. Don't open a hangar planet-side either, just in case there's an astronomer being nosey.'

'There's something odd with the population too, Captain,' said another of the bridge crew.

'In what way?' Whipper asked.

'Records of this planet from a few hundred years ago show a large population spread over the two main continents in many cities using mainly fossil fuels. They had flight but were non-spacefaring.'

'What's changed?'

'Everything, sir,' she said, her brow furrowing. 'Cities in ruins, no flight of any kind and a population a fraction of its original size all living in small primitive villages.'

'Perhaps they had a war or something,' said Whipper, as he watched an engineering ship leave one of the larger port hangars.

He turned suddenly as a shout from the opposite side of the bridge caught his attention.

'Multiple missiles incoming,' shouted one voice.

The huge vessel shuddered as dozens of heavy lasers struck their shields.

'Laser fire from at least twelve cloaked positions,' called another.

'What the fuck,' shouted Whipper, jumping to his feet. 'Where did all these come from?'

'Shields at forty-one percent and dropping,' came a call that the captain couldn't ignore.

'Pilot, emergency jump, now,' he bellowed.

The pilot was quick, but the ship still lurched to one side a fraction of a second before the jump took place. Alarms screamed their protests from more than half the bridge stations and an explosion at one console threw three crew across the floor.

'Are we away?' the captain called, clambering off the floor where he'd been thrown and sliding back into his seat.

'Yes, sir,' came a call from navigation.

'Get a medical team in here,' he shouted, pointing at the wounded officers on the far side of the bridge. 'Damage report?' he continued, turning to glare at the first officer.

'Multiple hull breaches, Captain,' was the reply, as the stern-faced officer stared at his screens. 'The array has taken a hit and propulsion is offline.'

'Do we have any idea who the hell that was?' Whipper asked.

'No, sir. There were at least twelve sizeable vessels, they were cloaked and using tycelerin warhead missiles. It was one of those that hit our shields as we jumped that caused the damage. If we hadn't jumped, we would most likely have been destroyed.'

Whipper glanced up at the holomap. It was glitching, fading in and out and showing very little.

'Are we safe here, wherever we are?' he asked. 'Are they able to follow?'

'The jump was un-embedded, Captain,' replied the navigator. 'We're fifty-six light years away in clear space, so they're likely to follow us and our cloaking is down.'

'Damn. Get engineering teams on-to this immediately, priority propulsion, the cloak and the array.'

'Yes, sir.'

'Who the hell would use tycelerin missiles?' he mumbled, as a medical team rushed in. 'They've been outlawed for generations.'

'Within the GDA worlds,' said the first officer. 'I have a feeling they weren't GDA. Only we have shipborne lasers of that power and they had top-notch cloaking too.'

'No wonder Loftt's ship was damaged,' said Whipper. 'I'm amazed he avoided all that in a gunship and was able to land the bloody thing.'

'Are we reporting the freighter as destroyed, sir?' a crew member asked.

Whipper thought about that for a few moments before answering.

'Send a drone back to Dasos with all the information we have, but don't confirm the freighter as lost quite yet. There was debris, but only a very small amount. Not enough to warrant an entire ship.'

'Understood. On its way, sir.'

'How are we doing on the hull breaches?' he asked.

'Temporary shield zones employed, Captain. Main shields are up and back to full strength.'

Whipper nodded and watched as one of the injured bridge crew was stretchered past him.

'Other casualties?' he asked.

'Several hundred injured and seventeen unaccounted for at the present time, sir,' came the subdued reply.

His brow furrowed as he watched the stretcher party leave the bridge.

'I don't know who these fuckers are,' he growled, 'but they're going to pay dearly for this. Have all weapons systems that are still operational charged and on full alert. The fighters out too.'

'All of them, sir?'

'Yes. If any one of those bastards follows us, give them everything we've got.'

'Are you authorising the nukes too, sir?'

'I did say everything.'

14

Battleship Heliotrope, *Ballenhyght, Dresse,*
Dresse system

'THE SHIP'S ASCENDING,' said Malic, staring out of the flyer's front screen.

Bache and Zaphir joined her and watched as the mountains visible in the distance fell away outside the huge hangar door, replaced by clouds rushing by vertically.

'Well, it wasn't the way I had envisioned

getting back into space,' said Bache. 'But it's probably done us a favour.'

'How d'you figure that?' Zaphir asked.

'If we were to steal one of those,' he pointed to the line of shuttles out the side window, 'we could just jump away now and not have to be vulnerable on the ascent into space.'

'That's if we can work out how to fly the bloody things,' moaned Zaphir, waving her hand at the control console.

'Haven't you noticed something?' said Bache, reaching over and touch-illuminating a screen on the left-hand side of the pilot's console. He opened a menu and even though everything was written in Guasse, he seemed to know what to press. After flicking through several screens, he grunted and smiled, flamboyantly pressing the last icon with a flourish. The language on the screen suddenly changed to Ellinika.

'Ta, da,' he said.

'Well, slap my thigh with a wet flannel,' exclaimed Zaphir.

'How did you know?' Malic asked.

'My father taught me the workings of GDA technology from an early age,' he said. 'I recognised the basic layout of the software even though it was in a different language and I'll wager those shuttles out there are using stolen GDA tech too.'

The lighting out in the hangar suddenly went a dull red.

'I think we've just cloaked,' said Zaphir. 'Shall we steal something a bit more useful?' while she cracked the flyer's door slightly and peeked out to check the coast was clear.

'What about these?' Malic asked, nodding at the bodies strewn around the floor.

'Leave them,' said Bache. 'They'll be out for a few hours yet. Visor down, Zaffie, remember we're escorting a prisoner.'

They jumped down from the flyer as a distant thudding noise started up from somewhere deep within the vessel.

'What the ancients is that?' Malic asked.

'Heavy lasers,' said Bache.

'Are they testing them or something?'

Before Bache could answer her, the back

hangar door swished to one side and dozens of soldiers in full battle armour poured into the room. He saw Zaphir beginning to raise her weapon and slapped his hand on top of the rifle, while shaking his head.

'We don't stand a chance,' he whispered, as the threesome stopped and stood very still.

Instead of surrounding them the soldiers made straight for the shuttles, bypassing them with barely a glance. They piled aboard the small ships, distributing themselves evenly across the twenty or so vessels.

'Where are they off to?' Zaphir called, above the sudden whine of antigravs on startup.

'That's a good question,' said Bache. 'We're in space now, it can only be to board another ship. They wouldn't come all the way up here, only to go back down again in smaller ships.'

Zaphir was silent for a moment before she turned towards Bache, her face obscured by the dark visor.

'Are you thinking what I'm thinking?' she said. The nervous edge to her voice caused Malic to turn and stare at them.

'What's going on?' she asked.

A bright flash from outside lit the hangar like daylight for a second and the distant thudding of the ship's heavy lasers stopped abruptly.

'It could've been the arrival of the *K2*,' said Bache. 'And that's what they were firing at. These are some of the boarding party preparing to take the ship.'

'You're kidding?' Malic said, looking back at the shuttles nervously.

'Fourteen cloaked warships of this size suddenly opening up on you would need some quick reactions from the bridge crew,' said Zaphir, as the clamour of the antigravs began to lessen again.

'I hope that flash wasn't the *K2*,' said Zaphir.

Bache glanced over at the nearest shuttle.

'The troops aren't moving,' he said. 'That's a good sign. Come on, we need to move so we don't look so conspicuous.'

The trio moved off again, this time towards the hangar exit. Bache turned his translator off and slipped it into a pocket, hoping the Skirmats only spoke Ellinika and not Guasse.

'We need to get to another hangar and find something to get off this thing,' said Bache. 'If that was the *K2*, Mr Whippy will be spitting fire right at this moment and plotting some serious payback.'

The red lighting in the hangar dimmed slightly as they reached the door. Bache looked over his shoulder to see the starfield fade into focus outside.

'We've just jumped,' he said. 'Probably chasing the *K2*.'

'Let's hope they don't...'

The whine of the shuttle's antigravs behind them started to increase again.

'Skata,' swore Bache. 'We need to hurry. The *K2* must be damaged if they've found her this quick.'

They began to run, turning right through the airlock and down a wide corridor. The thudding of the heavy lasers started up again causing Bache to swear under his breath. He was hoping the hangars were all on one level. About four hundred metres further down, they came to another airlock doorway slightly smaller than the one they'd passed through a few moments ago. Unlike that one, this one had both doors closed.

Looking through the porthole window didn't provide any answers, so he pressed what he hoped was the open icon on a recessed screen to the left of the door. A clunk indicating the locking bolts disengaging was encouraging and sure enough the heavy blast-proof door motored away to the right.

This time it was Zaphir who made it to the internal door porthole first. She whistled under her breath as she peered in.

'What have we got?' Bache asked.

'Maintenance hangar I think. It's dark in there,' she said, moving over so Bache could see in.

It was very dark inside, so he raised his visor. What he saw made him smile.

'What the crap is that weird thing?' Zaphir asked, raising her visor and peering over his shoulder.

'It's a cutter,' said Bache.

'A what?' asked Malic, taking her turn to peek inside.

'It's for repairing and replacing sections of hull, at least I think it is. Slightly different to the ones I've seen on GDA ships. That might prove really useful.'

'What are you going to do, cut the ship into little bits then?' said Zaphir, with a smirk.

Bache grinned at her. She stared back at him in disbelief.

'You're kidding, right?'

'Nope.'

The bridge, Katadromiko 2, approaching Dresse, Dresse system

CAPTAIN GASTION WHIPPER turned suddenly as a fresh alarm sounded behind him.

'What is it?' he asked, jumping down from his raised podium and approaching the line of defensive measures officers.

'They've found us, sir,' came the reply.

'Crap, that was quick,' he said, turning and pointing at the pilot. 'How long to an embedded jump, Lieutenant?'

'Seven minutes, sir,' the pilot replied, apologetically. 'Without the main array it takes longer to safely calculate.'

'How far away are they?' he asked, glancing up to where the holomap should be out of habit.

'Two hundred thousand kilometres, sir. There's two of them so far. No, make that three.'

'Are they cloaking?'

'No, sir.'

'They're over-confident, they think we're a sitting duck. Phase our shields in and out a bit,' he said. 'Make them think we're here for the taking and hold those fighters for a few moments. Let them come in close.'

Once the alarm had been silenced, it went very quiet on the bridge. Every officer in the room knew the vessel's very survival and the lives of forty-seven thousand crew depended on them doing their jobs quickly and accurately.

Whipper walked over to the offensive suite, a zone of control stations manned by operators wearing a plethora of direct eye apparatus, enabling them to direct their particular weapon targeting with eye movement.

'On my command, hit their lead ship with a narrow asteri beam with as much power as you can muster. Let's see how good their shields really are. And cannon operators, concentrate on any missiles they decide to launch and not on the ships. We can't risk another of those tycelerin missiles getting close again.'

'They're slowing, sir.'

'Range?'

'Ten thousand—eight—six—five. They're stopping, sir.'

The captain peered over the shoulder of one of the asteri beam operators and watched the three vessels spreading out. Weapons lock alarms began trilling as the three targeted the Katadromiko.

'Ugly bastards aren't they?' he said.

'Not familiar with the design, sir,' the operator said. 'Which one and where do I target?'

'I know you would normally target the array, but we don't know where it is on these ships, so hit the middle one dead centre and see if we can drain their shield generator.'

'Firing now, sir.'

The two metre-diameter bright white beam punched out from the *K2* striking the centre vessel's shields amidships. Immediately the ovoid and normally invisible barrier turned opaque, desperately attempting to dissipate the immense energy of the asteri beam. Though the beam initiator was more than three kilometres away from the bridge, the hum and vibration could be heard and felt through your feet. Even the lighting on the bridge dimmed slightly. The beam, as hot as the interior of a star, crackled around the vessel in vibrant displays of coloured lightning and blinded the ship's array and targeting systems.

Twenty-four of the Katadromiko's heavy cannons on the side facing the enemy also let fly with a barrage, similarly lighting up the other two enemy ships' shields.

'They've cloaked, sir,' came the call.

'Keep the fire constant and their shields will continue to fluoresce,' called Whipper. 'Kataligo missiles at the centre ship, now,' he called.

Sixty-two missiles flashed away, quickly disappearing into the backdrop of stars.

The other enemy ships hadn't delayed in returning fire. This time however there were only two of them and the laser operators on the Katadromiko were easily able to take out the missiles as they approached.

The ship shuddered as the enemies' heavy lasers pounded them however.

'Shields?' called Whipper, turning to point at the defence suite.

'Seventy-six percent, sir.'

'Jump time?' he asked, glancing at the pilot.

'Two minutes, Captain.'

He nodded.

Above him the holomap suddenly lit up, beautifully displaying the battle in three dimensions.

'Thank fuck for that,' said Whipper, as he watched in awe as their missiles reached their destinations.

Shielding his eyes from the flash, he looked back as he received from his left the shout he'd been waiting for.

'Their shields are down, Captain.'

Immediately turning to the asteri beam operator, he nodded.

'Do it,' he said, turning back to the holomap and feeling a twinge of remorse as he knew those two words had sentenced a lot of people to death.

The operator nodded in return and in the wave of his iris, cut the huge black ship in two. An explosion in its centre folded the vessel in half. Both the two and a half-kilometre halves crashed together, before hurtling away from each other, spilling debris, bodies and fluids from the severed ends. Internal explosions sparkled like distant stars, as the massive vessel's two parts began dismantling themselves. A handful of lifeboats could be seen punching out from the two halves, but not many.

An explosion on the right-hand enemy ship caught the captain's eye. But before he could speak, a voice told him the answer to the question he was about to ask.

'Their systems have just shut down, sir,' said

the young girl to his left. 'They're blind and defenceless.'

Whipper shook his head at the asteri beam operator who turned and raised his eyebrows.

'We don't need to kill everyone on that ship too,' he said. 'Just make sure its propulsion and weapons are taken out and everyone else concentrate your fire on the third ship now.'

As the captain watched, lumps of drive cones and cannon nacelles exploding out from the second ship, the third one began moving away, its cannon fire lessening as it turned and fled. It jumped away moments later.

A spontaneous cheer resonated around the bridge as the captain stepped back up onto his rostrum. He held his hand up to quieten everyone down.

'Well done, everyone, I'm proud of you all,' he said, holding a finger up. 'Remember, we're not out of this yet. We need to grab some of the survivors to interrogate and get away from here before the others find out what happened and they all turn up for revenge.'

He pointed at the pilot.

'Ready?'

'We are, Captain.'

'Okay, let's tractor in some of those lifeboats and get away from this mess.'

'Captain,' called one of the communications officers. 'I'm getting a very strange signal from the wreckage of the second vessel, sir.'

16
____

Battleship Heliotrope, *non-system space*

BACHE CLOSED THE OUTER DOOR, opened the inner one and stepped inside the small hangar. Walking over to the strange ugly machine, he rubbed a bit of dust off the front screen and peeked inside. He turned and grinned at Zaphir again.

'Room for three?' she asked.

'It'll be cosy,' said Bache, glancing at the wall to his right and pointing. 'We want that attachment on it too.'

'What is it?' asked Zaphir.

'A plasma torch,' Malic said. 'A very powerful one.'

'That's all well and good,' said Zaphir. 'But who's going to fly the thing?'

Bache dropped down underneath the cutter and opened the small cockpit pressure hatch. Climbing inside, he sat on the operator's seat and surveyed the touchscreen and joystick controls that faced him.

'I thought so,' he said, smirking, as Zaphir squeezed up beside him and eyed the controls warily.

'You're familiar with this operator layout aren't you?' she said.

'It's the same as my old skouter back home,' he said. 'At least the flying controls are. It'll be a little bit of hit and miss with the cutting torch, but I'm sure you'll get the hang of it.'

'Me!' exclaimed Zaphir. 'How would I know how to operate the bloody thing?'

'I can,' said a voice below them.

They both glanced down as Malic struggled

her way up into the tight confines of the cabin and surveyed the layout in front of her. She grinned and raised her eyebrows at Bache.

'That's really weird, it's the same design as the one I trained on for my category four space engineering certificate. Move over, you two.'

They did as she asked and after a bit of manoeuvring and swearing, they managed to get Malic into the operator's seat, with Bache and Zaphir squashed in at each shoulder.

'Right,' she said, touching icons on the panel, causing it to light up and a head-up display to appear on the front screen. A single noisy antigrav began spinning up behind them.

'Should be wearing a helmet with ear defenders really,' Malic shouted above the racket.

Once the motor was at optimal, she motored the door closed beneath them. An audible hiss sounded as the cockpit became airtight and she lifted the machine, turned it towards the torch hanging in its rack on the wall and expertly pushed the cutter into the four pickup points. A loud clack echoed around the cockpit as she locked it into place.

'I'm chuffed with that,' she shouted, raising a fist. 'Didn't lock it in first time ever during training.'

'Awesome,' said Bache, peering over his shoulder. 'Do you know how to open the outer door?' he asked, pointing behind with his thumb.

'No,' she answered, trying a few unfamiliar buttons and switches around the cockpit as the machine turned, that appeared to do absolutely nothing. 'But I do have a master key,' she said.

They all squinted as Malic lit up the bright white plasma torch and proceeded to cut the door out of its frame.

'Be careful with the…'

The machine jolted forward and crashed into the door, jerking the three of them forward savagely.

'…decompression,' grunted Bache, rubbing his wrenched neck muscles.

'Sorry,' said Malic. 'Forgot about that.'

Once the atmosphere had completely vented from the small hangar, she was quickly able to finish the job and push the door out in front of them. She triggered the tractor beam that would

prevent them being left behind if the ship ma-
noeuvred and dropped down the side of the
monstrous vessel.

'Okay, what do we do now?' Malic asked.

Before Bache could answer, the heavy cannons along the side of the ship opened up,
making them all jump.

'Bloody ancients,' said Zaphir. 'I'm glad we
weren't in front of one of those.'

Bache peered off into the distance, following the laser bolts as they flashed away. He
could see the faint glow of a ship's shields dissipating the energy many hundreds of kilometres
away.

'That's got to be the *K2*,' he said. 'We need
to work fast. Go underneath the ship and cut into
anything that looks like an array nacelle.'

Malic dropped down the side of the ship as
fast as the machine would go, giving the laser
cannons a wide birth and staying close to the
hull so they couldn't be targeted.

'There,' said Zaphir, pointing to a large protuberance on the underside as they rounded the
corner.

'There's another further down,' said Bache. 'Whatever they are they've gotta be important.'

Everything suddenly lit up around them, as if they'd been caught in a spotlight. They all froze, thinking they'd been spotted.

'It's okay,' said Bache, staring downwards and shielding his eyes. 'It's the big ship's shields fluorescing. We're taking fire from the *K2*.'

Malic carried on towards the first large nacelle, the plasma torch not looking so bright anymore against the huge amount of energy dissipating a hundred metres above them.

'That's a bit disconcerting,' said Zaphir, her knuckles white as she gripped the side of Malic's seat.

'Don't forget, Malic, if we get their shields down with the damage we're about to inflict, get us away from the ship as quickly as possible, as the *K2* will target it with everything.'

'I'll punch us away and disengage the drive so we float and tumble as if we're wreckage,' she said.

They arrived at the nacelle and Malic didn't waste any time. The torch flared and hacked into and through the hull plating as if it was paper. Sections of plating soon became separated and floated off, so she could cut into whatever was inside.

She backed off as an explosion from within almost enveloped them in flame.

'Go on to the next big one,' said Bache, as a second internal explosion showered them in debris that rattled around the outside of the small vessel and off its collection of manipulator arms. Peering around, he noticed several of the nearby cannons had gone quiet and reckoned they'd knocked out their targeting array.

Malic did the same thing when they arrived at the bigger protuberance. It stuck out many metres from the hull and had a range of flat shiny circular discs all over it.

'That's an array for something serious,' said Zaphir, as Malic set about it with the cutter.

A sudden flash and crack blinded and deafened Bache. It jolted the whole machine and when his eyes recovered one of the manipulator arms had disappeared.

'What the fuck was that?' said Zaphir, as

Malic turned the machine so they could see behind them.

An armoured soldier stood about fifty metres away, a large rifle of some kind cradled in its mechanical arms. The thing began clumping towards them, his magnetic boots keeping him attached to the hull plates.

'Shit,' said Zaphir. 'I take it this thing isn't armed?'

'No,' said Malic. 'It isn't. But we do have other things," as she released the tractor beam and aimed it at the approaching soldier.

He stopped as the powerful beam locked on to him and tried to remain upright as the attraction caused the suit to bend forward at the waist. He began raising the weapon again, but hadn't thought that through, as the beam was more powerful than his mechanical fingers and snatched it away from him. It hurtled across the void and stuck to the beam emitter on the upper side of the machine.

Malic smiled, returned the beam to grip the hull and using two of the finer manipulator arms, she grabbed the weapon, turned it around, found its trigger mechanism and fired at the soldier. He was backing away as fast as his boots would allow. The shot went wide but Malic quickly readjusted her aim and the second shot removed one of the suit's arms. The suit went limp as a mixture of mechanical and body fluids blasted out of the severed socket, pushed out by the suit's pressurised atmosphere.

'Oh, no,' gasped Malic. 'I killed him.'

Bache realising she was in shock, grabbed the joysticks and turned the machine back towards the array.

'Fire on the array, Malic,' he said firmly, thinking it would be a good idea to give her something else to concentrate on.

She did as instructed. The big laser weapon, too heavy to use without a mechanical suit, ripped into the big array and after three shots the whole section of hull exploded outwards, again showering them with shrapnel. This time the front screen took a hit and cracked.

Below or above them, depending on which way you looked at it, the lightning display vanished as the big ship's shields failed. The next incoming laser fire from the *K2* hit the outer hull, tearing into the vessel and removing huge chunks of superstructure.

'Get out of here, Malic,' shouted Zaphir. 'Quickly, get away from the ship.'

Malic didn't need to be told twice. She disconnected the tractor, turned towards a load of debris expanding out from the big ship and shut the drive off. The cutter immediately began rolling and tumbling similar to the shrapnel around them.

Bache winced as a particularly large piece clattered against them and he eyed the cracked screen with trepidation.

'Can you bring the arms up to protect the screen and then shut everything down?' he asked. 'I don't want a particularly trigger-happy gunner mistaking our power signature as a threat.'

Malic did as he requested, causing it to go very dark and the temperature in the little vessel to noticeably and very quickly become cooler. They all ducked instinctively as a laser bolt flashed past only metres away.

As the tiny ship tumbled, they were given a regular view of the condition of the battleship. Every rotation they could see it was rapidly getting more and more second-hand. Then the firing stopped, from both directions. It appeared the battleship was as good as dead. It was almost unrecognisable from before, every visible weapon system had been erased and it drifted randomly, seemingly without any helm control, only the occasional explosion on board altering its trajectory.

'Can you stabilise us, Malic?' Bache asked. 'I need to send a directional message towards the *K2* before they jump away. I don't want this lot picking it up.'

He extracted his tablet from inside his jacket and began typing.

17

————

The bridge office, Katadromiko 2, *non-system*
space

CAPTAIN WHIPPER READ the message on his personal screen next to his seat and rolled his eyes.

"This is a message for Captain Whipper from Lieutenant Loftt, Lieutenant Mye and Junior Engineer Malic. We are in desperate need of a ride, a hot dinner and sympathy. Sorry about the gunship, I can explain."

'Fucking Loftt,' the captain muttered under his breath and turned to face one of the array officers. 'Where are they?'

'In a cutter, sir,' came the reply.

'What—a plasma cutter?'

'Yes, sir.'

'Where the ancients did they get that from?'

'I believe it was from the second dead battleship, as they're amongst its debris, sir—and it might explain why that ship's shields suddenly failed.'

'You're telling me Loftt was running around inside that battleship's shields removing lumps of it with its own plasma cutter?'

'Would explain a lot, sir.'

'Ancients help us—we'll never hear the end of it,' Whipper sighed. 'Send someone over there to tractor them in before they freeze to death.'

'Yes, sir.'

The captain's office, Katadromiko 2, *hiding in system D37459/PT*

'I don't know whether to reprimand you or give you a fucking medal,' growled Whipper, as he reclined behind his desk, staring at Bache standing rigidly to attention in front of him.

'If it's any consolation, sir, all the decisions were made jointly, so I'm equally to blame,' said Zaphir, standing bolt upright next to Bache.

Bache glanced at her out of the corner of his eye, as what she'd said wasn't entirely true.

'Hmm,' grunted the captain, eyeing them sceptically. 'Load of bullshit springs to mind. But then again, we survived with minimal casualties and the loss of a gunship—they lost two of apparently fourteen brand new battleships.'

The captain stood up, sat on the corner of his desk and stared up at a holographic image of one of the enemy battleships rotating slowly above them.

'Stand at ease, you two. Do we have any

idea what these ships are for?' he asked, his tone a little less officious than before.

'It's an invasion fleet for something, Captain, but what for, we never found out,' said Bache.

'Do we know where the rest of the civilian crew of the freighter went?'

'No, sir, although they were taken off the freighter alive. They weren't spaced or anything,' said Zaphir. 'Well, at least we don't think they were.'

'This Malic, the junior engineer. Is she legit?'

'Absolutely, sir,' said Bache.

'She wasn't deliberately left aboard to infiltrate us when we turned up?'

'No, sir, she definitely would've died on the freighter and it was her operating the cutter that cost them a battleship,' said Zaphir.

'Hmm, right,' said Whipper, sucking on his top lip for a moment as he stared up at the holomap. 'This ship's going to be fully operational again in a few hours. The first thing we're going to do is sneak back in there through the back door and see if we can find out where those ships are going and what their intentions are.'

He turned and jabbed a finger at Zaphir and Bache.

'You two, however, are going to take a tug and tractor that bloody gunship off the red classified planet before the locals decide to reverse-engineer it.'

'I don't think it can be classified as red anymore, sir,' said Zaphir, shrugging. 'Not after what these grey felines have been up to.'

Bache inched away from Zaphir, expecting her to get a tirade from the captain after that comment. He was surprised when she didn't.

'I tend to agree with you, Mye,' Whipper said, sitting back at his desk. 'But that is a decision for the council to make and not us. I've sent another drone back to Dasos with all the present data and we will wait for their decision and act on it accordingly.'

'Are we planning to engage them again if they're still around?' Bache asked.

'I think you already know the answer to that one, Loftt,' Whipper said, giving Bache a withering look. 'We might be able to overcome a couple of those ugly monsters, but there's still twelve more. They're not going to underestimate the power of one of these again.'

'I'm surprised they did this time by only sending two,' said Bache. 'The technology and control systems in those ships is all GDA. Bearing that in mind, you'd think they'd know the capabilities of a Katadromiko.'

Whipper steepled his fingers, puffed out his cheeks and stared at Bache in thought for a moment.

'Those ships have GDA kit in them—like stolen kit?' he asked.

'No, not physically stolen equipment. They've built their own, but the designs are based on GDA technology,' said Bache.

'Almost identical,' added Zaphir.

'That's a worry,' said Whipper. 'The council are really going to need to know that.'

His eyes drilled into the two of them for a moment.

'Are there any other important gems of information you've forgotten to tell me?'

Zaphir and Bache glanced at each other.

'Erm, well, the locals said the purrers have been here for twenty years,' said Zaphir. 'They arrived with a damaged ship that needed repair, but something changed and they decided to hang around and build the fleet of battleships, two of which you've already met.'

'They got excited about something they found in the mountains, some ore or something, and they started using slave labour to mine it,' said Bache.

'Do we know what it was they were mining?'

They both shook their heads.

'I have a suspicion tycelerin was involved,' said Whipper.

'What!' exclaimed Bache. 'That stuff's so dangerous—and illegal.'

'That's what did the damage to us. We need to beware,' Whipper sighed.

'They would need to be mining other ores too,' admitted Bache. 'You can't build fourteen starships of that scale without a lot of resources. The surviving indigenous population are scratching a living in the dirt. If their planet has mountains of all the elements required to construct advanced vessels on that scale, then they should be extremely affluent.'

'Well, the existence of other sentient humanoid civilisations is well and truly blown on that world,' said Zaphir. 'I'm sure the council will see sense and rapidly bring them into the GDA family. It would improve their wellbeing and prosperity tenfold.'

'Don't bet your life on it,' said Whipper. 'I've witnessed some very strange decisions made by the council over the years.'

He stood up, rounded the desk and, shaking both their hands, he nodded towards the door.

'Now, you two go and get a meal and some rest. I want that gunship off the surface as soon as we get back there.'

18

Maintenance hangar 59, Katadromiko 2, *non-system space*

TWELVE AND A HALF hours later Zaphir lifted one of *K2*'s heavy tugs off the deck and turned it towards the outer door, through which they both saw one of the system's stars rise up from behind Dresse and flood the hangar in sunlight. She paused and hovered for a moment, the tug's four huge antigravs thundering their disapproval behind.

'Nice view,' she said, tilting her head to one side.

'It is,' said Bache, rolling his eyes. 'But we're not on vacation, so can we go?' He peered out one of the side windows. 'The boss isn't too happy with you hanging around.'

Zaphir followed Bache's gaze to find the hangar supervisor waving at them frantically to get out the door.

'He's wearing ear defenders,' said Zaphir, shrugging. 'What's his problem?'

'Four class five antigravs in a confined area,' said Bache, sinking back into his seat with a smirk. 'Have you never stood near one of these as it sparks up?'

She shook her head as she ensured all its various exterior tools and manipulator arms were in their retracted positions, before squeezing the vessel through the only-just-big-enough doorway. The atmosphere shield buzzed around them as they emerged into the bright sunlight.

Deploying the heat shield below them, Zaphir dropped the ship bottom-first into the planet's night side.

Katadromiko 2 had arrived in the Dresse system again less than an hour ago and uncloaked as they approached the planet, the pilot's finger hovering over the jump icon with an embedded co-ordinate already programmed. Nothing happened. No battleships attacked. No planet-based cannon opened up. It was quiet and seemingly deserted.

Whipper immediately despatched four marine teams down to Ballenhyght. Scans had indicated a lot of smoke and dust and not much else, as the indigenous rock in this region proved extremely dense and scan-resistant.

On the opposite side of the planet, Zaphir and Bache sat back and watched the firework display ripping past the tug's carbon glass windows as they dropped lower into the darkness of Dresse's early morning.

'The marines get a nice sunny day,' whinged Zaphir, folding her arms and letting the automated systems guide their descent.

'It won't be dark for long,' said Bache. 'And anyway, we shouldn't need to land at all.'

'We will,' she said. 'I deployed a ground anchor when we landed and if you remember you set the anti-tamper to full power too.'

'Ah, yes, there is that,' he admitted. 'Best land first and shut those down.'

'Good plan, Lieutenant Obvious.'

Bache hadn't realised he'd dropped off for a while, when the sudden clunking of the ground struts deploying brought him to his senses.

'Bloody ancients, are we there?' he said, sitting up with a start.

'Just as well the pilot's awake, eh?' Zaphir scoffed, as she ignited the floodlights below them and swung the ship around in a big loop.

'I was just giving my eyelids an internal inspection,' said Bache, hopefully.

'Hmm,' grunted Zaphir.

'Don't you start doing that,' said Bache, scowling at her.

On seeing the coast was clear she came in close to the gunship and settled the tug down to the ground.

'Doing what?' she asked.

'Going "hmm", like Mr Whippy.'

'Oh, crap, I didn't, did I?'

The tug settled into the soil and tilted a little to starboard. They both sat for a moment to ensure it wasn't planning on toppling over. There was a thump from below and the tug lurched the other way.

'You'd best stay here and keep the motors hot,' Bache said, jumping to his feet. 'I'll pop across and turn everything off. Where's the ground anchor?'

'Flashing red icon on the bottom right of the pilot's console, press it so it goes green.'

Bache nodded, grabbed a laser pistol, ensured it was on medium stun and dropped down to the airlock on the port side.

As soon as he opened the outer door he wished he'd put a coat on, as the early morning chill went straight through his thin ship suit.

'Shit it's cold,' he shouted up to Zaphir.

'Shut the bloody door then,' she replied, stretching to turn the cockpit thermostat up a notch.

The tug's spotlights lit the small clearing like it was daylight, but Bache couldn't see anything beyond the tree line. He jumped down, his boots squelching on the wet ground. He squinted into the light drizzle and checked around to ensure he was alone, then grimacing at the noise of the tug's motors thundering above and behind him, he strode over to the gunship. He was careful not to touch the ship before he'd keyed in the code that disarmed the security field running through the hull, then he hurried inside the airlock as soon as the two doors motored away into their housings. Once inside, he leapt up the stairway to the cockpit. It didn't take him long to find the ground anchor release icon as it was the only one illuminated.

The ship juddered and tipped to starboard as he released it. He paused, his finger hovering over the icon as the vessel's struts sank into the sodden ground on one side. It continued to tilt and, realising the gunship was in danger of tipping over, he quickly reactivated the anchor.

The gradual tilting ceased and he called Zaphir.

'You're going to have to pull it up to the *K2* with me in it, Zaffie,' he said. 'I can't release the anchor without it collapsing.'

'That's against all regulations,' she replied. 'If the tractor fails, you're dropping in a dead ship.'

'I trust you,' he said. 'But I will fire up the environmental systems. It's bloody freezing in here.'

'If Whippy finds out, we're both up for a disciplinary, a big one.'

'Never a truer word spoken, Lieutenant Mye,' said Captain Whipper, his booming voice echoing around both cockpits.

Bache chuckled to himself and leant forward to peer through the front screen. He could see Zaphir in the tug's cockpit cringing.

'You've got nothing to laugh about, Loftt,' Whipper continued. 'You may have broken my expensive antigravs, but the cockpit cameras are working just fine.'

'Yes, sir,' he said, quickly adopting a straight face. 'Any ideas how we stop this ship rolling over without the anchor?'

'As a matter of fact I do,' replied the captain. 'Initiate the gunship's tractor too, you both lock on to each other and get that bent ship up in orbit as quickly as possible.'

'Is that okay as far as regulations go, Captain?' Zaphir asked.

'It is if I say it is, Lieutenant,' Whipper snapped back. 'And don't drop him—I know Loftt is a pain in the backside, but he can be a useful pain in the backside, occasionally.'

Bache smiled at the comment as he listened to the tug's huge engines spooling up. He sat in the co-pilot's seat, closed the airlock and brought the gunship's tractor online. He watched the tug lift up and hover above him, the gunship shivered as Zaphir locked the powerful tractor onto his hull. He did the same onto hers and reached across to deactivate the anchor again.

'Go, Zaffie,' he said, as soon as he felt the ship shake again as the anchor released its attraction to the ground.

Outside the cockpit, he watched the trees, hillside and ocean drop away as they thundered upwards and sat back in his seat.

He nearly jumped out of his skin as four Gata soldiers were suddenly standing either side of him. He froze as he felt the coldness of metal against his neck. He looked over to his right as a fifth Gata came into view, one he unfortunately recognised and who spoke to him in Ellinika.

'Good morning, Mr GDA,' the priden growled. 'Perhaps you'd like to reacquaint me with my fucking uniform.'

19

GDA marine gunship, upper atmosphere,
Dresse, Dresse system

'You do realise where you're going to be in a few minutes?' said Bache, turning slowly to face the priden.

'Exactly where I want to be, young GDA,' the Gata replied. 'Exactly where I want to be.'

This wasn't the reply Bache was expecting and his confusion was compounded when Zaphir called from the tug.

'We've got company—oh shit.'

The priden purred, sat on the pilot's seat and glanced up at the holomap, smiling.

'Oh dear,' he gloated as Bache followed his gaze to find the *K2* surrounded by the twelve remaining Gata battleships. 'It seems your captain made an error returning here.'

Bache frowned and wondered why the *K2* hadn't jumped away to safety.

'You're wondering why your vessel hasn't jumped away, aren't you?' said the Gata in a sad patronising tone.

Bache slowly dropped his eyes to meet the priden's, knowing something bad was about to happen.

'We call it a trypex zone,' he said smugly, as he sat back and folded his arms across his chest. 'Disrupts any attempt to achieve a jump envelope.' He pointed at the *K2*. 'Around about now, your captain is being given the option of surrendering his vessel or face complete annihilation.'

'What are you doing here? asked Bache. 'What is this all about?'

'Retribution for wrongs committed a long time ago,' was the Pride's reply.

Movement in Bache's peripheral vision caused him to turn as someone else entered the cockpit.

'Welt,' exclaimed Bache, as he noticed the soldiers didn't seem remotely concerned about his appearance. 'So it was you that betrayed us and your people.'

Welt ignored Bache's comment and stared straight at the priden.

'You have what you wanted,' he said, nervously. 'We made a deal.'

'The deal is fulfilled when I say it is,' the priden snapped back.

'I want to see my family,' Welt blurted, puffing out his chest and glaring at the priden.

Bache swore he'd never seen a Gata move so fast. One minute the priden was sitting on the pilot's seat and in a blur of movement, Welt was on the cockpit floor with the Gata looming over him. Blood oozed from three claw gouges on the left side of his face. Welt wiped it with his hand and looked at the blood with horror, before nervously glancing up at the priden.

'One more comment from you and that'll be your throat, followed by an airlock,' the Gata hissed, moving casually back to take his seat.

Bache reluctantly felt sorry for Welt. They'd obviously taken his family, forcing him to provide them with information. From what he'd seen of the cruelty of these Gatas, he doubted Welt's family were still alive at all, they were just playing him along.

'Bache, the *K2*'s just dropped its shields,' Zaphir called, the worry evident in her tone. 'Why haven't they jumped away to safety?'

The priden reached across, seemingly familiar with the control console's layout, and touched the reply transmit icon.

'You will take both vessels into your designated hangar as normal,' the priden demanded.

'Who is this?' Zaphir asked.

This time Bache leant forward over the co-pilot's console and toggled the same icon and unseen by the priden, flicked the safety cover off one other.

'Better do as he says,' said Bache. 'Just make sure it's as soft as our water landing earlier. Don't want the ship damaged any more do we?'

There was a momentary pause before she replied with just one word.

'Understood.'

Bache watched closely through the front screen as Zaphir steered them along the port side of the massive Katadromiko and in through the gaping allocated hangar entrance. He realised immediately that she'd understood his misdirection. Climbing, she took the two ships up as high as possible without actually scraping the ceiling. As soon as they were in the middle of the hangar and it was clear below, Bache leant forward again, this time hitting two icons on the console and sitting back firmly in his seat, pressed a third icon on his arm rest. Immediately a set of crash belts whipped around him and pulled him firmly back into his seat.

'Now, Zaffie,' he shouted.

'What are you doing?' the priden screamed. It was the last thing he said before the gunship dropped like a stone and hit the hangar floor with an almighty bone-shuddering crash and rendered the Gata unconscious as his head slammed into one of the arm rests.

Bache had disengaged the artificial gravity field which had made the impact so much more abrupt. Smoke began drifting up from below and he heard a cough from behind him. Turning his head, he found the soldiers were equally in a state of disarray. Only one appeared conscious, but was in no state to do anything with what looked like a broken leg and arm. Bache released himself from the crash harness and rolled sideways onto his hands and knees. Every part of him ached as if he'd been hit by a skouter. He crawled to the stairs, keeping below the smoke, and glanced at Welt, who was breathing at least. His eyes blinked and looked back at Bache.

'What the fuck did you just do?' Welt croaked, the gouges in his face glistening with blood.

Bache shrugged and pulled himself up into a sitting position using the door frame and sat for a moment assessing his fitness. The sound of weapons fire from below focussed his attention and as quickly as he could he disarmed all the soldiers, placing their weapons well out of reach.

He reacquainted himself with his rifle, which had slid under the control console and half lying, half sitting, he waited.

The sound of something crashing down heavily in the loading bay replaced the laser fire and after a short wait, boots came thudding up the stairs. His finger hovered over the rifle's trigger as he waited to see if there were more Gata soldiers on the way up.

'Bache, are you there?' asked a familiar voice.

He breathed a sigh of relief and coughed. The smoke was getting worse. Zaphir peered in over the top step, the muzzle of her rifle hovering in front.

'I'm here, Zaffie girl,' he wheezed, crawling over to meet her.

She glanced around at the state of the Gatas lying haphazardly around the cockpit.

'Where the hell did they all come from?' she

asked. Then she noticed Welt struggling to sit up. 'You,' she snarled. 'It was you, wasn't it?'

'He had no choice, Zaffie. They had his family,' said Bache, knowing he would have most likely had to do the same in similar circumstances.

She sneered at the native Dressen and grabbed his collar.

'Whatever the reason, you're coming with us,' she said.

'I don't know if I can walk,' he whinged.

She stuffed the muzzle of her rifle up his nose and suddenly Welt found the ability to stand. Bache did the same and, stooped low below the worst of the smoke, they both hustled Welt down the stairs.

The lower deck was a mess. Partially crushed by the impact, Bache could see what Zaphir had been using her laser rifle for. The rear ramp had twisted and she'd used her weapon to melt the locking mechanism on both sides, causing it to crash down out of its bulkhead housing.

'Crude but did the job,' she said, noticing

Bache eyeing the ramp. 'The side airlock was completely crushed, it was my only way in.'

'I'm impressed,' said Bache, limping off the gunship. 'We'll make an engineer of you yet.'

'Yeah, the Zaphir Mye school of engineering,' she said, rolling her eyes. 'Just shoot it and it'll be right.'

Eight marines with weapons up suddenly burst into the hangar and approached them warily.

'We understand your vessel was compromised, Lieutenant,' said the sergeant, aiming the question at Bache.

'There's five of them in the cockpit,' he said. 'You'll need a medical team.'

The marine raised his eyebrows.

'You should've been a marine, sir,' he said, signalling his men to board the wreck. 'That's impressive.'

'I played a part too,' said Zaphir, indignantly.

The comment was ignored as the sergeant scuttled off and followed his troop inside the gunship.

'Sexist fucking grunt,' Zaphir grumbled, as they made their way to the rear hangar door.

Bache made sure to keep his expression neutral.

'You never told me why the *K2* didn't jump away to safety,' she said. 'Surely Whippy can't expect to take on twelve of those bastards?'

'They have some sort of anti-jump field,' he replied. 'Whippy had no choice, I believe they're going to attempt to take the ship rather than destroy it.'

The buzz of the atmosphere shield interrupted him followed by the scream of antigravs. They turned to see a Gata troop carrier turning and dropping, its rear ramp already opening.

'Skata, they're here already,' Bache blurted. 'Run.'

20

Katadromiko 2, *orbiting Dresse, Dresse system*

THEY BURST out into the corridor, the airlock gradually closing behind them and shutting out the noise of the antigravs and laser weapons as the marines made the newcomers welcome.

It was warmer inside the ship for which Bache was thankful. It was always cold in the hangars as the absolute zero of space always permeated the atmosphere shield.

Half escorting, half dragging Welt in the

higher gravity of the vessel to the nearest tube stop, they boarded the awaiting carriage.

'How big is this bloody ship?' questioned Welt, as he peered through the concave front and back screens and down the lit tubes that disappeared off into the distance in both directions.

'Fourteen kilometres,' said Zaphir, pointing to a seat.

'What's a kilometre?' he asked.

'Let's just say it's a big ship,' said Bache, punching in an obscure deck as the terminus.

Zaphir frowned, noticing their destination.

'Aren't we going to the bridge?' she questioned.

'That'll be the main target along with central engineering for the boarding parties,' he said. 'This is somewhere they won't find us…at least for a while anyway.'

The carriage zipped aft through the tunnels on a magnetic cushion, stopping frequently to become an elevator and drop down countless levels.

'This can't be a spaceship, surely?' muttered Welt, glancing dubiously at Zaphir and Bache.

A moment later the carriage stopped and the door slid silently up into its housing. Bache leant out, checked both ways were clear, and nodded at Zaphir. She slapped Welt on the back of the head.

'Move,' she said, grabbing his arm.

He shrugged her off, stood and seemed suddenly quite capable of walking unaided, although the higher gravity than the world he was used to did slow him somewhat.

'Does your planet have gravity this vicious?' he asked.

Bache was surprised that a man who came from a planet with no space exploration of any kind would be knowledgeable about planets with differing gravity fields.

'Mine doesn't, but Zaffie's does,' he said, giving Welt a knowing eye. 'So don't try and outrun her.'

Welt glanced nervously at Zaphir who winked back and tapped her rifle with a forefinger.

Bache stopped suddenly, causing Welt, who was still looking at Zaphir, to bump into the back of him. The hum of the alma drives was loud here. As the monstrous engines were only a couple of decks above, it was an area of the ship that no one spent time in.

'What's up?' asked Welt, leaning round Bache to stare up the corridor.

'We're here,' he said.

'We are?' said Zaphir, seemingly equally puzzled at why they'd stopped in the middle of a nondescript passageway.

Bache brushed his hand along a black stripe on the wall at about head height. It wasn't anything unusual on the ship, almost all of the many kilometres of corridors had the black line.

'What are you looking for?' Zaphir asked in a slightly impatient tone.

A numbered key panel lit up within the stripe and Bache smiled.

'This,' he said, tapping in a six-digit code and holding his wrist against the panel.

A clunk below them had Welt and Zaphir stepping back anxiously. A section of the decorative panelling sank inwards and slid to one side.

'What the fuck is this?' Zaphir asked, stooping to peer inside.

A room around five metres square appeared as wall lights flickered to life.

'It's an ROR, a remote operations room,' said Bache, waving for them to squat down and enter.

Once inside, he entered a code into a similar panel on the opposite side of the wall. The door slid back and clunked away from them and back into place. The room had a single control panel similar to several found on the bridge. Eight unlit screens hung above the two seats. On the opposite wall was a set of two bunkbeds. Welt staggered over and made use of the lower one. The third wall opposite the door contained rows of cupboards and drawers, with a door to a tiny bathroom.

'Why didn't I know about this place?' Zaphir asked, sounding a trite miffed.

'Err, senior officers only,' said Bache, grimacing and keeping his back to her, as he knew that wouldn't sit well with her.

'Then why did you know?' came the inevitable snappy reply. 'Don't tell me,' she said before Bache had a chance to open his mouth. 'Your father told you?'

He nodded as he sat in one of the two chairs in front of the control panel.

'He was on the design team for the Katadromikos. It was something he always thought was missing on the earlier Kidemonas class cruisers.'

'He gave you the access codes too, then?'

'Actually no, he didn't, but I did have his and it's probably best Mr Whippy doesn't know I'd downloaded them either.'

Zaphir shook her head and rolled her eyes.

'I'm not even going to ask,' she said. 'Plausible deniability and all that. I see you still have that illegal wrist implant then?'

'Maybe,' he said, as he touched a few icons on the panel.

The eight screens lit up and went through their boot up routine.

'Okay,' said Bache. 'Where do we want to see first?'

'Bridge,' she said. 'I'm sure Whippy will have a plan of some kind.'

The lower left screen lit up with a view of the bridge from a camera that must have been mounted just above the main door. They both scanned around the room for a moment before Zaphir spoke.

'Where is he? And who's that sitting in Whippy's seat?'

'A stand-in,' said Bache. 'It's Deedahaye, she's wearing the captain's insignia. Mr Whippy will be in one of these hidden rooms, most likely the one nearest the bridge along with First Officer Falenthraite. It must be standard procedure for an aggressive boarding.'

'What about all the marine detachments on board?' Zaphir asked. 'Are they going to come out all guns blazing?'

'Depends what the captain ordered,' replied Bache. 'If there was a fire fight for every room and deck, it would take forever and destroy half the ship.'

He began flicking through random camera views around the huge vessel.

'Where is everyone?' Zaphir queried, staring at the screens with a puzzled expression, as view after view of empty corridors and public areas flashed in front of them.

'He's probably confined all except critical personnel to their cabins,' Bache said, shrugging. 'It'll mean fewer casualties and lead the Gatas into a false sense of security. At some point they'll have to drop the anti-jump beam thing and that'll be Mr Whippy's chance to make a big embedded jump somewhere remote. He can then concentrate on retaking the ship and the Gatas won't have any backup.'

'How d'you know all that?' Welt asked in a muffled voice from the lower bunk, while holding a wad of tissue over his wounded cheek.

Bache turned to him and sighed.

'I don't,' he said. 'But that's what I'd do.'

Movement on the screen showing the bridge caught their attention. They both turned to see around twenty Gata soldiers pour through the main bridge entrance. Circling around the outside of the room, they kept their weapons up and positioned themselves at regular intervals, the bright bridge lighting reflecting menacingly off their dark helmet visors.

Understandably, the bridge crew sat motionless, their hands laced on top of their heads ensuring they gave the enemy no excuse for unnecessary violence.

Another Gata entered the bridge, this one Bache recognised as wearing the uniform of a priden.

'Have we got sound?' Zaphir asked.

Bache searched around in the menu and after a few moments, found what he was looking for.

'…will do exactly as ordered and nothing more,' the priden's booming voice was instructing after stepping up onto the captain's central dais. 'You will all now stand and be escorted to your locked cabins where you will remain until further notice.'

'What about food?' a voice called from behind the priden.

'Stand up,' the priden ordered, turning and stepping down towards the young lieutenant as he slowly stood.

The priden's laser pistol fired once, the lieutenant dropped like a stone with a hole the size of a fist in the centre of his chest and an expression of total shock frozen on his face. A collective gasp sounded around the bridge as blood coursed from the wound, pooling around the body in an ever-increasing circle.

'Anyone else have any questions?' the priden shrieked across the room, his left eye twitching involuntarily.

21

Katadromiko 2, *orbiting Dresse, Dresse system*

'THAT MURDERING BASTARD,' spat Zaphir. 'I'll rip his flea-ridden head off and kick it out an airlock.'

Bache just sat there clenching his fists until his knuckles went white.

'Now you know why I did what I did,' mumbled Welt, from behind them.

'You can just shut up,' Zaphir hissed, turning and jabbing a finger at him.

Bache glanced over, realising Welt was about to say more and unseen by Zaphir, he shook his head at him. He knew only too well not to antagonise her when she was severely pissed and didn't want her taking her frustration out on him.

Welt luckily took the hint, kept quiet and lay back on the bed again.

They turned back to the screens to see the bridge crew being escorted away. Bache counted twelve new un-uniformed Gatas filing onto the bridge and taking up positions behind some of the consoles.

'They seem quite familiar with the layout,' said Bache, watching as they immediately began tapping away at their relevant stations.

'I told you that Gata flyer's controls on the surface was of GDA design,' said Zaphir. 'Someone, somewhere has undertaken some espionage and given these grey bastards our technology.'

'Well, let's not worry about that for the moment,' said Bache. 'We need to help Mr Whippy get his ship back and find some way to counter that anti-jump thing.'

Zaphir nodded and glanced up at the ceiling.

'Is there a holomap generator in this room?' she asked.

'No,' he said, pressing a couple of icons and pointing at a screen in the centre of the group. 'But we do have a three-dimensional map on there.'

An image of Dresse and the surrounding region appeared on the screen, slowly turning and showed the *K2* still in orbit and surrounded by the twelve Gata warships.

'At some point soon they're going to want to go somewhere,' said Bache. 'These ships must have been built for a specific job, it's taken them years to do this and when they go wherever they're going, they'll need to turn the anti-jump zone thing off.'

'Does it affect them too?' asked Zaphir.

'It must do,' said Bache. 'The priden stated it impeded a jump envelope being generated, which has to affect them as well. What I need to do is quietly feel around with the main array and try and pinpoint what sort of beam or frequency they're using to enable this.'

'Won't Whippy be doing the same?'

'He may not know what we know. He won't have spoken to anyone before retreating to his ROR and he certainly won't know why his escape jump didn't eventuate.'

'Can't we contact him and ask?' questioned Zaphir.

'Possibly, but I don't want that piece of shit detecting the communication,' Bache replied, pointing at the screen showing the priden strutting around the bridge.

'Aren't these rooms connected independently?'

'I have no idea. I'd like to think so, but I can't take the risk of him finding out about us. He's already murdered one crew member for just asking a question.'

'Mr Whippy must be doing his nut,' she said. 'I'd hate to be locked in one of these with him right now.'

Bache grimaced, knowing exactly what she meant. Putting that thought out of his mind, he began going through the camera feeds from the engineering decks.

'Ah,' he grunted, finally finding what he was looking for.

A screen had lit up with a scene from the main engineering deck and offices showing a contingent of Gata soldiers standing guard over Chief Engineer Catams and a handful of her staff. Bache had known Desme Catams for years as his father had trained her, an experienced officer and although quite a shy girl, her intimate knowledge of the ship's systems was quite extraordinarily detailed and guaranteed to be accurate.

They were all sitting on the floor in her office with the door closed. The furniture and computers had been removed. Bache could see several Gata soldiers standing guard outside and again, the same as on the bridge, a few civilian grey Gatas in the background sitting at the main engineering stations.

'Hmm, I was afraid of that,' said Bache.

Zaphir looked across at him quizzically. He

noticed her raised eyebrows and took it as a cue to explain his comment.

'If you have complete control over the bridge and main engineering,' he said, 'then you pretty much have the vessel. They know what they're doing, or at least they think they do.'

'When d'you think Whippy will make a move?'

'The earlier the better, it gives them less time to establish and fully infiltrate the ship. Although he can't do anything until he can jump the ship away from that fleet and that's where I can try to help.'

Zaphir watched as he brought up a screen that showed the standings of the various arrays. The main one and a couple of the secondary arrays were in use by the Gatas, so he chose not to use those in case it was noticed. A smaller array, normally used for geological surveys of planetary bodies, was sitting dormant.

Bache hoped the enemy crew were engrossed in their own tasks and not paying any attention to this peripheral piece of equipment stuck out on a spur at the stern of the vessel.

Delving into the arrays menu, he changed its function to a wide spectrum of frequencies and keeping the range local so the Gata fleet were less likely to detect his snooping, he scanned for anything anomalous.

After a few minutes, he sat back in his seat, rubbed the back of his neck and groaned with frustration.

'Nothing?' questioned Zaphir, her face mirroring his look of disappointment.

'No—nothing,' he said in almost a whisper. 'I must be missing something.'

'Perhaps it's a field that only initiates as an envelope is developing,' said a quiet voice from the other side of the room.

They both turned and stared at Welt lying on the small bunk with his back to them.

'Didn't I tell you to shut up?' Zaphir snarled. 'What would anyone from your primitive planet know about jump dynamics? You haven't even got into spa…'

Bache put his hand up to silence Zaphir and spoke.

'Actually, he has a point,' he said. 'It could

be a dormant field.'

'How d'you mean?' Zaphir asked, giving the back of Welt's head a penetrating sneer as she turned back to Bache.

'Well, if you were to use your permanent array feedback to signal the development of an envelope in a designated zone, the anti-jump system could then flash something out to kill it.'

'There's enough time to do that as the envelope is developing is there?'

'Oh, yes, definitely,' he said, a little more enthusiastically now. 'It takes over a hundred milliseconds to form…plenty of time.'

She shook her head and rolled her eyes.

'Only you would know that shit,' she replied.

'Didn't you cover the theory of jump dynamics in your pilot training?'

She shrugged.

'I was probably asleep through all that nerdy crap.'

Bache gave her an exasperated gaze before sighing again and turning back to the console.

'If there was some way of initiating an envelope and scanning as its forming, we might be able to detect what the hell we're dealing with,' he said, sitting back in his seat again and crossing his arms despondently.

'Can't we programme a drone to do that?' Zaphir asked.

Bache stared straight ahead silently for a moment.

'They'd detect it though and probably start torturing the crew to find out who did it,' he said, eventually.

'Not if it was made to look like an automated function,' she said.

'Hmm,' he grunted, turning to look at her and then back at the console. 'That could be done. The only drawback is someone would have to go to one of the drone hangars, pull one off the rack and retrieve its programming code.'

'The drones are all automated though... aren't they?'

'Most are,' he said. 'But the jump-capable drones are expensive and apparently, years ago, when Mr Whippy was a chief engineer, he caught someone secretly trying to launch one to their home planet to wish her partner a happy birthday. The captain blamed him because they all come under the chief engineer's remit. So ever since, on his ships, all the jump-capable drones have to be manually authorised from the bridge and they're not left flight-ready.'

'Shit,' she mumbled. 'Well, you need to be here to programme it, so it'd better be me that goes.'

'I'll go,' said Welt, turning over to face them and sitting up.

'No you fucking won't,' snapped Zaphir. 'I'm not putting my life and the lives of this crew in your hands.'

'How will I ever prove to you that I'm not your enemy?' he whined.

'With difficulty,' said Bache. 'And with an operation this critical, I need someone I can trust implicitly.'

He turned to Zaphir.

'I wish there was someone else trustworthy to send instead,' he said. 'But needs must. I want you to promise me you'll take no unnecessary risks.'

'I won't,' she said.

22

Katadromiko 2, *orbiting Dresse, Dresse system*

Zaphir stepped quickly out into the corridor, stood to her full height and watched as the door sank back into place. Suddenly feeling very exposed, she hurried off aft towards the nearest emergency stairway.

Using the tube trains would be way too risky, so they'd decided the safest way to get to hangar 171 was on foot, using stairways and service corridors. It was around two and a half kilometres through the ship and the chances of getting all that way undetected were low. So Bache had decided that checking ahead of her on the internal cameras and talking her through the route was the way to make it a lot safer.

'Stairway on the left,' Bache's voice whispered in her ear. 'Go down to deck ninety-two.'

'I thought the hangar was on deck ninety-one,' she whispered back.

'It is, but deck ninety-two is mostly taken up by equipment storage and is a lot more likely to be deserted than one of the main hangar decks.'

'Ah, okay,' she said, quietly opening and closing the stairway door before listening for any noise above or below.

'Stairway is clear going down, turning the cameras off now,' said Bache.

She made her way down quickly and silently, stopping every so often to listen again. Down and down she went, floor after floor and about halfway down her earpiece started buzzing.

'Bache, I'm getting interference on the comms,' she whispered.

'Th……urn…of……int……..oms… eep….go…g,' was the garbled reply.

She got the gist of it though. Internal communications had been turned off and the small headset she was using that normally piggy-backed onto this system as you moved further away had now run out of its limited range.

'Ah crap,' she mumbled under her breath.

Continuing down a little more cautiously now, she removed the headset and stuffed it in a pocket to enable her to hear her surroundings more clearly.

Finally reaching deck 92, the first thing she noticed was the smell of machinery oil was strong here and the background hum of the ship was considerably more invasive.

'No one would want to be down here then,' she said to herself, trying to allay her fear of discovery. She slowly approached the door, which had a small circular window that presented a peculiar fisheye view of the corridor beyond. Watching for a few moments, she detected no movement, so she cracked the door slightly and peeked through the narrow gap.

She could see nothing, but the whine of vehicle motors was unmistakable somewhere in the distance.

'Who the hell would be driving around down here?' she asked herself, as she opened the door a little wider and stuck her head out just far enough for one eye to see down the wide passageway.

In the distance, she could see a column of military fighting vehicles being moved from their internal garaging into what must be one of the larger external hangars and of course it was the way Zaphir needed to go.

'Wherever they're going involves a ground offensive then,' she said to herself. 'Unless they're just stealing the equipment.'

Closing the door again, she descended to the level she actually wanted and repeated the process. The smell of oil was gone here, but strangely replaced by the pungent odour of burning plastics.

The reason was just the other side of the door. Two marine armoured suits lay crumpled in the corridor, both still smoking from recent and fatal action. Zaphir recoiled away from the window when she noticed blood dripping from the helmet of one of them.

She descended again.

'This one better be deserted,' she moaned, glancing left and right through the fisheye window.

Again, after detecting no movement, she cracked the door and peered both ways. She shivered as the coldness of this level surprised her and nipped at any unprotected skin.

'Shit, it's cold here,' she grumbled, now ruing the decision to leave her jacket in the control room.

The passage was clear in both directions though and hugging her rifle close to her chest, she turned right out the door and hurried off into the cold. She kept close to the right-hand wall, periodically glancing over her shoulder as she ran. Every couple of hundred metres she'd stop behind a bulkhead and listen, the steam of her breath fogging around her.

She knew the emergency stairwells were every five hundred metres and the fourth one would be the one she needed. The drone store and hangar should be just down the corridor to the left on the level above.

Zaphir soon realised the reason for the coldness as she passed storeroom after storeroom of frozen foodstuffs. Her stomach rumbled at the thought and she decided to pop back down here afterwards and find supplies to take back to the control room. Anything would be better than the dried rations in the cupboards there.

Finally reaching the fourth staircase, she caught her breath and ascended the one level back to where she wanted to be. Praying there wouldn't be any dead soldiers lying outside, she went through her usual peeping routine. Thankfully, it seemed clear.

She smiled as she noticed the door opposite read Hangar 172, so Bache had been correct, the hangar was indeed to the left. She was also thankful the burning smell of death hadn't permeated this far up the corridor as she made her way purposefully towards hangar 171.

She stopped suddenly twenty metres from the hangar airlock as a whirring noise from inside surprised her. Flattening herself quickly behind a bulkhead pillar, she watched in horror as the door slid slowly away and two Gata soldiers emerged warily. They checked both directions up and down the corridor were clear before walking off in the other direction.

Zaphir breathed a sigh of relief and while their backs were to her, she quickly ran on tiptoes and slid through the airlock door just before it closed. Opening the second door, she waited to see if anything moved. It didn't, so she stepped cautiously into the hangar.

Inside the lighting was low and as the second airlock door clunked shut behind her it took her eyes a while to adjust. When she was confident she wouldn't walk into anything, she ventured deeper into the hangar.

The first thing she saw were four jump drones removed from their racks and lined up on trolleys in front of the atmosphere shield. Circling around them, she noticed something about their shape was different. It was difficult to see in the low lighting. Bending down, she read the lettering on the side of some sort of cylinder recently and perhaps slightly amateurishly strapped to the underside of the drone.

She gasped as she recognised the coding. These were nuclear warheads, the most powerful and destructive ones too. One of these could lay waste to half a continent and they were about to send four somewhere.

23

Katadromiko 2, *orbiting Dresse, Dresse system*

ZAPHIR WISHED she had some way of contacting Bache. He would know how to disable the nukes without it being noticed.

Turning, she quickly made her way over to the racks and, selecting one of the drones on the bottom row, she pushed a trolley underneath it and engaged the latches. She was halfway through freeing it from its wall cradle when the airlock door motor made her jump by starting to open again.

She quickly ducked down and slid behind the drone before swiftly climbing up and concealing herself behind the one above.

Three Gatas strode in after the airlock had cycled and, stretching her neck around the drone, she was able to determine it was the two soldiers from before accompanied by a priden.

They approached the drones and after circling around them once, the priden nodded his approval and pulling out a tablet, proceeded to tap away while the soldiers released the trolley latches.

The quietness in the room was quickly shattered by four antigravs spinning up and Zaphir swore under her breath as she realised they were about to launch the drones.

Feeling the weight of her laser rifle slung across her back, she made her decision in a split second. Bracing herself with her legs, she swung the weapon around, made sure it was set to heavy stun and shot the priden before any of the drones lifted off their trolleys. Luckily, the two soldiers were caught completely by surprise and she nailed one of them as he turned, a look of complete shock on his face as he joined the priden on the floor. The other soldier, however, managed to duck down behind the drones and activate his rifle. He popped up and snapped a shot in Zaphir's direction, but luckily, as she had concealed herself again, he had no clue as to where she actually was. She did however notice his weapon wasn't set to stun.

Watching closely, she knew she had to get him quickly, before he could call for backup. She couldn't fire indiscriminately in his direction because of the nukes. Instead, she set her rifle to full power and targeted the maintenance bench on the far side of the hangar. She knew there were always pressurised containers involved in maintaining anything with an antigrav drive. Sure enough, her third shot hit something containing a flammable liquid, which exploded out in a maelstrom of burning droplets directly behind the Gata. Cats detest fire and Gatas are no exception. He jumped up, frantically slapping his clothing where flaming droplets of oil had caught him.

Zaphir wasted no time in returning her weapon to stun and targeting the soldier, where he soon joined his unconscious colleagues on the floor.

She climbed down. The automatic fire suppression system activated suddenly and she found herself choking on the noxious gases. She dived across the hangar and grabbed one of the self-activating emergency breathing masks. Once it was on, she snatched three more and returned to fit one to each of the unconscious Gatas. The masks weren't designed for fur-covered faces, but she did her best and hopefully they would keep the men from suffocating.

Time was of the essence now, so she ran back to the drone she'd been preparing before, unlatched it, heaved it across the floor into clear space and made a note of its launch coding. After releasing its trolley latches so it could fly, she snatched up the priden's tablet on the way to the airlock.

She hopped from foot to foot willing the airlock to cycle quicker. They always seemed to go slower when you were in a hurry.

Her rifle was up and ready as the second door rumbled slowly away, but instead of the empty corridor she was hoping for, two armoured marines stood menacingly in the corridor and they had activated laser cannons pointing directly at her head.

'Put down your weapon and the tablet. You will come with us,' demanded an intimidating electronic voice.

Zaphir had no idea which suit had spoken, but what she did know was if she didn't comply it would be game over in the blink of an eye.

She slowly lowered the rifle, bent down and dropped it beside her along with the tablet. Standing again, she raised her hands, palms out and slowly and deliberately turned in a complete circle to show she was now unarmed.

One of the suits clumped by her, picking up the tablet as it went and cycled itself into the hangar.

'Do you realise how many people could die if you launch those?' she said to the expressionless and sinister black visor of the remaining suit.

'The prisoner will remain silent,' it snapped.

Zaphir shrugged and waited. A few minutes later the second suit cycled its way back through the airlock.

'Walk to the right, Lieutenant Mye, and continue down the hallway until we tell you to stop,' the electronic voice from the newly returned suit ordered.

She didn't know what made her more nervous, the fact that they knew her rank and name or that she didn't know what side they were on. They might just be taking her to the nearest airlock for all she knew. But of course she complied, she had no choice.

She found the continuous whirring and clunking of the suits behind her quite intimidating, and found herself holding her breath as they passed the first airlock. But pass they did and the next and the next. After about twenty minutes, she realised they should be coming up to the stairway door and the two smouldering armoured suits. But the corridor had been cleared, the only evidence remaining was a couple of scorch marks and a bloodstain visible on the floor as she passed. Shortly after, when they reached a tube station, she was finally instructed to stop.

A carriage was waiting, and she was ushered inside and told to sit. She was beginning to think they were perhaps on her side after all, but when she saw one of the suits enter the destination as the bridge deck, her heart sank. She remembered the bridge officer being executed for just asking for food—what chance would she have facing that psychotic priden?

The carriage swept through the enormous vessel. It didn't stop at any other stations but still took seventeen minutes to get all the way up to the bridge deck. Again, she was instructed to walk in front as they headed up towards the closed bridge doors. Four Gata soldiers guarded the double doors and they didn't seem in any hurry to move as they approached.

'Saboteur for the captain,' stated one of the suits.

They still didn't move, but one of them

spoke quietly inside his helmet and then seemed to be waiting for authorisation. It must have come through, as he nodded and they all stood aside as the double doors swished apart.

The lighting inside was more subdued than in the corridor and carried a reddish hue. It reminded Zaphir of a bar she used to frequent on her home planet of Shand.

It was also quiet and apart from the faint hum from all the control panels, the clumping of the armoured suits behind her sounded even louder and more forbidding.

She was ordered to stop in front of the captain's dais. With the high-backed chair on top facing away from her, she didn't know if there was anyone sitting in it.

That question was swiftly answered as the seat slowly rotated to reveal just the person she didn't want to see. She also felt the coldness of one of the suits pressing into her back, preventing her from fleeing.

'Lieutenant Mye, I understand,' murmured the priden, smugly. 'Our little saboteur from hangar 171.'

He stood up from the chair, drawing his laser pistol as he rose.

'It appears my clear demonstration of supremacy earlier didn't provide enough clarity to the situation now at hand.'

He glanced over at one of his operators.

'Ensure this is on the screens in all the cabins,' he said, before looking up to where the cameras were. 'Anyone thinking of further challenges to our or my authority will also be awarded the same immediate retirement.'

He turned to the second armoured suit, which had placed itself facing the rest of the room.

'Dispose of the body out the nearest airlock, soldier,' he said as he raised the weapon.

Zaphir glared at the Gata and, knowing there was no chance of getting out of this, she realised for the sake of the GDA and the rest of the crew that she had to remain stoic to the end and not let this bastard have the pleasure of seeing her break down and plead for her life.

She thought of Bache, probably freaking out back in the remote control room, and hoped he would be all right. She thought of her home planet and how she'd meant to but not visited for years, and lastly, she thought of her fellow crew members of the *K2*, having to watch this and hoping they didn't suffer nightmares for years to come.

She defiantly raised her chin and closed her eyes. The report of the laser weapon was loud. She felt electricity pulsing around her, then darkness.

24

Katadromiko 2, *orbiting Dresse, Dresse system*

BACHE SCREAMED at the monitors in the remote control room as the two he had covering the bridge suddenly went black.

'No, no, no,' he shouted, banging his fists on the desk. 'Zaffie—oh, please no.'

Even though the screens had gone black, he could still hear the sounds of rapid weapon fire and see the flashes of laser energy bolts criss-crossing the room. Screaming, lots of screaming.

The more he listened, the more he realised the weapons firing were laser cannons, they had a deeper boom when discharged than a pistol or rifle, and he reasoned it was the armoured suits that were doing the majority of the firing. Light suddenly cascaded across the bridge as the main door swished open and as Bache watched from the camera above the same door, the four soldiers from outside piled in with guns up. In a split second, four cannon bolts met them, decapitating them with blood and limbs flying back through the door or ricocheting off the door bulkhead.

He squinted as the lighting on the bridge suddenly came back on and his heart missed a beat as he could see Zaphir lying on the floor in the same place she'd been standing only moments before. The two armoured suits stood back to back either side of her, their twin cannon barrels mounted on their shoulders roaming the room for more targets. From what he could see, all the Gata soldiers that had been lining the outside of the room had suffered the same fate as the four coming in the door. Bache knew those suit-mounted weapons could track and eliminate multiple targets in milliseconds.

Grabbing a data chip from its housing on the control panel and his rifle, he lunged for the door control. Once outside and he'd closed the hidden room up again, he sprinted for the nearest tube station.

Annoyingly, once there, he had to wait for a carriage. He punched the door in frustration, ruing the decision to let Zaphir go on her own down to the hangar. He also decided he'd rip those marines' heads off for using Zaphir as bait to get them onto the bridge. The carriage came, he piled in and set the destination as the bridge deck, entering an officer's code that ensured it went non-stop.

He didn't sit down for the fifteen-minute journey, he paced up and down the ten-metre tube, muttering to himself and gripping the rifle so tight his knuckles were white. He glanced at the rifle setting and considered changing it to full power, so he could murder any Gata he came across. The humanitarian side of him won over though, as he realised giving in to that amount of hate would make him no better than the monster who'd just killed his colleague, best friend and occasional lover.

As the small train arrived at its destination, he was through the door before it was even half open. The smell of death hit his nostrils as soon as he ventured up the corridor. He wrinkled his nose and averted his gaze as he passed the rather gory sight around the bridge doors. Entering the room, he saw the armoured suits had lined up all the Gata crew and were in the process of searching them. He headed straight for the dais where Zaphir had been and was surprised not to see her. There was very little evidence of blood on the floor here either, though there was plenty on the captain's dais and chair, along with the gruesome remains of the priden. He looked over at the suits, one of which had stopped what it was doing and was staring at him.

'We put her in the captain's study, Loftt,' the emotionless electronic voice told him.

Bache turned in the direction of the office, took two paces, stopped and glanced back at the marine.

'Don't think for one bloody minute I'm going to let you get away with using my colleague and friend for bait,' he snarled, jabbing a finger at the black faceplate.

Surging into the study a few seconds later he slammed the door behind him and stopped in the centre of the small room looking for a body on the floor.

'For fuck's sake, Bache, do you have to make so much noise,' said a voice from the small bunk in the corner.

He froze to the spot, whipping his head around towards the voice.

'You look a right twat with your mouth hanging open like that, doesn't a girl get a hug then?' said Zaphir, sitting up and running a hand through her blood-splattered hair.

'Fuck the ancients,' was all Bache could utter, as he stumbled towards her and enveloped her in his arms.

A few moments later when Bache finally released the pressure, Zaphir found she could breathe again.

'You took your bloody time,' she said, wiping a tear from his eye with a forefinger.

'There was a train strike,' he said, causing her to smile for the first time in a while.

'Those bastards out there used you as bait to get on the bridge,' he carped. 'I'm going to have them up on a disciplinary for mentally abusing a senior officer.'

Zaphir smirked and looked over Bache's shoulder.

'It's not funny,' he said. 'I thought those boneheads got you killed.'

She nodded towards the door and Bache turned to see one of the suits had opened the door behind him.

'I don't care if you just heard that,' said Bache, waving the finger at the marine again. 'You can't go around risking the lives of senior officers.'

The armoured suit brought up both arms and depressed the release catches for the helmet.

There was a slight hiss as the internal life support pressure matched that of the ship and the helmet was lifted away.

'I'll think you'll find it was a junior officer,' said Captain Whipper sporting a wry grin. 'You can report me to me if you like, but I fear the complaint might get mislaid and if it's any consolation, the first officer stood up close behind her and incorporated her in his personal shielding. Although, I will be having words with him about how much priden he managed to distribute all over my fucking chair. Also, there's always the question of what you were doing in a senior officers-only remote operations room?'

Bache's mouth had been hanging open again and Zaphir pushed it shut with a clop.

'Lieutenant Loftt is very sorry for what he said and I'm sure on reflection he won't be filing any charges. Isn't that right, Mr Loftt?' said Zaphir, nodding vigorously.

'Err, shit yes, I mean no, Captain,' he stammered, not quite believing what just went down.

'Hmm,' grunted Whipper, giving Bache one of his knowing glares. 'Now, if you'll excuse me, I'm busy ensuring the rest of this bloody fleet doesn't find out what just happened and find some way of jumping this ship out of danger.'

Bache suddenly jumped up, retrieved the data chip from his pocket and waved it in the air.

'I might just be able to help you with that, Captain,' he said with a hopeful grin.

25

Katadromiko 2, *orbiting Dresse, Dresse system*

THE FIRST THING the captain had done was initiate a complete communications block from within the ship. He released his detachments of marines locked in their cabins and had them rounding up the surprisingly small number of Gata forces aboard the vessel. The Gatas had managed to utilise a number of the armoured suits, but as the two on deck 91 had found out, they didn't have the codes to initiate the personal shields or laser cannons, which left them extremely vulnerable.

The detachment in main engineering put up a bit of resistance, but once they'd suffered serious losses and discovered they had no backup or ability to communicate with their own ships, the remainder wisely surrendered.

'Was that the drone that launched from hangar 171 while I was in there?' Captain Whipper asked, looking up at Bache from his private office desk.

'Yes, sir,' Bache replied.

'I thought you said you'd lost communications with Mye. How come you had its launch code?' Whipper asked.

'She'd written it on her hand and when you apprehended her she put her hands up with her palms facing the corridor cameras.'

The captain glanced at Zaphir, standing next to Bache.

'You're quite frighteningly smart sometimes aren't you, Mye?' he sighed, shaking his head.

'Yes, sir, thank you, sir,' she replied, with a demure expression.

'Hmm,' he grunted, shifting his gaze back to Bache.

'And Loftt, you say transmitting this frequency as we initiate a jump should invalidate their anti-jump field thing?'

'It's untested, sir. But it seems they're using a particular high phonon frequency that only triggers when an envelope begins to form. The invisible quantum fluctuations are such…'

'No need to go into all of that, Loftt,' the captain interrupted, waving his hand as if swatting a fly. 'Will your blocking field work, is all I'm interested in?'

'Yes, sir.'

'Sure?'

'Yes, sir.'

'Because if they see us attempt a jump that doesn't work, we're in the mire.'

'I also know which of their ships is transmitting the field,' said Bache. 'And it seems to be only one.'

'Really?' said Whipper, his eyes lighting up as he turned to his personal holomap. 'Which one?'

'That one there,' Bache said, pointing to one of the closest enemy battleships. 'It's transmitting from an extra field projector just here. None of the others have it.'

'So I see,' said Whipper. 'I'll target that ship with all of their converted drones.'

'You're going to use them then?' asked Zaphir, her eyes wide.

'They wanted them, it'd be rude to deny them,' said Whipper, a malevolent tone to his voice.

Zaphir looked worried.

'You do realise what will happen to a ship hit by one of those?' she said.

'If they find out they no longer have this ship, they will destroy it,' he said, staring straight into her eyes. 'It's them or us. Excuse me for seeming selfish, but I'd rather it was them.'

Zaphir turned to Bache.

'Do you agree with that?' she asked, quite forcibly.

Bache sighed and nodded.

'I'm afraid so.'

'Come on then,' said Whipper, standing suddenly. 'Let's get the hell out of here.'

The cleaning on the bridge was almost complete as they filed out of the captain's study. You wouldn't have known of the slaughter that occurred in that room only an hour before. The bridge crew had returned and sat behind their stations, some rectifying changes made by the Gatas and others waiting patiently for orders.

Bache went directly to one of the main array operators and worked with him to set up the particular frequency he believed would counteract the anti-jump field.

The captain handed the tablet from hangar 171 that had the launch codes for the four nuclear drones to his chief weapons officer and indicated they were to be jumped in close proximity to the enemy ship transmitting the anti-jump field and detonate them two seconds apart, the plan being that if that turned out to be the command ship too, it might disorientate the rest of the fleet if it was damaged or destroyed.

Captain Whipper stepped up onto his dais and glanced around the room.

'Is everyone set and happy with what they have to do?' His deep voice resounded around the bridge.

A sea of nodding heads replied that they were. He pointed at the weapons officer.

'Take those four drones out of the hangar and deploy.' He turned to Bache.

'Transmit as soon as they're away and, pilot, jump as soon as Lieutenant Loftt gives you the nod.'

The bridge crew watched the holomap as the four drones exited the hangar at the rear of the ship and vanished. Bache hit the transmit icon activating the beam and nodded at the pilot.

The first drone detonated on the port side of the enemy vessel. The shock wave reached them in a split second and shook the ship even through its shields. The pilot hit the jump command, his face going white as he turned to the captain.

'Jump failed, sir,' he shouted just as the second drone exploded. Again the cruiser shook.

Captain Whipper turned to Bache.

'Loftt, what happened?'

The third nuke detonated before he had a chance to reply and again the ship reverberated as the huge shock wave passed over them.

'Their shields are down,' came a call from an array officer just as the fourth drone blew the huge enemy battleship into three pieces. The massive sections hurtled away, spinning and shedding debris amongst the fleet.

Bache couldn't believe his beam hadn't worked, but the transmitting ship was gone now, so he pointed at the pilot to try again.

The pilot did as he instructed.

'Jump failed again, sir,' he said, looking worriedly at Bache and then at the captain.

Meanwhile, within the enemy fleet, ships were going in all directions trying to avoid the debris and bringing weapons online.

'We're being targeted by multiple ships, captain,' called a weapons officer. 'Missiles now incoming.'

'Full shields,' shouted Whipper, giving Bache a glare. 'Fire at will.'

Bache quickly realised there must've been at least one other ship transmitting the anti-jump field.

'Widen the beam to incorporate all the enemy ships,' he said to the array officer. 'It'll weaken it, but it might just be enough.'

Bache nodded at the pilot for a third time, just as their shields lit up with multiple missile strikes from the enemy fleet.

'Shields at thirty-one percent,' came the call as the Katadromiko shuddered much more violently this time.

The pilot grimaced and waited for the ship to stabilise and the jump icon to illuminate. But again, enemy ordnance cascaded against their already badly weakened shields and the jump light remained dark.

'Shields dropping, captain.'

'Everyone brace for impact,' shouted Whipper, sitting quickly and grabbing his seat arms.

'Shields down, imminent multiple impacts, three, two, one…'

As the shield failed, its influence on the vessel had also diminished and the huge ship momentarily settled, causing the jump light to illuminate. The pilot wasted no time and mashed the icon.

The *Katadromiko 2* jerked and then went perfectly still, the busy holomap changed to an empty starfield and everyone on the bridge exhaled and sat back in their seats, staring straight ahead for a moment, until the captain broke the silence.

'Damage report?'

26

Katadromiko 2, *arriving at Dasos, Prasinos system*

ZAPHIR DIDN'T SPEAK to Bache for the entire trip back to Dasos. He wasn't sure whether it was because he'd sided with the captain over the use of the nuclear drones or because the ship had almost been lost. But, whatever it was, he missed her, although not her frequent and sudden mood swings.

The full report of the episode had been sent ahead to Naval Command by jump drone and Bache knew it was down to people way above Whipper's pay grade who would be making the final decision on their futures now. It could be a medal or just as easily a demotion. The new admiral of the fleet was Candor Henns, who'd at one time been the captain of the ship Bache's father had been chief engineer on and that had most definitely not been a happy professional relationship. So he hoped it wouldn't be him.

The *K2* was unusually given clearance to dock on Stathmos Vasi space station. It was connected to the planet's capital city of Kentro below by a two thousand kilometre-long space elevator or kordoni. Predominantly a civilian station, it was rare that a military vessel was permitted to dock there, especially one the size of a Katadromiko.

Captain Whipper and Lieutenant Loftt had reservations confirmed on the elevator as soon as they had docked. They both knew this was a slight, as normally the captain of a Katadromiko would use his personal shuttle to fly directly to Naval Command in the east of the city.

Today they sat in their dress uniforms surrounded by tourists giving them strange looks.

'I hope you brought your thick skin, Loftt,' said Whipper. 'Something tells me we're going to need it today.'

'Do you know who we're meeting yet?'

'Guess?'

'Oh, great.'

'Hmm, your father's best buddy, I remember.'

'Don't remind me.'

'Henns always was a bloody liability,' groaned Whipper. 'Ancients knows who he sucked up to to get the bloody top job.'

'His wife's a council senator.'

'Oh, really? Hmm, I didn't know that.'

They both went quiet and squinted out the thick curved window of the elevator as the brightness of the planet's horizon slowly turned from a crescent into an almost flat line and then disappeared as they dropped into high cloud.

They sunk deeper into their seats as the kordoni slowed dramatically and suddenly the cloud was above them and a spectacular view opened up across Kentro City to the snow-capped mountains in the north.

Disembarking a few minutes later, they were both glad to see a naval flyer waiting for them. The pilot had them in the air within seconds and rose straight up and into the fast lanes, using a military code to bypass the queue of civilian aircraft waiting for clearance.

'Here to see the delightful new boss, sirs?' the pilot asked over his shoulder as soon as he had lane lock.

'Wanting to fly ore loaders on Garag, Lieutenant?' snapped Whipper.

'To be honest, sir,' he said, shrugging, 'the pay would be four times as much and it would get me away from Mr Grumpy Pants. So I just might.'

Bache scoffed.

'I take it you're referring to our illustrious new admiral?' he asked, before Whipper could strangle him.

The pilot nodded and faced front again.

'Admiral's personal pilot, it was the job of my dreams until I met him…and his psychotic wife.'

Bache and Whipper glanced at each other.

'She's here a lot then?' Bache asked.

'A lot! She practically runs the place. Everything has to go through her. Grumpy Pants doesn't get a look in.'

'But she's a civilian,' said Whipper. 'Everything that goes on in Naval Command is classified. She can't be anywhere near the place.'

'I'll let you tell her that, sir,' said the pilot, switching to manual and dropping down towards the sprawling military complex below.

He landed them as close as possible to the building they needed due to the light drizzle.

'Welcome to smiley town, sirs,' he said as they jumped down.

'Should be reprimanded for his attitude,' grumbled Whipper, scowling back at the flyer as they quickly trotted towards the main administration building.

'He's a pilot and probably a good one,' said

Bache. 'They're always opinionated. Just look at Mye.'

'Hmm,' Whipper grunted as they entered reception and approached the main desk.

'Captain Whipper and Lieutenant Loftt for the admiral,' Bache announced to the one male and one female unsmiling security guards.

'I'm sorry, sirs,' the male guard said. 'The admiral is unavailable today.'

'You have a rescheduled appointment tomorrow morning,' said the female. 'We've taken the trouble to book you into the Gateway Hotel for tonight.'

'The Gateway, eh,' grunted Whipper, as his tablet buzzed. He retrieved it and stared at the screen for a few moments, before tapping a reply and sending.

Bache knew something was wrong as the captain's face had gone purple.

'Something wrong, sir?' the male guard asked.

Whipper threw him a glare that made the man physically shrink back into his chair.

'I've decided to turn down your offer of accommodation,' he said, through gritted teeth. 'My shuttle is on its way down and I'll be spending the night back on board my ship, as will Lieutenant Loftt,' he said. 'Instruct the admiral I'll be expecting him on board at first bell tomorrow morning.'

The guard's eyes opened wide, as Whipper met Bache's gaze and nodded towards the front door. The two of them turned on their heels and marched towards it.

As Bache put his hand on the door handle the locks engaged with a clunk. They turned to find the male guard walking purposely towards them.

'I'm sorry, sirs,' he said, a little more forcibly than before. 'I'm not permitted to let you leave.'

'On whose fucking authority?' Whipper boomed.

'Mine,' said a voice off to the right.

Admiral Henns stood scowling at them from a doorway.

'My authority is not to be questioned, now get in here you two,' he demanded, before turning and disappearing back inside the room.

'That was First Officer Falenthraite on the tablet,' the captain whispered, as they crossed the concourse. 'There's a bunch of private security trying to appropriate the prisoners.'

Bache had questions but had to remain mute as they were at the door. It wasn't the admiral's office, just a reception meeting room. It had a large table in the middle and a screen on the wall. Bache guessed the admiral had been watching and listening all along.

He was sat behind the big table with a smartly dressed woman who had her back to them and was staring out the window.

'Ah,' said Whipper. 'You're in a meeting with a civilian. We'll wait outside until it's concluded.'

'No you won't, Captain,' he said. 'This is Council Senator Henns and she has every right to be in this room as she is part of the naval advisory board.'

'Sorry, Admiral, but that's incorrect. Section 42 of the confidential and classified military information act clearly states that in the matter of galactic security, no civilians are permitted to be a party to military, in this case naval affairs.'

'The only exception is the President,' interjected Bache. 'We cannot discuss anything involving naval affairs while the civilian lady is in the room. Senator or not.'

Admiral Henns's glare went from Whipper to Bache and across to his wife.

'It makes no difference,' he said, sitting back in his chair. 'After recent events involving loss of personal and serious damage to a naval vessel, Captain Whipper, as of immediate effect you are relieved of command and on permanent leave pending further enquiries. Lieutenant Loftt, you are demoted to ensign with a posting immediately to the *Dirtmire*.'

'Sounds amazing,' said Bache, smiling. 'What is it?'

'An ore carrier out of Garag,' said the Senator, turning away from the window and giving Bache a strange look.

'Fabulous,' he said, glancing at Whipper. 'I can go with the pilot.'

'Is that everything?' said Whipper, cheerily and seemingly going along with Bache's chipper demeanour.

The admiral nodded slowly. Bache noticed him exchange a perplexed expression with his wife as the two of them turned and left the room, grinning and fist bumping.

'There's something very odd going on in this building,' said Whipper, once they'd closed the door. 'It's normally humming with activity. Just look at it.'

The entrance concourse was again empty, with just the two security guards sitting behind the reception desk and observing them with what Bache thought was more than just casual scrutiny.

'They're not authorised to do that are they?' Bache asked, as they strolled towards the door.

'Absolutely not,' said Whipper. 'There are strict disciplinary protocols that have to be adhered to. Admiral or not, he doesn't have the authority to hire and fire at will.'

'D'you think they have something to do with what happened in the Dresse system?'

'I'm not ruling it out, but that operation there had been underway for decades, long before these two had any seniority.'

'I do have a niggling impression that the *K2* perhaps wasn't expected to return.'

'Hmm,' grunted Whipper. 'I can't for one minute believe that to be true, but then again I'm told the prisoners do seem to be extremely shocked they didn't get the ship.'

'Do you think it was part of the plan?' said Bache.

'What d'you mean?'

'That a Katadromiko was supposed to turn up all along and get commandeered?'

'Someone screwed it up then,' said Whipper. 'I don't suppose they envisioned losing three of their shiny new battleships in the process.'

This time the door was unlocked and they exited back out into the drizzle, and heads down they jogged through the rain towards the flyer.

Four men stepped down from inside the aircraft as they approached, all armed and pointing their weapons at Bache and the captain. Three of them wore plain black jumpsuits, but Bache recognised the uniform the fourth man wore. He'd had dealings with them before. Sure enough as they got close the eagle insignia sewn into the man's forearm swung into view. A Skirmat Eagle, a member of the GDA's notorious secret police.

'Good morning, Kyyt,' said Whipper cheerily. 'Still not man enough to join the navy and do a proper job then?'

'Shut it, Whipper,' he snapped, waving his pistol at the flyer's door. 'I've waited a long time for this, now get in.'

'Still having to threaten people with a gun to promote authority then?'

'You can abuse me all you like, you're both under arrest and going to Fort Dagster,' he said, grinning.

'Fort Dagster?' said the pilot, overhearing and turning in his seat. 'I'm not bloody flying there.'

One of the other three armed men turned and shot the pilot. He slumped over the controls with a shocked expression frozen on his face and slid unconscious to the cockpit floor.

Bache realised at that moment that he and the captain were in serious trouble. The situation had escalated out of all proportion and he had no idea why.

27

Naval Command, Kentro, Dasos, Prasinos system

THE SUDDEN SCREAMING of antigravs above made them all jump. Looking up, Bache witnessed a marine assault craft dropping with alarming speed directly overhead. He was just considering running to get out of the way, when Whipper grabbed his arm and shook his head.

The ship ceased its rapid descent only about thirty metres above them, turned and continued down to land a few metres away. It was shrouded in its own cloud of steam as the rain evaporated off its still red-hot heat shield. The puddles on the carboncrete pavement below the ship fizzed and boiled, creating more clouds of vapour that drifted towards them on the breeze. Bache thought they couldn't have made it look more sinister if they'd tried.

Its rear ramp powered down with a clunk, creating swirls of steam as it dropped. Four armoured marines emerged, their shoulder-mounted cannons traversing around selecting and locking potential targets.

'What the fuck is this?' exclaimed Kyyt, his bravado waning slightly.

'You're going on holiday, Patreyous,' said Whipper. 'I have a special cabin waiting.'

'I'm not going anywhere,' Kyyt said, taking off back towards the buildings.

Whipper nodded towards the running figure and a marine hit him with a stun shot. Kyyt dropped like a bag of rocks and the same marine clumped over and picked the unconscious body up.

The Skirmat's three colleagues stood frozen, not daring to move. They would all be acutely aware of the capabilities of armoured marines and they were seriously outgunned many times over.

Bache peered back into the flyer.

'Bring the pilot too,' he shouted above the noise of the antigravs, and pointing inside the aircraft. 'I think he'll be wanting a redeployment when he wakes up anyway.'

He trotted over to the assault craft with Whipper, through the clouds of steam and straight up the ramp, his exposed skin warmed considerably from the ship's underside heat shield as he boarded.

The assault craft was only on the ground for thirty-eight seconds, its four powerful antigravs had it vertical and over the speed of sound within eight seconds of lifting off again. The pilot cloaked the vessel and side slipped across to follow the space elevator cord closely just in case someone could still track them and considered taking a shot. As soon as they were in space, the small ship jumped.

'Aren't we going back to the *K2*?' Bache asked.

The captain's intonation darkened.

'We are, only it's just not attached to the station anymore.'

Bache picked up on the captain's sudden change in disposition.

'Problems?' he questioned.

'While we were on the kordoni earlier a large number of non-military security turned up at the ship to escort the Gata prisoners away.'

'Yes, you told me. I take it there was a problem with that?'

'The first officer felt something wasn't quite right when they insisted on boarding the ship. He kept them waiting at the airlock while he did a facial recognition check.'

'Don't tell me—mercenaries?'

'All arrived on the station an hour before us and with fake credentials.'

'What ship did they arrive on?'

'That's where it gets even more suspicious. The docking log and camera feeds for the time they arrived were supposedly mistakenly deleted and when the error was rectified, that particular ship's data had been, surprise surprise, permanently lost.'

'Don't tell me—the ship was mysteriously no longer on its jetty?'

'Dock was empty. I reckon it released, cloaked and hid underneath one of the large passenger liners leaving at the time.'

'So, did they get the prisoners?'

'Nope.'

Bache smiled.

'I have a feeling we have something or someone they want back, badly, and I think I know a way to find out who it might be.'

The sound of the landing struts extending ended the conversation and the buzz of the atmosphere shield against the hull told Bache they had arrived at the *K2*.

The first officer was waiting as the rear ramp lowered.

'Are we away securely?' the captain asked.

'Yes, sir,' said Falenthraite, saluting the captain as they disembarked. 'Do you think the admiral is involved? There appears to be a lot going on here that we're not a party too.'

'I don't know, Hegg,' said Whipper. 'Henns has always trampled on anyone smarter than him to get a promotion.'

'Or his wife has,' interjected Bache.

They both turned to stare at him and he thought he was about to get reprimanded for disrespecting a council senator.

Whipper shrugged and adopted a rueful expression.

'Loftt's right,' he said. 'She does appear to be calling the shots.'

'She was there then, was she?' Falenthraite asked.

'Hmm,' grunted Whipper. 'We seem to have a civilian running the navy.'

'The question is,' said Bache, 'is she running it for the benefit of the GDA or her own agenda?'

'Ancients only knows,' said Whipper. 'But I'm sure as gravity going to find out in the very near future.'

'What's our next move?' Falenthraite asked.

The captain turned to Bache.

'Young Loftt here has an idea of how to find out who amongst all our prisoners was the reason for the elaborate rescue attempt.'

'You think we have someone important within the group?' said Falenthraite, raising his eyebrows.

'Someone went to a lot of trouble and took a big risk to try and recover those men. I don't think they would've attempted that to recover a few foot soldiers,' said Bache.

'Loftt does have a point,' said Falenthraite, looking at the captain. 'What's the plan?'

The canteen had been set up with extra cameras and microphones that covered the room from every angle. The ruse was that the prisoners were about to be handed back over in a secret rendezvous, authorised by Naval Command. They were to be given a final meal together in the canteen shortly before the handover.

A small team of psychologists watched the

camera feeds intently as the prisoners were informed of this and led into the room. They were looking for anyone who didn't quite fit in with the rabble, someone given a little extra space or perhaps kowtowed to in the slightest of ways as to give up their seniority.

Halfway through their meal an announcement was made that their return had been cancelled as the senior Gata commanders had decided they were expendable and no longer required. They would now be going to a GDA military penal mining colony.

This was the moment the watchers had been waiting for and sure enough many of the prisoners glanced over at one particular table. One even approached the table and began remonstrating with one of the three Gatas sitting there. He was quickly bundled back to his seat by two others.

Bache, sitting in the observation room next door, smiled. He didn't need the psychologists to tell him who they were looking for now.

Captain Whipper grunted and raised his eyebrows at Bache.

'You were right, Loftt,' he said. 'Let's separate that one and the one that had a go at him. I'm sure he'll let us know who he is. Take them individually, without the other's knowledge, and keep them well separated. I want to see the senior one's face when we know his name and rank.'

Bache nodded.

'I'll have it done in the middle of the night,' he said. 'Then, when we get to question them in the morning and they've been sitting alone in an interview room for half the night, they'll be tired and more likely to slip up.'

'Good idea,' said Whipper. 'We'll resume at first bell.'

Katadromiko 2, *stationary in non-system space*

BACHE WAS in high spirits as he strutted into the interview room the following morning. 'Greetings,' he chirped, sliding into the chair opposite the Gata.

The Gata's head slowly lifted off the table. He'd been cuffed to the only other chair in the room for seven hours and his half-open catlike eyes regarded Bache coldly.

'What the fuck is this?' he hissed, rattling the restraints that held his wrists to the chair arms. 'I've been like this for bloody hours.'

Bache half smiled and studied the Gata from the opposite side of the table. He glanced up at one of the cameras.

'Captain's orders,' he said, dropping his gaze back to stare straight into the prisoner's eyes. 'You've already murdered enough of his crew.'

'That wasn't me was it?' he spat. 'I'm a civilian engineer, not a bloody soldier—or one of those fucking deranged pridens.'

'Like the one you threatened in the dining hall?'

'You saw that, huh?' he said, cackling suddenly. 'Of course you did.'

His chin jerked up, his expression changing to one of distrust.

'That was a set up wasn't it? All that handover crap was just a ploy to get us to reveal who was in charge, wasn't it?'

Bache didn't answer the question, but asked one of his own.

'What's your name?'

'Gadd,' he said. 'Jillcott Gadd, Nkris.'

'Okay, Gadd,' said Bache, as a close-up of the incident in the dining hall came up on a wall screen to their left. 'I take it he's the only priden left amongst you then?'

He pointed at the frozen image.

Gadd laughed.

'Priden!' he scoffed. 'He's no priden.'

Bache said nothing. He just raised his eyebrows and jutted his chin, making it evident he wanted the prisoner to continue.

Gadd grinned and sat back in his chair.

'Oh, no,' he said smugly. 'That sort of information has a price.'

One of the two marines guarding the door took a step forward, activated his rifle and pointed it at the Gata's head.

'At ease, Corporal,' snapped Bache, turning to glower at the soldier. 'That's quite unnecessary.'

The marine slowly returned to his position by the door, his face obscured by his dark helmet visor and the barely audible whine from his activated rifle ceased, returning the room to complete silence once more, until Bache spoke again.

'I am in a position to make your life a lot more comfortable,' he said, calmly. 'But remember, at the end of the day, you're still a prisoner of war.'

'I want a private cell,' he said. 'Away from those other warmongering Nkris.'

'That can be arranged.'

'You don't realise, I didn't come on this operation willingly. None of the non-military did.'

'I understand,' said Bache.

The Gata stared at the table top for a moment, contemplating.

'Better food,' he continued, suddenly looking up again. 'Not that slop you obviously think we eat.'

'Anything else?'

'An entertainment screen.'

'Right, okay,' said Bache, with a slight smirk. 'You do realise it'll all be human stuff on there?'

The Gata shrugged.

'Anything's better than staring at the four walls.'

'Okay, deal,' said Bache. 'But I want to know everything you know, and I mean everything.'

Bache lowered his tone and continued.

'If I find out you withheld anything, you'll be straight back in with your warmongers and they'll be informed what you did.'

Gadd's eyes widened and his grey face went a shade lighter.

'He's the Patrician,' he blurted.

'And that is?' asked Bache.

The Gata looked at him strangely and exhaled loudly in irritation.

'The Grand Leader—President—King, or whatever you want to call him in your weird human languages.'

'And his name is?'

'Histermain,' he said. 'Patrician Koll Histermain.'

'What's the operational reason for the fleet of battleships?'

'To take a home world for the Nkris.'

'Where? And what was wrong with the one you were on?'

'Too remote and not amongst the Gata worlds.'

'So the plan is to take one of the existing Gata home planets?'

'Yeah. It's always been our destiny to return and the Nkris to rule the Gata Realm.'

'Which planet? There are eight of them now, I think.'

'No idea, way above my pay grade.'

Bache raised his eyebrows and leant forward, staring straight into the Gata's eyes, but saying nothing.

'No, really,' Gadd said, nervously. 'I don't think even the pridens know that. Only the Patrician and the Guardians have that information.'

'Guardians?' Bache questioned.

'Err—regional commanders would be a fair translation,' said Gadd. 'Although I have no idea if it'll be happening now the Patrician's here and he's lost his flagship. The captain that took control of this ship is a Guardian.'

Bache decided not to tell the prisoner he no longer existed.

'So, one of the destroyed battleships was his flagship?' he asked instead.

'No—no, no, not one of those,' said Gadd, shaking his head and pointing at the ceiling. 'He was promised a GDA cruiser. It would arrive and he was given extensive instructions of how to take it. This vessel was to be his flagship.'

'The Katadromiko?' Bache asked, struggling to keep the excitement from his voice. 'You were expecting a cruiser to turn up all along? And given instructions on how to commandeer it?'

'Uh, huh,' said Gadd, looking a little contrite. 'He was very pleased when one of these turned up, although it did arrive sooner than we expected. We weren't ready. The jump disrupter plans had turned up later than promised and we'd only been able to build and install it to one ship and it was still on the surface.'

Bache glanced fleetingly up at one of the cameras, knowing the captain would have heard that.

'Where did the disrupter plans come from, Gadd?' he asked, turning his attention back to the Gata.

'We were never told that. Every now and then a drone would arrive in system and we had to retrieve it and download its encrypted data.'

'How long had this been going on?'

'Oh, erm—it must be about eighteen years I suppose,' he said, thinking hard. 'I was quite young when we crash-landed on the planet and it was a couple of years after that.'

'Are the drones still on the planet?'

'No, they were all—actually the last one might still be there,' he said, staring at the wall. 'We had to download the data and send them back, but I don't think that last one was returned because of the freighter arriving really quickly.'

'Where were they sent back to?'

'No idea, only the Patrician and the Guardians would have that information.'

'Why did you remove the crew of the freighter?'

'We didn't, they'd been paid for the last container, they transferred onto the other freighter and left.'

Bache glanced at the camera again. This was getting more interesting every minute.

'They forgot the girl in the medical room though,' he said.

'No, she had to be there to send the distress drone.'

Bache stared at him in disbelief.

'Her crew left her there to die?'

'I suppose so—I was just on one of our ships to retrieve the containers.'

'Containers? I thought there was only one you wanted?'

'One on each trip the freighter made.'

'What was in the containers and how many deliveries were there?'

'Tycelerin ore,' he said, looking sheepish. 'Hundreds over the years. That freighter's crew must be hugely rich.'

'Gadd, tell me more about this Patrician, Koll Histermain. What kind of leader is he?'

Gadd sighed heavily.

'He's not really a leader for the people. He's a dictator. He rules over the Nkris with an iron fist. Anyone who dares to question him or go against his wishes is met with brutal punishment. As will I if anyone finds out I've talked to you.'

Bache leant forward, his eyes narrowing.

'I can protect you, Gadd. But I need to know more about this Patrician and his plans. Which planet's he after and what do you think he's going to do with the surviving indigenous population once he takes it?'

Gadd shifted uncomfortably on his chair, his eyes darting around the small room.

'I don't know. As I said before, he doesn't share his plans with anyone other than his Guardians. But I suspect it won't be good for the Gata clan involved.'

Bache leant in closer, his eyes intent on Gadd's face. The Gata's pointed ears flattened against his head and he shrank back into his chair.

'Can you tell me more about his methods of

punishment?' Bache asked, his voice low and steady.

Gadd hesitated for a moment, his eyes flicking towards the door before he spoke in a hushed tone.

'Death is the most common form of punishment for those who cross him. But he's also been known to subject people to horrific experiments and torture.'

Bache's brow furrowed and he sat back regarding the Gata.

'What about the Guardians? Who exactly are they?' he asked, trying to shift the direction of the conversation away from the Patrician for a moment.

'The Guardians are the Patrician's most loyal and trusted officers. They oversee the pridens and enforce the Patrician's will on the clan. They're powerful and respected among the Nkris, but at the same time greatly feared.'

Bache took a deep breath, his mind racing with the information Gadd had given him. He knew that this was all very interesting but not the breakthrough they needed to find out where that fleet were heading. The Gata home worlds were spread out over hundreds of light years and if they didn't narrow it down to one planet quickly, hundreds of thousands could die in the invasion.

29

____

Katadromiko 2, *stationary in non-system space*

CAPTAIN WHIPPER PUFFED out his cheeks and grunted as he watched the interview wrap up. They'd learnt a lot from the young engineer, but their attention now had to be on this Patrician character. He thought he'd leave it to Bache to tell Malic her crew had only hired her to die on the freighter. Or perhaps they shouldn't tell her. Knowing something like that could have serious mental health consequences. Probably best to let the medical team make that decision.

A knock on his study door interrupted his thoughts. Glancing left at a small screen recessed into his desk, he saw Lieutenant Loftt waiting outside.

'Enter,' he called. 'Just the man I want to see,' he added, as Bache closed the door behind him and approached the desk.

'I have something I want to run by you, Captain,' Bache said, standing bolt upright in front of him.

'At ease, Lieutenant,' he said, waving at a chair to Bache's right. 'You want to have a crack at the Patrician, I take it?'

'Actually, no, sir,' said Bache, sitting on the front edge of the seat. 'I think he'd eat me alive and rather die than divulge any information.'

'Then, what?' Whipper asked, leaning back in his seat and crossing his arms.

'I want to go back to Dresse.'

'Are you mad? Absolutely not. If it's slipped your mind, there were twelve battleships hungry for a fight the last time we were there.'

'Yes, sir, but I don't believe they'll be there now. My guess is they'll be on the way to Gata space.'

'For what possible reason would you want to go back there anyway?'

'To secure that last drone, Captain,' he said. 'If it's still there, it may have information of who sent them still programmed into its data core.'

'Hmm,' grunted Whipper. He rubbed his chin as he considered Loftt's proposal. It was true that any information they could gather on the drones' origins would be hugely valuable, but was it worth risking a valuable member of his crew and another ship? However, Bache was one of his best young officers, and he trusted his judgement.

'All right, Lieutenant,' he said after a moment. 'You can take a small ship back to Dresse, but you'll have to go alone. I can't risk any more of my crew on this mission.'

Loftt nodded and turned to leave, but suddenly stopped and turned back.

'Could I take the pilot we picked up on Dasos?' Bache asked. 'He's technically not a member of the crew, a better pilot than me, and I would like to have someone covering my back.'

Whipper rolled his eyes and nodded slowly.

'Permission granted,' he said. 'Just bring him and the ship back in one piece this time.'

'Do you know his name?' Bache asked.

The captain touched a few icons on his recessed desk screen and read the result.

'Pilot Officer L'Clers,' he said, glancing back up again.

Bache nodded, his excitement barely concealed.

'Thank you, sir. I won't let you down.'

'I know you won't,' Whipper said, with the hint of a smile. 'Just be careful. And remember, if it's too dangerous, cut your losses and get back here. I'm sure we'll get to the bottom of this mess with or without that drone.'

Bache nodded again, standing up from the chair. 'Understood, sir. I'll leave as soon as I'm ready.'

Whipper watched as Loftt saluted him and left the room before turning his attention back to the screen on his desk. It was a risky move, but if the lieutenant could retrieve the drone and find its source, it could change the course of their mission.

He hoped this time they'd have a bit of luck.

Bache was back at hangar 41 again. Because of the operational situation the lighting was dimmed to a dull red glow and it took a few moments for his eyes to adjust from the bright white light in the corridors. It was cold too and he shivered as he climbed inside a considerably smaller and older gunship than the one he'd been given last time. Probably captain's orders after the state of the new one he returned previously. This he knew wasn't so much of a bad thing, as this model had the Mark II Jaxion antigravs. Bigger and much more powerful, but alas they were noisier. It also had a multi-barrel rail gun that could be fired fore and aft, alongside the laser cannons.

Bache checked the items he'd requested had

been loaded onto the lower deck, but was surprised to see L'Clers already in the cockpit, undergoing a full systems check.

''Allo, boss,' said a grinning L'Clers, glancing over his shoulder as Bache stooped to enter the snug cabin.

'You didn't waste any time getting here,' Bache replied, squeezing himself into the co-pilot's seat.

'I've not had a bang in one of these before, so I thought I'd better attune myself to her foibles,' he said.

'Is that so?' said Bache, raising his eyebrows. 'Going bang in this is something I'd personally like to avoid. What's your first name by the way?'

'Handis,' he said. 'But everybody calls me Clunk.'

'Clunk?'

'Ah,' L'Clers grunted, pulling an awkward face. 'I landed a fully laden freighter a tad heavily on a small space station in the Fal'it system a couple of years ago. Almost knocked it out of orbit. It took them two days to jack the landing struts out of its deck.'

'Ouch,' Bache uttered and was about to say more, when he was stopped by a voice from behind him.

'My services not good enough for you anymore?' snapped Zaphir, from the cockpit door.

Bache turned, thinking she was joking, but the expression on her face said otherwise.

'Err—it was captain's orders, Zaffie,' he said, in the most genuine voice he could muster.

'You're a lying bag a crap,' she hissed, thrusting a forefinger at him. 'I hope you don't fucking come back.'

With that, she turned and stomped down the stairs. The two of them in the cockpit turned and watched her through the front screen as she marched across the hangar and left without looking back.

'Nice girl,' said L'Clers, giving Bache a slow eye roll. 'Know you well, does she?'

Bache said nothing, just the glower he gave L'Clers was enough to persuade him to not continue on that particular line of inquiry. It was silent in the cockpit for the next few minutes as L'Clers completed his flight checks.

Bache sat quietly staring at the closed hangar airlock door wondering if he should pursue her and explain. But he'd known Zaphir a long time and when she was in one of those moods it was always better to leave her well alone.

'Ship's all ready, boss,' said L'Clers, waking Bache from his thoughts.

He nodded and pointed towards the gaping hangar door, where hundreds of distant stars sparkled.

'Clunk, let's get out there and call me Bache for ancients' sake.'

30

GDA gunship, arriving in the Dresse system

CLUNK WOKE Bache as he undertook the final jump into Dresse space. Materialising behind and as close to one of the systems stars as safety protocols permitted, he cloaked the tiny ship and engaged the alma drive.

By the time Bache had motored his seat to the full upright position and rubbed the sleep from his eyes, they were emerging from behind the star.

'Let's see if anything's changed,' he said, as the holomap updated with Dresse around one hundred million kilometres distant.

It was quickly evident there were no uncloaked vessels in the system or anywhere near Dresse. But as Bache knew, that didn't mean they weren't there, hiding somewhere. He paid special attention to the upper atmosphere of the Dresse system's single gas giant, some four billion kilometres further out—a favourite concealment ploy for ships' captains since the beginning of time.

An hour later as they approached Dresse, Bache asked Clunk to stop the ship a hundred thousand kilometres shy of the planet and remain stationary while he tried something.

'What are you up to?' Clunk asked, as Bache unfolded himself from his chair.

'A little bit of tomfoolery,' he called, while clumping his way down to the main deck.

He unstrapped something tall attached to the deck and pulled off its cover to reveal one of the GDA's smaller attack drones. Pushing it on its cradle into the airlock, he activated it and shut the inner door. Returning to the cockpit, he grinned at Clunk and retook his seat.

'Now, let's see if anyone's lurking,' he said, waking up his control console and cloaking the drone, before opening the airlock and flying it out and away towards the planet.

It didn't have jump capabilities like the bigger ones, so they had to sit and wait as it eventually got into a high orbit using its small conventional drive. After tapping away on his console for a moment, Bache looked up at the holomap which panned in to show Dresse and its close surroundings.

'Knock, knock,' said Bache, pressing a final icon.

The drone immediately began turning and firing its cannon on automatic in every outward direction. Hundreds and hundreds of bolts zipped away into space. It mimicked a firework display and they both sat and watched, waiting to see if just one of those bolts touched the shielding of a cloaked ship, causing it to fluoresce.

'If one of those hits us, it'll give away our

position too,' said Clunk, ducking as a bolt went close overhead.

'I omitted our exact position,' said Bache. 'So they'll get close but not touch our shields.'

Clunk nodded, but judging by the expression on his face he wasn't totally convinced.

'As I expected, the fleet seems to have moved on,' said Bache, with a grin.

The smile disappeared as a bright flash and explosion, causing them both to squint, lit up the holomap as the drone vaporised.

'Ancients alive!' exclaimed Clunk. 'What the fuck was that?'

'Hmm,' grunted Bache. 'It seems their land-based cannon is still operational.'

'You didn't tell me they had one of those bloody things,' Clunk moaned. 'D'you know what that monster could do to us?'

'We wouldn't know much about it,' Bache replied. 'Can we pop around to the other side of the planet for insertion now please?'

'With pleasure,' Clunk replied, eyeing Bache anxiously. He turned and accelerated the gunship quickly against the spin of the planet to get out of the cannon's range as fast as possible.

Once they were safe from instant vaporisation, Clunk dropped them into the atmosphere, levelling out at twenty thousand feet. Bache had given him the coordinates for the Ballenhyght Caverns and they proceeded there at fourteen times the speed of sound.

Once there and remaining cloaked, Bache scanned the region from high above, ensuring their noisy antigravs wouldn't be heard.

'Is it clear?' Clunk asked.

'On the outside, yes,' said Bache, not looking up from his screen. 'But the rock is very dense here, so who knows what or who's lurking inside the construction caverns.'

'Where's that cannon?'

'Somewhere well hidden. Remember, this was supposed to be a katapato red planet, so everything is well concealed under rock.'

After a few minutes and detecting no movement other than indigenous fauna, Bache gave Clunk the order to descend and find a suitable landing spot.

'What about in the caverns themselves?' said Clunk. 'It'll hide the ship from above.'

'I was thinking that too,' said Bache. 'Take it slow and be ready to backtrack if anything moves.'

Clunk nodded slowly and began dropping the ship down towards the mountain range. Bache watched closely, mostly on his array screen, but occasionally out of the front screen.

'Stop,' he said, suddenly and after scowling at his monitor for a moment, he pointed out the front screen. 'Turn to port a few degrees and creep forward slowly.'

'Movement?' questioned Clunk.

'No, an intermittent power source.'

A clean and dry rocky peak was dead ahead, which normally wouldn't have been unusual amongst all the other rocky peaks dotted around the region. This one, however, was the only one without a covering of snow on the top.

'No snow,' said Clunk.

'Exactly,' replied Bache.

His screen pulsed again for a millisecond.

'Ahh,' he exclaimed. 'I think we've found our land-based cannon.'

Bache activated the bow rail gun, targeted the location of the power source and sent a volley of slugs into the mountainside. The reaction was instantaneous, as a section of the peak slid to one side, revealing the tip of a huge cannon barrel. As they watched, the weapon motored upwards, its metres-wide barrel traversing and attempting to lock a target.

'Fuck the ancients,' said Clunk. 'That's a monstrous thing. Can we disable it?'

Bache was already targeting the weapon and within seconds the rail gun spoke again. This time the result was a little more spectacular. The cannon had been prepped to fire and the colossal amount of charged energy about to be unleashed into the heavens exploded outwards, sending lumps of the weapon and the mountain top cascading out in all directions.

'Woah,' shouted Clunk, backing the gunship away as quickly as he could.

They had been quite a distance away, but

they still witnessed a lot of shrapnel ricocheting of their shields.

'Move again, quick,' snapped Bache. 'The dust is giving away our location.'

Clunk dropped the ship again, seeking shelter and a hiding place.

Bache saw the snow-capped peaks rise up and disappear above as Clunk carefully positioned the gunship in the middle of a narrow steep-sided valley that led into the wider one with the caverns.

'Well, I'm glad to see the back of that fucker,' said Clunk. 'Biggest one I've ever seen.'

'That looked like the model fitted to the planet protection satellite ring around Dasos,' said Bache, the concern evident on his face. 'That's more secret GDA technology we've found here.'

It was silent in the cockpit for a few moments before Clunk spoke again.

'Are we looking for a specific cavern?' he asked, while concentrating hard on their narrow surroundings.

Bache knew the ship had terrain avoidance

overrides, but he also knew pilots were a proud bunch and took it personally if the software had to take control of the vessel.

'The Gata told us if the drone was still here, it would be in cavern eight,' said Bache.

'Do we know which one that is? Cuz I bet they're not going to have a big sign above the entrance.'

'I remember they're in a line stretching from south to north, but all the entrances to the caverns are slightly different because they're all originally natural. They were enlarged inside by the Gata to hide and build their fleet. I've been inside number twelve before and I might recognise that one.'

Bache studied his screen again.

'I'm still getting no movement or power sources locally, so take us slowly out into the main valley and let's see if I can spot it.'

Clunk did as he requested, emerging about halfway along the valley.

Bache leant forward in his seat and craned his neck left and right. He didn't know at what point in the valley they'd emerged, so he was trying to spot where the first or last cavern was and then work it out from there.

He also checked his monitor closely too, just in case the explosion on the nearby mountain top had attracted any attention. All seemed quiet though.

'Go that way,' said Bache, pointing right.

'D'you know where you are then?'

'No, don't have a clue, but right is as good a choice as any,' he said, with a shrug.

Clunk smirked, more nervously than humorously, and turned the ship to starboard.

They travelled north watching the cavern entrances closely as they passed, but detected no movement. When they could see the final opening, they backtracked six, presuming that to be number eight and with the bow floodlights on flew inside the massive gaping entrance.

'Bloody ancients,' exclaimed Clunk, when he saw the scale of the cavern. 'So, let me get this straight, only one of their ships could fit in here?'

'Hmm—yeah,' said Bache, with a sigh. 'Big black evil-looking things.'

They both had their eyes out on stalks as Clunk flew down the left side, shining the powerful lights into every nook and corner as they went.

'How big is this drone?' Clunk asked.

'If it's the model I'm thinking of, about six metres tall and stands on four struts. It's based on the same chassis as the manned maintenance tractors they use in most of the servicing space stations.'

'Ah—right, I know them.'

GDA gunship, Ballenhyght Caverns, Dresse

THEY'D GONE AROUND TWICE, inspecting every corner of the five kilometre-deep cavern. There was plenty of abandoned equipment lying around the walls, but no GDA-issue drones. They were about to give up, when Clunk suddenly pointed at the cavern wall on the left-hand side.

'That just moved,' he said.

'What moved?' said Bache, following the direction of Clunk's finger. 'What d'you mean?'

'The wall, sort of swayed.'

'Take the ship back slowly.'

Clunk crept the gunship backwards and this time Bache saw what he meant. A small section of the wall wobbled slightly, probably caused by the back-draught of the antigravs.

'That section of wall isn't solid,' said Bache, standing up. 'Set us down here—I want to have a look at that.'

The ship clunked down heavily on the solid rock floor, dumping Bache back in his seat again. He threw an exasperated stare in Clunk's direction.

'I can see where your moniker came from, still haven't perfected the landings then?'

'New ship,' he replied, with a shrug. 'I'll get the hang of it.'

'Please do that,' said Bache, standing again. 'Come on, let's see what that is,' he added before disappearing down the stairs.

Clunk shut the motors down and followed. Bache met him in the loading bay. He'd donned a warm marine-issue jacket and a weapon. He handed a jacket to Clunk.

'It's freezing out there, so you'll need that and grab a rifle too.'

Bache bypassed the safeties and opened both airlock doors. They jumped down, lit their rifle lights and moved towards the weird wall. Apart from the ticking of the cooling antigravs, the cavern was silent, cold and very dark.

The cavern wall was only thirty metres away and Bache reached out an arm and pushed it when he arrived. It moved back slightly and something rattled off to the right. He followed the noise with his light and discovered a crudely made latch about two metres away.

'It's a door,' said Clunk, stepping up and lifting the latch.

It opened inwards and he was able to push it back inside a three metre-wide tunnel. They both shone their lights inside. It stretched away into the gloom, further than their lights could penetrate.

'Perhaps it's a connecting tunnel to the neighbouring cavern,' said Clunk.

'Yeah, could be,' said Bache. 'I've been thinking—perhaps this isn't cavern eight. We didn't start at one and count up, we started at what we presumed to be fourteen and counted back. What if there were more than fourteen caverns?'

Clunk looked at Bache and then down the tunnel.

'It could be that one down there then?' he said, emphasising the point by flashing his light down the tunnel again.

'Or the next, or the next. We really don't know how many of these things there are do we?' said Bache, dejectedly.

'Do we go back out, head south to the first one and then count back eight?' asked Clunk.

Bache looked back at the gunship and then turned to stare down the tunnel again. Deciding on a course of action, he retrieved the remote activator from his pocket and pointed it at the ship. The airlock closed and sealed, the vessel cloaked and was then completely invisible in the gloom.

'Come on then,' he said. 'Let's stretch our legs and see where this leads.

'You said they had other ships besides the fourteen big ones?' said Clunk, as they walked.

'Yeah—they have some medium-sized freighters and gunships and so on.'

'Well, they would've been built somewhere too. You could only get one battleship in that cavern and if all these caverns are around the same size, then there must be more.'

A door in the left-side wall appeared out of the shadows. Clunk tried the handle.

'Locked,' he said and went to walk on.

'I have a key,' said Bache, holding up his rifle.

Changing the setting from stun to full power, he lined it up with the mechanism and gave it the good news. The report of the laser rifle sounded louder than usual in the confined space, as it echoed around the tunnel. It had the desired effect though. The circular hole where the lock had been glowed red as Bache kicked the door. It swung inside and crashed against the internal wall.

Shining their lights inside they immediately took a step back, as dozens of faces stared back at them from behind three high bunk beds, all shielding their eyes with their hands from the brightness of the lights.

'Fuck the ancients,' blurted Clunk. 'Who are these guys?'

'They're locals,' said Bache, recovering quickly from the shock and recognising the facial features and clothing.

'They're so skinny,' Clunk said. 'How many are there?'

Bache fumbled inside his pockets for his translator and set the language for Guasse.

'We are GDA—not purrers,' he said and waited for the translator to do its work.

'Who are GDA?' croaked one man, stepping out from the darkness. His clothes were no more than rags and they hung off him as if five sizes too big. His hair was long, grey, matted and framed his gaunt lined features.

'That's a long story, but rest assured we are your friends,' Bache answered. 'How many of you are there?'

The man watched Clunk nervously checking up and down the corridor with his rifle.

'You're not with them?' he said, a little more confidently this time.

'Absolutely not,' said Bache.

'Two hundred and forty-one in this dormitory.'

'There are more like this?'

'Hundreds of dormitories,' he said. 'We have to build ships. Ships gone now. Left us here to die.'

'You're free now,' said Clunk, as they both stepped back into the corridor and gestured for them to follow.

The line of human misery traipsed past one by one and turned right, back towards the cavern with the gunship.

'What's that way?' Bache asked, pointing in the other direction as the man who'd spoken approached them.

'Command cavern,' he said, stopping in front of them and giving Bache a concerted stare. 'I'll come with you as you release the others,' he added, sternly.

Bache realised that was more a challenge than anything else. He smiled and nodded.

'What's your name by the way?' he asked.

'Elder Parsic,' he said, confidently.

'You're one of your villages elders?' said Bache, nodding his head in a respectful bow. 'I'm very pleased to meet you. Now, if you'll show me where they are, let's get the rest of your people out of this prison.'

Parsic nodded at both of them, turned and marched off up the corridor with a surprising gait considering his weakened condition.

Over the next hour they opened and released twenty-four more dormitories. Parsic would enter and explain the situation, before they all traipsed out, or were carried out and went always in the same direction. They were to grab tools from the cavern and the fitter ones carry on through all the caverns and release the other prisoners in that direction.

'Surely, we must be nearer that cavern now?' said Clunk, pointing in the opposite direction. 'Wouldn't it be quicker to go out through that one now?'

Parsic stopped, his expression darkening.

'For years, anyone dragged off to the command cavern was never seen again. There were rumours of torture and horrific murders,' he said. 'Whether it was true or not, nobody knew, but just the threat of going in this direction was enough.'

'Is it also known as cavern eight?' Clunk asked.

Parsic nodded.

'And the cavern of skulls,' he said, his eyes dropping to the floor. 'Both my brothers went there some years ago.'

'You haven't seen them since?'

This time he shook his head, before taking a deep breath and looking back up at them.

'I'm coming with you,' he said. 'Someone's got to cross over and organise releasing everyone in the other caverns.'

'Are you up to it?' asked Bache.

'I have to be,' he said, turning and marching off again.

Bache and Clunk exchanged a glance and trotted off to catch him up.

______

32

Approaching cavern eight, Ballenhyght Caverns, Dresse

BACHE WAS surprised at how quickly the elder could move down into the darkness. But the more he thought about how long they'd been living down here, and judging by the almost total lack of light fittings, it was obvious his night vision had become extremely pronounced. All the others had disappeared off in the other direction into complete darkness seemingly quite confident as to where they were going.

It wasn't long before a faint glow ahead had him slowing, then coming to a dead stop and turning to face them with a perplexed expression.

'Was cavern nine illuminated when you entered the tunnel?' he asked.

'No it wasn't,' said Bache. 'Just the faintest of luminescence from the main entrance.'

'Hmm,' grunted Parsic, glancing back at the glow in the distance. 'Well, that one still is. We need to be wary.'

Bache turned his rifle light off and signalled Clunk to do the same.

'Don't want to advertise our approach if they're still in there do we?'

They carried on with Bache and Clunk leading this time and at a slightly reduced pace.

Bang.

'Ouch!' blurted Clunk as he walked into something in the darkness. 'What the fuck is this? And what's that bloody smell?'

Bache inched his way over and felt around the obstruction. It was a rectangular container of some kind, roughly a metre high and two metres long. It had a faint glowing red light on the far side. He'd smelt that odour before and his eyes went wide when he remembered what it was.

'Ancients save us,' he muttered, as he bent down by the small red light.

'What is it?' asked Clunk, rubbing his knee vigorously.

'You two shield me from the cavern,' he said. 'I want to turn my light on and inspect this.'

They both passed him and stood between him and cavern eight, which was only about two hundred metres away now.

Bache whistled through his teeth as he lit his rifle light. A primed explosive device was attached to the side of the box. Luckily, it was a recognised GDA self-adhesive detonator and Bache had seen and used them before. He held his breath, pressed the arming button and the red light went out.

'Woah!' exclaimed Clunk. 'Did you just disarm a bomb?'

'Uh, huh,' he said, exhaling and pulling the detonator away from the box.

'What's in the box?' asked Parsic.

'That's what that smell is,' said Bache. 'Tycelerin.'

'Tycelerin!' blurted Clunk, glancing around Bache at the size of the box now illuminated by Bache's light. 'Oh, shit—you can blow a cruiser in half with a cupful—there's enough there to move the planet.'

'Indeed,' said Bache. 'They're intending to bring the entire mountain range down to cover their tracks.'

'D'you think there are more of these?' Clunk asked.

'They had another whole space freight container delivered only recently and they've been getting them regularly for years. So my conclusion is, yes.'

'We need to find and disarm them all,' said Clunk. 'If we miss just one…'

'So, they were going to bring the whole mountain down on top of us,' said Parsic. 'Quicker than starving to death I suppose.'

'They still might,' said Bache, standing, turning his light off and slipping the detonator device into one of his large jacket pockets. 'Come on, the lights might mean they're still here and haven't finished the job yet.'

They made their way down the remaining couple of hundred metres cautiously as the door to the tunnel was open out into the cavern. As they got closer, they could hear the whirring of motors and a strange clattering sound.

Luckily, there was a collection of machinery, packing cases and piles of old spacecraft parts piled around the entrance to the tunnel. Bache waved for the other two to hide in cover while he crouched down and crept forward to see what was going on.

He stopped behind a pile of old worn anti-grav spoolers and peeked around the left-hand side.

A Gata ship sat a few hundred metres down

the cavern. He recognised the design as a sister ship to the one he and Zaphir had dumped in the ocean on their first trip here. It was quite large and had obviously undergone considerable use. Its once white exterior was badly faded to a shade of dirty grey and the tell-tale scorch marks of many planetary re-entries lined all sides.

Its freight ramps were down and the rattling they'd heard was a collection of electric freight loaders running containers up inside the ship. He could see a couple of Gatas organising the loading and then he saw it.

The GDA drone was sat on its struts at the back of the equipment they were in the process of loading.

'Fuck,' mumbled Bache to himself. 'So close.'

He crept back to the other two and reported his findings.

'Can't we make some kind of diversion, while you get over to it and download its data core?' said Clunk.

'That could be like poking a gattle nest with a stick,' said Bache.

'What's a gattle?' asked Clunk.

'A particularly aggressive insect on Dee-latayne,' Bache explained. 'There might be only one or two visible before you poke a stick in the nest, but thousands will suddenly appear and they're always mad as hell.'

'What's so important about that thing anyway?' asked Parsic, as he stretched his neck around the corner to survey the cavern he'd never seen.

'Someone within our organisation has been providing the purrers with our technology,' said Bache. 'That drone could have the details of who that is.'

'A traitor.'

'Yeah—and we need to identify them quickly.'

Parsic gazed across the cavern.

'Can you see if the dormitory passage gate is open across the other side?' he asked.

Bache brought his weapon sight up to his eye and zoomed in directly across the cavern.

'It's open, but there's no way to get there unseen.'

Parsic was looking back over his shoulder at something.

'That's not entirely true,' he said. 'Do you have a spare weapon for me to open the dormitory doors?'

Bache hesitated for a second.

'I'm not going to bloody shoot you with it,' said Parsic, raising his eyebrows.

Bache nodded, opened his coat and pulled out a small hidden laser pistol and handed it to the elder.

'I didn't know you had that,' whined Clunk. 'Where's mine?'

'It was presented to me by the President when I saved the universe from crazy androids,' said Bache, then he turned his attention to Parsic. 'So look after it, don't lose it.'

Parsic smiled for the first time.

'It seems some humanoids in this galaxy aren't so bad after all,' he said, patting Bache on the back and staying crouched, made his way through the nearby equipment in the opposite direction to the Gata ship.

'What's he doing?' Clunk asked, moving in beside Bache.

'I'm not sure,' said Bache. 'But whatever it is, I think we'd better be ready to move on that drone.'

They moved deeper into the cavern towards the drone, using the discarded equipment as cover, until they came to a void. There was a gap with no cover between them and their target within plain sight of the Gatas.

'Crap,' said Bache, peeking over a pile of old environmental filters.

The two Gatas were engrossed in their loading duties, when one of them suddenly looked up and pointed down the cavern.

Bache looked too and saw another of the un-manned loaders motoring across the cavern, having come from where Parsic was last seen. The two Gatas seemed to be having a conversation involving a lot of gesticulating and pointing. Finally, they seemed to come to some sort of conclusion, with one of them jumping on an electric cart and motoring off towards the errant loader.

'Will he make it?' whispered Clunk.

'I don't know,' said Bache, noticing the other Gata was watching his colleague and had his back to them. 'I hope no one's watching from the ship—stay here.'

He gave Clunk the gunship remote activator, stood and sprinted on tiptoes towards the drone. Seemingly reaching it without drama, he dived down behind the drone and quickly pulled out his tablet. Glancing to his left, he saw the Gata on the cart quickly catching the loader and pull alongside. Using his rifle sight again, he watched to see what the Gata would do.

The loader stopped and he saw Parsic stand up from behind it. He'd been hanging on the opposite side to remain hidden. Bache watched him point the pistol and blow a hole in the Gata's chest.

The report from the weapon reached him a split second later and the Gata standing next to the ship's ramp must have presumed it was the other Gata firing to stop the loader, as he did precisely nothing.

Bache looked through his sight again and

watched Parsic kick the Gata off the cart and zip away towards the dormitories, only much quicker now.

He puffed out his cheeks and continued bringing up the software he needed to download the drone data bank. Once it opened he entered his GDA officer codes and was able to connect to the drone's systems. He swore to himself, as he found the data core was doubly encrypted.

Shouts from the ship caught his attention, as about a dozen armed Gatas spilled out from the ship and he shrank back into the shadows. They weren't coming in his direction though. He glanced across to where Clunk was hiding and was pleased to see no sign of him. The Gatas weren't going in his direction either, they fanned out and began running in towards the dormitory passage.

Suddenly the huge antigravs on the Gata ship began spooling up and a loud siren sounded. The armed Gatas stopped and began retracing their steps back to the ship.

'Oh, shit no, not yet,' muttered Bache as he realised they were just going to bug out and blow the whole mountain range into dust as soon as they were clear. He'd only disarmed one of them and if there was one for every cavern, there'd be enough tycelerin to vaporise the entire region for a hundred kilometres or more.

33

Cavern eight, Ballenhyght Caverns, Dresse

THE ARMED GATAS sprinted back up the loading ramp and inside the large vessel. Its antigravs continued thundering their way up towards equilibrium with the planet's gravity.

Bache gritted his teeth as the noise became deafening. You wouldn't normally be anywhere near a ship of this size on take-off, especially in an enclosed space.

'Come on, Bache, think,' he shouted at himself. In a few moments, himself, Clunk, Parsic and all the thousands of locals still trapped within the caverns would be reduced to a cloud of gas.

He stepped back and looked up at the small unmanned ship and then it struck him as to what he had to do. Moving away from the drone quickly, he set his tablet down on a stack of unused pallets and began tapping away.

The drone's systems weren't encrypted, only the data core was. It also still had an intact weapons cache. Activating its flight controls, while the small antigrav began spooling up, Bache brought its weapon systems online.

In his peripheral vision he saw the Gata ship begin to lift.

'Shit—come on,' he shouted at the tablet, as if that was going to speed things up.

The big ship turned lazily, the pilot had to be careful not to hit the ceiling. It seemed to be what was called a hybrid vessel, part freighter, part warship. Normally, a ship of this type would be used for trade runs into the more seditious corners of the galaxy. Bache knew, even without its shields up, which couldn't be activated while still in the cavern, its armour was thick and it would take pin-point accuracy to bring it down.

Finally, the drone lifted off its struts and Bache, flying it through its forward-mounted camera, sent it left and towards the quickly retreating Gata ship. It was halfway down the cavern now and Bache knew he had to be quick and because he couldn't get above or below the big ship, he couldn't target the antigravs or its array. He instead targeted the rear loading ramp. Knowing he only had six kataligo missiles, he thought he'd first try and penetrate the ramp with the laser. If he could do that, he'd send the missiles inside the ship.

He hit the big door over and over with everything the small cannon had but only managed to punch a few small holes in the outer skin. He had no idea if it had penetrated through inside the ship and anyway the vessel hadn't changed its course or speed one iota.

He sent two missiles towards the points where the ramp pivoted up, hoping they were a weak point. When this didn't do anything, he sent two more at exactly the same points. This time he was sure the ramp flexed and sending one more at the left hinge point, he finally had a result. The ramp disconnected at that side and swung down which twisted the right hinge which also snapped. Flapping open, it dropped, caught the floor of the cavern and tore itself off.

Bache wasted no time and sent the final missile towards the open freight deck just as the ship cleared the cavern and disappeared upwards. He screamed in frustration as the missile lost its lock and sailed straight on across the valley floor.

'FUCK,' he bellowed, punching and kicking the pile of pallets in frustration.

The drone was still a kilometre from the exit when he saw something on his screen drop past the cavern, followed by an enormous explosion on the valley floor.

'What the hell was that?' he muttered. He was convinced it couldn't have been the Gata ship, as it was nowhere near damaged enough. Then he saw something he couldn't quite believe. A GDA gunship nosing its way down from above and into the cavern.

It quickly bypassed the drone, that Bache had landed, and arrowed up the cavern towards him at breakneck speed.

'Can't be mine, surely,' he said, wondering if he should hide behind the pallets again.

The gunship approached at speed, braked late, turned and landed with a teeth-jarring crunch fifty metres away, confirming to Bache it certainly was his gunship.

'How the hell did he pull that off?' Bache said to himself, scratching his head and glancing to where he had last seen Clunk.

Both side airlock doors opened together. The sound of loud music pumping out from the interior hit him. Clunk then appeared, jigging about to the beat in the doorway.

'Bring it on,' he shouted, continuing to jump around and punch his fists to the beat excitedly. 'I just shot down a fucking freighter.'

Bache approached, stopped and stared up from the bottom of the steps.

'I really have no idea how in the name of the ancients you just did that,' he said.

'Top killer pilot, me,' said Clunk, his grin almost as wide as the airlock.

'But you were just there a minute ago,' he said, pointing to where he'd left him.

'As soon as I heard their ship starting up, I realised we'd all be dead if they got it out of the cavern. So I sprinted back to the gunship. They emerged from this cavern at the same time I did from next door. I was able to take out his motors before he got his shields up. Although, I think I might've scratched the top of the ship trying to exit the other cavern.'

'I'll let you explain that to Mr Whippy,' said Bache. 'You did well though, we'll probably never know how many lives you just saved.'

Clunk beamed and leant out from the airlock, staring back down the cavern. Bache soon realised what he was looking at, as the sound of an electric cart grew in volume.

Bache lifted up his weapon and gazed through the sight, but he soon lowered it again when he realised it was Parsic. He swung around the gunship, approached and stopped a few feet away.

'Have they all gone?' he asked, glancing at where the big ship had been.

'Oh, they've all gone all right,' said Clunk. 'You're welcome.'

Parsic listened to the translation and looked at Bache quizzically.

Bache showed him the drone footage of the Gata ship dropping and exploding out on the valley floor. His eyes widened when he saw it.

'You killed them all?' he said, the shock evident in his tone.

'They would've detonated the big bombs and killed all of us if that ship had got enough altitude,' said Bache.

Parsic seemed to think about that for a moment, glancing back towards the cavern entrance.

'And anyway, you didn't hesitate with that Gata driving this thing,' said Bache, indicating the cart that Parsic was sitting in.

'He was a priden and a particularly cruel one,' replied Parsic. 'He murdered a few of my friends over the years. So I knew it would be me or him.'

'What's happening with your people?' Bache asked, peering over in the direction of the dormitory tunnel.

'They're going down the line of caverns and releasing everyone,' he said, turning to follow Bache's look. 'None of them will come this way, and that reminds me.' He stooped down and picked another detonator off the floor, giving it to Bache. 'There was another of those big crates down that tunnel too,' he said. 'I showed them how to deactivate and remove the detonator.'

'Good,' said Bache. 'Make sure you find all of them.'

'What do we do with them?'

'Nothing, don't touch them. I'll organise a disposal team to come here and get them off your planet as soon as possible.'

'Did you get the information you wanted from the drone?' Clunk asked.

'It was doubly encrypted,' said Bache, rolling his eyes. 'Someone was certainly being careful.'

'So we came all this way for nothing?' Clunk said, dejectedly.

'Not necessarily,' Bache replied. 'We can still send it on its way, as they were probably about to do when they got it into space.'

'What, and follow it?'

Bache nodded with a wry grin.

'That's brilliant,' said Clunk, peering around the cavern. 'Where is it anyway?'

Cavern eight, Ballenhyght Caverns, Dresse

GETTING the drone into the gunship had proved a lot more of an issue than Bache had envisioned. With its struts deployed, it was too tall to squeeze through the airlock and into the payload bay. They'd had to construct a thin pallet from bits and pieces lying around the cavern and then fly the drone inside the ship and carefully settle it down on the contraption.

'Well, that's half a day I won't get back,'

whinged Clunk, strapping the drone down so it didn't move around on the flight back into space.

'Worth the effort though,' said Bache, ensuring there was nothing else loose on the deck. He stuck his head out the airlock when he heard the sound of an electric vehicle approaching.

Parsic waved and this time he wasn't alone. Four other locals were with him, although Bache could see by their nervous expressions, they weren't overly thrilled at being in cavern eight. Decades of ingrained fear of the place had clearly taken its toll.

Bache stepped down as they arrived and greeted them all as they stepped down off the small truck.

'These are a few other surviving council elders,' Parsic informed him. 'We thought it only right we should thank you for everything you've done for us before you left.'

'You're more than welcome,' said Bache. 'Is everyone getting home okay?'

'The ones from the local area have left on foot or calloppe, but the people from further away have found a broken-down flyer the purrers left behind and are attempting to fix it.'

'Have they got everything they need?' Bache asked. 'I'd give them shuttle rides home with this but there's thousands of them and time is of the essence for us now.'

'We understand,' said Parsic. 'To be honest, we've got all we need and they're quite enjoying the work. For the first time in years they're doing something for themselves instead of an alien with a big whip.'

'More help will come,' said Bache. 'Just give us a chance to thwart whatever it is the purrers are planning on doing with that battle fleet. I'm sure at some time in the future, you'll be given the chance to join the galactic council.'

'I look forward to the day, and remember you're always welcome here, Lieutenant,' he said, as all five of them bowed and clambered back onto the cart.'

Parsic went to pull away but seemed to remember something. He jumped back down from the cart and approached Bache again.

'I nearly forgot,' he said, pulling out Bache's

laser pistol and handing it over. 'Thank you for your trust.'

He stepped away and alighted the truck before Bache could say anything and powered away with a wave.

Bache stood and watched the cart until it disappeared down the dormitory tunnel before turning to find Clunk watching him from the airlock.

'D'you think they'll recover from this?' he asked.

'I don't think there's any doubt about that,' said Bache, stepping past Clunk, closing the two airlock doors and resetting the safeties. 'Come on, let's see where that thing's going to take us,' he added, nodding at the drone.

Two hours later, they sat in a high orbit above Dresse. It had been a tight squeeze, but the drone had just fitted in the airlock and now sat stationary two hundred metres off the bow of the gunship.

'Ready then?' Bache asked, raising his eyebrows at Clunk.

'Oh, absolutely,' Clunk replied, with a smirk. 'Light it up, boss. Let's see who it points the finger at.'

Bache touched an icon on his tablet and looked up to witness the drone disappear. He turned to Clunk and raised his eyebrows.

'Have you a trail?' he asked.

Clunk didn't look up from his console, he just nodded and jumped the gunship in pursuit.

One thing Bache had been able to do, was disable the drone's ability to embed its jump signatures, enabling Clunk to detect and copy the emergence point into their own navigation computer. They both looked up at the holomap as they winked back into existence forty-six light years away. It was in non-system space but when you extended the line from the Dresse system to their present location and onwards, it pointed straight towards GDA space.

'Well, that's no surprise,' said Bache, watching the drone powering off on the same trajectory and charging for its next jump.

'Might as well get your head down for a while, boss,' said Clunk. 'This could be a long trip.'

Forty-two hours and several shift changes later, Bache reached over and shook Clunk's shoulder.

'Wake up—we might be here.'

'Where?' Clunk asked, wiping the sleep from his eyes and powering his seat upright.

'Well, it's kinda nowhere really,' said Bache, pointing up at the holomap. 'The drone took an unusually small jump into non-system space and instead of powering off, it stopped and is remaining stationary.'

Clunk squinted at the holomap and then surveyed his screens.

'It was only a three light year jump,' he said. 'Aren't we going closer?'

Bache shook his head and sat back in his seat.

'No, this could be a test to see if it's being

followed. Let's just hang around here and see what happens.'

It took four hours for Clunk's patience to start wearing thin.

'Fuck's sake, don't they want the bloody thing?' he griped, folding his arms. 'All the crap we went through to get it.'

'They're just being careful,' said Bache. 'And we must be too.'

He'd hardly got the words out of his mouth when they detected a ship jumping in and powering towards the drone.

'They're not bothering to cloak,' Clunk said, suddenly more animated.

'They can't,' said Bache. 'That's a Killonian civilian vessel, it doesn't have cloaking technology.'

'Is that right? How d'you know that?'

'My dad was tasked with improving the design for their drive buffers years ago. That and the fact it says so there,' he said, pointing to one of his screens.

'Ah, right, so it does,' said Clunk, leaning

over and reading the information out loud. 'Killonian Gaad class, mark four freighter.'

He sat back again with a perplexed expression.

'Weren't the Killonians from a system adjacent to Gata space?' he asked, turning to Bache with a quizzical look.

'Uh, huh,' grunted Bache. 'It doesn't mean it's a Killonian crew though. They're one of the most peaceful races in the galaxy, so I'd be very surprised if they were knowingly involved in all of this.'

They watched as the two red signals on the holomap merged and became one.

'When they leave, follow at a distance,' said Bache. 'We don't want to spook them. It shouldn't be too difficult either, those ships are pretty basic and leave a trail a junior cadet could follow.'

'No pressure then?' replied Clunk, as he prepared the gunship for a jump.

The freighter only initiated two jumps, the second into Gata space and a system called

Berge in the middle of the Lynkas group of worlds.

The habitable planet also called Berge was one of the Gata worlds. Medium-sized, slightly lower gravity than Dasos and with two moons. The nearer one, Galle, was still whole and round and normal unlike the outer one, Brakk, which at some point in its history was hit hard by something colossal and the twelve thousand-kilometre satellite fractured into several pieces. Due to gravitational forces that no one could quite understand, the massive fragments, almost like segments of an orange, had remained bunched together. They now moved around seemingly randomly, with the gaps between them ranging from almost nothing to many hundreds of kilometres. It took a brave pilot to attempt to navigate through the forever-shifting fissures, which explained the reason Bache's knuckles were white as he gripped his seat arms and his eyes bulged in disbelief.

'Did you just jump inside a moon?' he asked, staring though the front screen at walls of rock seemingly only centimetres away.

'Outrageous, huh,' replied Clunk, almost casually. 'I always wondered if that was possible.'

'Well, next time you wonder something, make sure you're the only one who could die as a result,' Bache spluttered, inwardly reassessing his choice of pilot for this mission.

Clunk barely acknowledged what Bache had said as he was busy concentrating on cloaking the vessel and powering the gunship out into clear space without getting crushed.

'There we go, all tickety boo and right in the thick of it,' Clunk said, pointing at the holomap showing the freighter in clear view, sitting in a high orbit around Berge. 'Now we know we haven't missed anything.'

'I'm glad I didn't have any breakfast, or I could be missing that,' Bache mumbled, as he joined Clunk watching the Killonian ship closely.

35

GDA gunship, hiding in the Berge system

THEY WATCHED the freighter sit undisturbed for several hours, quietly and indifferently orbiting Berge every forty-nine minutes. To any casual observer, just another trader ship amongst several dozen other trader ships, at any given time, awaiting clearance to descend and land.

'They've been there a while now,' said an impatient Clunk. 'Plenty of ships that arrived after them have landed. What are they waiting for?'

'They might not have to land, just transmit the data from the drone.'

'Aren't you scanning for that?'

'Yep.'

'And have they?'

'Nope.'

'So, wouldn't they have done that by now?'

'It could be paranoia,' said Bache. 'They could be watching and listening to everyone else. Checking for anyone paying them unwarranted attention.'

'Like us?'

'Exactly.'

'Won't they detect our array sweeping over them?'

'No, because I'm piggybacking our scans into Berge's planetary defence satellites that scan everything every fifty milliseconds anyway.'

'Clever.'

'Thank you.'

Clunk rolled his eyes and sat back, lacing his

fingers behind his head. He stared at the holomap above, willing for something, anything to happen, and then it did.

A GDA destroyer jumped in only a few hundred metres from the freighter, something flashed from one to the other and the destroyer was gone again.

'What the fuck just happened?' yelped Clunk, swinging upright again. 'Did they just fire on that warship?'

'No,' said Bache. 'That was a drone being handed over.'

'So we need to follow that destroyer?'

'No.'

'No?'

'No, it was a drone being handed over, but not our drone.'

Clunk looked up at the holomap again.

'So, that was just a ruse?'

'Yep, but a worrying ruse all the same.'

'Yeah—what's a GDA warship doing involved in all of this? Do you know which ship that was?'

'It wasn't transmitting any identification,'

said Bache, tapping away on his tablet.

'So, you don't then?'

'I didn't say that,' answered Bache, waving his wrist at the underside of the tablet.

Clunk must have witnessed it, because he turned in his seat and stared at Bache.

'Have you got one of those illegal dermal chips?' he asked, in an accusatory tone.

'Don't know what you're talking about,' said Bache, holding his tablet up so Clunk could see the screen. 'GDA destroyer *Vasilias*, supposedly destroyed several years ago above a planet called Quillon III.'

'How d'you know that?'

'Because I was one of the only survivors.'

'Several years ago?' questioned Clunk. 'What, while you were a recruit?'

'No, I was still a civilian then.'

'What the hell was a civilian boy doing on a GDA destroyer in a war zone?'

'It wasn't a war zone and anyway it's a long story,' said Bache, making it obvious by his tone that he wasn't going to say more.

'So, you're saying someone's supposedly

rebuilt a lost navy destroyer under the noses of the GDA?'

'It's the only explanatio—they're moving,' Bache blurted, suddenly glad to be changing the subject and pointing at the holomap.

The freighter had turned and begun dropping in towards the planet, bringing its bow up to offer its armoured underbelly to the friction of planetary insertion.

'Do we follow?' Clunk asked, his hands hovering over the gunship's flight screens.

'Get over there,' said Bache. 'But remain in space for now. I want to see where they put down. Watch out for traffic though. Remember no one can see us.'

Clunk had the gunship out of the shadow of the fractured moon and powering towards Berge in seconds as Bache kept an eye on the freighter's whereabouts. It took twenty-two minutes to get to a position in space directly above and following the movements of the Killonian ship. By this time it was in the lower atmosphere, hidden below layers of cloud shrouding the planet's surface from view.

Bache knew, however, the freighter was descending towards one of the major cities rather unimaginatively called Bergess. From what he could see, the town was set in a vee between two converging rivers, one considerably larger than the other, then both flowed out into an ocean.

The freighter pulled up at about a thousand metres and turned, following the smaller tributary inland. Where the city's outer suburbs finally ended, desert took over and stretched onward for around eighty kilometres. The desert ended in a range of snow-capped mountains stretching east-west all the way down the majority of the northernmost edge of the continent.

The ship turned again, crossing into the desert and headed south towards the hills, before stopping suddenly in the middle of nowhere and hung motionless.

'What are they doing?' asked Clunk. 'Are they lost?'

'No, I think they're just paranoid about being followed,' said Bache.

'D'you think they've detected our scans?'

'I'm using the city's arrays to keep tabs, not

ours, so they certainly won't know about us up here. They're watching for suspicious activity behind them.'

As Bache finished speaking, the ship suddenly took off again, completed a U-turn and headed at speed back towards the city. It descended again as it approached a series of larger buildings in an industrial area right on the furthest edge of the town.

'Okay, Clunk, take us down—but quietly.'

'I'll drop us in over the ocean,' Clunk replied, his eyes already closing as he concentrated on his omniscient vision display and dropped the gunship into the gravitational pull of Berge. 'There's plenty of cloud cover too, so our trail should go unnoticed.'

Thirty-four minutes later, with the sound of the heat shielding popping and ticking as it cooled below them, they dropped out of the cloud cover and could see Burgess city sprawling away to the south.

'Stay high and watch for traffic,' said Bache, as he engaged the forward-mounted cameras and panned in on the far edge of the town.

The location of the freighter wasn't hard to find. Its heat signature stood out from everything around that area, especially on such a cold day. It sat on a landing pad not much bigger than itself and gently steamed away in the light drizzle falling on its still-hot hull.

Even from this distance, Bache could see the main freight side door was open and a few bodies could be seen milling around between the ship and an adjacent building.

'Can you see the drone?' Clunk asked.

'No, not yet,' replied Bache. 'The prevailing wind is coming in off the coast so stay south of them and come down to about a thousand metres just under the cloud base.'

The excellent sharpness of the cameras meant the detail was becoming very good now and facial features were quite discernible. The only problem was, most of them were wearing coats and hats against the rain, although Bache could see that some of the personnel weren't Gatas. But many of them were and he'd forgotten that Gatas had super-sharp hearing. Several turned in their direction, peered up and pointed. A couple of the humans turned and looked up too.

'Oh—hello,' said Bache, his eyes wide as he zoomed the camera feed in on the upturned faces.

'Someone you know?' Clunk asked, concentrating on the flying and not able to see what Bache was seeing.

'Pull back quickly,' Bache said. 'The locals can hear us.'

'Shit, really?'

'It's this noisy bloody thing,' Bache moaned, as the gunship backed away. 'Crap, that's going to have them on alert now.'

It turned out to be much worse than that, as almost all the ground crew drew weapons and began firing randomly in the rough direction of where they'd been only a few moments before.

'They're trying to fluoresce our shields,' said Clunk.

'Get back into the cloud,' said Bache, as a section of the roof of the large building powered back, revealing a ground-based laser cannon that immediately began panning around searching for a target. 'Ah—shit, not another one of those bastards.'

The cloud enveloped them and Clunk quickly fired the ship out over the ocean again and up towards space.

'Are we hanging around here?' he asked, opening his eyes and glancing at Bache.

Bache was studying the last good image of the faces from below. A second one caught his attention, this one a local, shortly before the facial recognition system confirmed his gut feeling of having seen that face before.

'The GDA's in big trouble,' he whispered. 'We need to get away from here and fast.'

'Who was down there?' Clunk asked.

'That Skirmat from Dasos,' he said.

'What, Kyyt—the bastard who had me shot?'

'Uh, huh.'

'Well, that doesn't surprise me.'

'There was someone else—who he was talking to.'

'Well?'

Bache took a deep breath.

'Desulet,' he said, almost spitting the name.

'What, as in GDA Minister for Defence, Hitten Desulet?'

'Uh, huh.'

'Oh, fuck—you're right—the GDA is in big trouble.'

36

___

*GDA gunship, en route to a rendezvous with
the K2*

AN ENCODED PING had placed the *Katadromiko 2* in open space near the Kraxx system and after leaving Berge, Bache and Clunk headed there as quickly as possible.

Bache knew very little about Desulet and had never met the man. The data bank on the gunship confirmed he was a senior Gata from

Junnee in the Flin'dr system. It just so happened this was the closest system to Berge at only seven light years, which Bache thought might be pertinent and could have some bearing on the current situation.

He stared at the picture of Desulet, noticing he had some grey streaks in his facial fur. Although the man was senior in age, Bache couldn't remember any ageing Gatas he'd known before going grey as they aged.

'He's as miserable as Henns,' said Clunk, glancing at the screen. 'Don't think I've ever met a cheerful Gata.'

'No, I have to disagree with you there,' said Bache. 'There was a Gata in my recruit intake—he told me a joke once.'

'Was it funny?'

'Thinking about it now—no, it wasn't.'

'There you go—race of whiners the lot of 'em.'

'I'm sure there's a happy one somewhere,' said Bache, glancing up at the holomap as Clunk jumped them into a remote jump zone in the

Kraxx system and powered the small ship out towards the *K2*.

Clunk cloaked and pinged the *K2* again, then adjusted his route as the reply included an exact course and hangar designation.

'I'm looking forward to my proper bed for a change,' said Bache, stretching and setting his seat in the upright position. 'These seats have seen better days.'

Clunk was able to relax a bit now as the automated systems took over and flew the gunship up to the *K2* and inside the hangar, setting it down in a spot near the rear hangar airlock.

They gathered their things, opened the side airlock and were met by a contingent of six marines.

'We're to take you straight to the captain,' said one of them sporting sergeant's insignia.

'I'm not surprised, but don't worry, I know the way to the bridge,' said Bache, immediately getting an inkling that something wasn't as expected. He'd never before arrived to be confronted by a marine escort on his own ship.

'He's not on the bridge,' the curt reply stated.

'He's not on the bridge, sir,' Bache corrected him, sternly. 'I let you get away with it once, but twice appears to me like deliberate disrespect.'

The sergeant flinched slightly and adopted a sneer.

'You are to come with us—SIR,' the marine hissed.

Bache turned to Clunk, who remained standing in the gunship's airlock.

'Wait here,' he said. 'I'll be back shortly.'

'Both of you—SIR.'

Bache noticed a couple of the other marines' hands hovered towards their weapons, confirming this wasn't a friendly escort.

'Are we under arrest for something?' he asked, staring straight into the sergeant's face.

'You must come with us—SIR.'

'On whose order exactly?'

'Mine,' said a voice coming from the rear hangar airlock behind them.

The sergeant stiffened as Bache turned to be

confronted by the chief engineer and two more marines.

'Captain,' said the sergeant snapping to attention.

'Captain?' questioned Bache. 'What's happened to Captain Whipper?'

'Under arrest for deliberately disobeying the admiral and endangering the ship and its crew. Those are just two of the many crimes committed by the previous captain,' stated Chief Engineer Desme Catams, stopping in front of Bache with her hands on her hips. 'The admiral's instructions were quite clear and he chose to completely ignore them.'

'You were trained by my father,' said Bache. 'Surely you can see there's something not quite right going on here?'

'I'm not jeopardising my career over a junior lieutenant's hunch,' she replied.

'The admiral is involved,' interjected Clunk. 'And Desulet.'

Catams laughed and shook her head in disbelief.

'That really does prove you've lost your

minds,' she said, stepping aside and nodding at the sergeant. 'Take them away—and make sure they're in separate cells. Don't want them thinking up more crazy conspiracy theories.'

They were taken to the nearest security station, searched, scanned and locked up. The cell Bache found himself in was actually quite comfortable. It had a main room with seating and a table to eat at, a bedroom and a small bathroom. There was even a holographic entertainment system. The door was an invisible shield, the guards could pass through but the prisoners couldn't. Bache found it fluoresced and gave you a slight shock if you touched it. He heard Clunk swear somewhere off to his right as he most likely tested the door shield too.

A guard sat at a desk about five metres away in the centre of the reception room. He glanced up and nodded at Bache when he realised he was being watched.

'Lunch will be in an hour if it's food you want,' he said, his expression remaining neutral.

'It was my tablet I wanted,' said Bache, knowing it was a long shot.

'No tablets, Loftt,' he replied. 'Captain's orders.'

Bache grunted, turned and went back to the seating. He knew he'd have to be patient and wait for an opportunity to escape, but first he had to find a way to send a discreet communication.

37

Katadromiko 2, *unknown location*

BACHE HAD SET a quiet alarm for the middle of the ship's night period and slipped out of bed as soon as it woke him. He crept into his main room and peeked across to the guard's station across the hall. He didn't really have to check, you could probably hear the guards snoring from the next system. Once he confirmed it was the guard making the racket and not a Dasonian tractor, he stepped over to his entertainment keyboard and touched his wrist to its receiver node.

Many years ago, Bache's father had been on Paradeisos and negotiated a little secret deal for a couple of the Theo-designed organic dermal data chips, giving one to his son. Although technically illegal, they were almost impossible to detect and any standard scans would fail to find it hidden under the skin. It had already proved invaluable and had saved Bache's life on more than one occasion.

A menu opened up, enabling him to quickly run through the ship's systems. Finding the listings for security station 8, he shut down the door field on cell 3 and exited the menu hopefully before his electronic intrusion could be detected.

The guard was still sawing wood as he crept past, silently exited the station and headed directly for the nearest tube station. He had expected the ship to be quiet at this hour and was able to get to the quartermaster's deck in a little under fifteen minutes. Keeping his head down from the cameras, he was pleased to see the storerooms were deserted. Again using his dermal chip, he let himself in and headed directly for the military section. Selecting everything he wanted and putting it on, he was about to leave when he had a thought. Searching for and finding a decent-sized backpack, he went back down the lines of shelving and picked another identical uniform and stuffed it in the pack. The sizes he had to guess, but knowing the recipient well, he didn't think he'd be too far out.

Retracing his steps to the tube, the next part of his plan wasn't a given. He arrived at the hangar where they'd left the gunship and peeked through the airlock porthole. He breathed a sigh of relief when he saw it was still there and even the outer airlock was still open.

The hangar unfortunately wasn't deserted. A crew of mechanics were working the late shift on a freighter and all turned to look in his direction as he cycled through the airlock.

This was going to be the first test for his new marine officer's kit. He'd deliberately chosen a set of basic operational armour as this came with a helmet that obscured most of your face, which was now a real necessity as he'd worked with a couple of these guys before.

'Something you need, sir?' asked the one who must have been in charge as he had clean overalls and was standing back with a tablet.

'Captain's orders—sent to search the gunship over there,' he said, changing his voice down an octave and striding past them as if he didn't have a care what they thought.

'Oh, that's a relief,' the mechanic said, grinning. 'I thought we'd done something wrong.'

Bache strode purposefully over to the gunship and entered. His and Clunk's weapons were where they'd left them. He checked they were both set to a low stun and stuffed one into the backpack. He waited a few minutes before running the gauntlet past the nosey mechanics and quickly headed out the hangar back to the tube.

The next part of his plan was the most dangerous and had several ways for it to go spectacularly wrong.

As the tube train reached his next destination, he took a few deep breaths, exited the carriage and walked resolutely towards security station 3, hoping to hell his target hadn't been moved since he checked the detention logs.

Relieved to see, as with his security station, just the one guard on duty—only this one was awake. He entered, made sure he closed the door firmly and strode over to the desk.

'Captain wants to see the prisoner on the bridge,' he said, firmly.

The guard eyed him suspiciously and raised his eyebrows.

'Does he now?' the guard scoffed. 'Considering the captain only left here a few minutes ago and it's the middle of the night, tells me that might not be entirely true.'

Bache saw his hand move across the desk and down, but before the smug guard could press the panic button that Bache knew was there, he stunned him with a shot to the chest. He collapsed backwards, his chair on wheels scooted out from under him and crashed noisily into the back wall.

'Shit,' said Bache, glancing over his shoulder and hoping no one was walking past the station as that happened. He jumped as a voice boomed at him from his left-hand side.

'Could you make any more bloody noise, Loftt?' said Whipper, standing just the other side of his cell door field. 'Would you mind turning this fucking thing off?' he added, running his eyes around the frame of his door.

'Sorry, Captain,' said Bache, trotting around the desk and switching the field off and dragging the guard's unconscious body over to the cell as Whipper stepped out.

'Put this on,' he said, unpacking the other light armour suit from the backpack.

'A lieutenant,' Whipper sneered, as he saw the suit's rank. 'D'you mean I have to be an equal rank to you?'

'I was in a bit of a hurry,' said Bache. 'Think yourself lucky I didn't grab a corporal's kit.'

He got a glare as the captain donned the uniform.

'You're welcome,' said Bache, as he reset the cell door field so the guard couldn't raise the alarm.

'Did you bring one for the first officer?' he asked, pointing towards another of the cells.

Bache shook his head, as they both stared at an empty doorway.

'Dumb-arse could sleep through a nuclear exchange,' said Whipper. 'We'll come back for him later.'

'What's first on the agenda, boss?' Bache asked.

'The bow ROR,' he said, squeezing his helmet on. 'Couldn't you find a smaller hat for ancients' sake?'

'Sorry—I didn't know you had such a big head.' Bache couldn't see the captain's eyes, but he knew he was getting glared at. 'A remote operations room?' he questioned, changing the subject quickly. 'Isn't that the first place she'll look?'

'There are circumstances at play presently that you're not a party too,' said Whipper.

'Would that have something to do with the chief engineer's visit not so long ago?'

'The less you know, the better for you when all this comes out in an enquiry one day.'

'At a guess, she's playing both sides?'

'No comment—come on,' he said, striding towards the door.

'Did you know Desulet is involved?'

The captain stopped dead and turned to face Bache.

'And how do you know that?'

Bache explained what he and Clunk had witnessed on Berge.

'You're absolutely sure it was him?' said Whipper.

Bache nodded. 'One hundred percent.'

'Do you have video evidence?'

'On the gunship.'

'And it's still in one piece and not in bits on some red katapato planet somewhere?'

'No, it's all in working order and in hangar 41.'

'It's a miracle,' Whipper muttered, rubbing his chin in thought. 'We need to go there first and retrieve it.'

'No need, boss,' Bache said. 'I've already sent the footage to the President.'

'What?—when in the name of the ancients did you do that?'

'A few hours ago.'

'But the communications officer would've intercepted it.'

'Not if it was hidden inside an array sweep that passed over a communications satellite somewhere,' said Bache.

'You're kidding.'

Whipper stared at Bache for a moment, his expression hidden behind the helmet visor. Finally, after a moment of silence he looked down and rubbed the inside of his wrist before whispering a name.

'Tirexian Loftt.'

'My father's got nothing to do with this,' said Bache, the surprise evident in his voice at the mention of his dad's name.

'He gave you a Theo chip too, didn't he?'

Bache opened his eyes wide.

'You have one too?' he asked.

'I was wondering how you got out of your cell so easily,' said Whipper, shaking his head. 'You wait till I see him.'

38

Katadromiko 2, *unknown location*

THE BOW ROR was in a maintenance corridor not far from the bridge. Because of the early hour, they'd only passed a couple of crew on the way who'd paid them no attention at all. The lighting had dimmed slightly at one point, indicating the ship had jumped.

Once inside and sealed up, the captain took the central seat and awoke the systems. Bache took the side seat and glanced up at the screens as they came online.

'We're on the periphery of Gata space,' said Bache, pointing. 'That's the Berge system there.'

A ping sounded indicating another ship had jumped into the vicinity.

'It's a private yacht,' said Bache. 'A very expensive one too.'

They watched as it approached and entered the captain's hangar adjacent to the bridge.

'Who's coming calling at this hour?' said Whipper, selecting a view of the bridge on one of the other screens.

'That's a busy bridge considering the hour,' he said. 'It's almost as though we're on a war footing.'

'It could well be Berge that's the target for all those battleships,' said Bache. 'Desulet could've been there making sure they had no inkling of what was looming.'

'Or organising sabotage,' said Whipper.

Movement on the bridge caught their eye as several Gatas entered the bridge.

'Well, well,' said Whipper, as he recognised Desulet as one of them. 'We've been taking commands from that treacherous bastard for years.'

Bache leant in and tapped a couple of icons to enable sound from the bridge too.

'…rning , Minister,' Catams was saying as the sound came online.

She stood up from the captain's seat and offered it to Desulet.

'Good morning, Captain, and congratulations on your promotion, albeit so short-lived,' answered Desulet.

'I'm sorry, sir?' Catams said, obviously confused.

'We knew all along your sad allegiance to Whipper would be the death of your career,' he said, rummaging inside his robes.

'What?—I, I arrested him as you ordered,' she stuttered.

'Indeed you did,' Desulet said, with a smug edge to his voice. 'But that was before you conspired with him in his cell not so long ago,' he added, nodding to the communications officer and getting a nod in return.

'Fucker,' mumbled Whipper. 'That's his career down the toilet.'

'So, I'm demoted already?' Catams said nervously.

Desulet smiled, stepped up to her and put his arm around her shoulders.

'Yes, you're right, it's time for you to go,' he said and with the smile still on his face, his other hand emerged from his robes and thrust a long curved blade under her rib cage, piercing her heart.

She screeched, stiffened, before slumping in his arms.

'NOOO,' thundered Whipper, his chair hitting the bunks behind them. 'Murdering fucking piece of shit.'

Bache just sat, his head in his hands.

The captain paced up and down the small room for a few moments and kicked the wall twice, before leaning over the desk again and tapping away.

As he was doing this the proximity alarm pinged again several times.

'The Gata fleet is here,' said Bache, as the twelve battleships emerged from wherever they were hiding.

The hardened face and cold eyes of Major Riccs, the most senior marine on board, appeared on a side screen. Bache reasoned from the bunks visible behind him that he was in one of the other RORs.

'Seen enough?' the captain asked.

'I'll rip his traitorous heart out with my bare hands,' Riccs grizzled, his stony expression not faltering.

Bache made a mental note not to ever cross that man.

'You know what we talked about?' said Whipper.

'I do.'

'Execute it now.'

'Understood.'

'I'll neutralise all the cameras in the vicinity and I'm sending Lieutenant Loftt down to help.'

'Roger that.'

'Good luck.'

'You too, Captain,' Riccs said with a sharp salute as he vanished from the screen.

The captain turned to Bache. His face seemed drained of colour and it appeared to Bache the man had aged in the last few minutes.

'Do you really have the personal ping code for the President?' he asked, almost whispering.

'I do,' said Bache. 'But can I respectfully request you forget that fact when this is over, sir?'

Whipper nodded slowly.

'Send him that footage,' he said. 'Then report to Riccs in hangar 81.'

'Yes, sir,' said Bache, loading the evidence into the array buffer as he had before. It would send itself buried in the next array scan initiated from the bridge. He stood and checked the corridor camera before opening the small door.

'And Bache,' the captain said, softly. 'Don't get caught.'

Bache flashed him a half smile as he donned his helmet.

'Good luck, sir, I won't,' he said, as he ducked out and was alone in the corridor.

———

Bache marched smartly without running to the nearest tube. He was relieved the carriage was empty and hoped it would remain so all the way to deck 376. A handful of crew got in and out during the journey aft, seemingly completely oblivious to the drama unfolding on the bridge.

As he stepped out on deck 376, he glanced at a couple of the cameras. Their active lights were off, so it seemed Mr Whippy had done what he promised.

A sudden electronic voice behind him made him jump.

'Identify yourself.'

He spun round to be confronted by two armoured marines stepping out from alcoves.

'Lieutenant Loftt,' he said. 'Here to report to Major Riccs.'

'Remove your helmet.'

He did so, and a light scanned him from head to toe.

After a short delay, the suit spoke again.

'Proceed down the corridor, the major is waiting.'

The two armoured suits backed into the recesses in the wall and out of sight again.

When he reached the airlock, the outer door was already open. Two marines waited inside, this time in light armour.

'Lieutenant Loftt reporting…'

'We know who you are, sir,' said one, interrupting Bache. 'The major is waiting for you.'

They cycled him into a hangar Bache couldn't remember visiting before. As soon as the inner door opened, he had to let his eyes adjust to the much dimmer lighting inside.

Twelve gunships stood in two rows of six. Bache noticed they were older models, similar to the one he and Clunk had flown recently. Strange-looking military equipment and vehicles lined the walls of the hangar, things Bache had never seen before and didn't know what they did.

'Welcome to my man cave,' said a gruff voice from his left.

Bache turned to find Major Riccs leaning against an auto trolley eyeing him warily.

'Ah, hello, sir,' he said, feeling a tinge of apprehension. 'I had no idea this place existed.'

'Senior officers and marines only, son,' said Riccs. 'So you wouldn't have—come with me.'

Bache followed the major across the hangar to a small mobile office parked against the wall. Climbing inside the rectangular box, Bache saw a wall of screens with six personnel sitting behind them, all wearing POKs, or GDA gunship flight helmets.

'The captain informs me you may have the ability to infiltrate the enemy battleships' shields,' said Riccs, raising one eyebrow sceptically.

'Huh,' grunted Bache. 'That might be possible. I take it from the twelve gunships out there, you're intending to remotely fly them inside the battleships' shields and attack their arrays or something?'

'Close, but no cigar,' said the major. 'Each of

those gunships is having a nuclear device loaded inside that will detonate on contact with the hulls. It should cripple all twelve vessels, then the captain and myself in our RORs will isolate the *K2*'s bridge and be able to finish off any that continue to demonstrate any aggression.

'A good plan,' said Bache. 'But I think I can improve it.'

Katadromiko 2, *unknown location*

THE HANGAR LIGHTING flickered indicating another jump. Bache was still preparing for a transmission he had to make.

'Where are we?' he asked, looking quickly from screen to screen searching for the *K2*'s new location.

'The Berge system, sir,' came a call from one of the remote gunship pilots.

'Shit, it is Berge then,' he mumbled to himself. 'Major, are you and the captain ready?' he called through to the major's ROR. 'We need to go now before they launch the attack on the planet.'

'Affirmative, bridge will be isolated in ten seconds,' came Riccs's reply.

Bache counted the seconds down in his head, and as he got to zero, the lighting in the cabin went red and he began his transmission to all twelve Gata battleships.

'This is the communications officer on *Katadromiko 2*. Minister Desulet has chosen your vessel as his command ship, please make immediate provision and flightpath for his personal gunship into your bridge hangar. There will be decoy vessels deployed. *Katadromiko 2* out.'

Bache took a deep breath and sat back nervously. He'd been flushed with excitement when Riccs and the captain had agreed to his plan; now, as they all waited to see if the twelve captains took the bait, he was positively anxious.

'There's mine,' said one of the pilots as he received the shield code and flightpath.

'Mine and mine,' said two more, sticking their arms up.

Four, five, six and seven came abruptly together, followed by four more.

'Come on—just one more,' Bache called.

'Got it, twelve,' called the final pilot.

'GO—GO,' shouted Bache, covering his ears as twelve gunships wound up outside and screamed out of the hangar.

He stood and paced up and down behind the busy pilots, although once locked on to the provided flightpaths they had very little to do until landing them inside their designated battleship. Walking back to his seat, he spoke to Riccs again.

'Stand by to move the *K2* away from the fleet.'

'Affirmative,' came the usual curt marine reply.

Bache watched the twelve small icons on the monitor in front of him gradually close the distance to their targets. He wished they could hurry, but it would look odd. Some were travelling a little faster than others, but only because they had a little further to go and they wanted them all to arrive about the same time to avoid scrutiny. It only needed one to shout foul and the game could be up.

Finally, after what seemed like hours, but was in fact only six minutes, the first gunships started entering their hangars.

Bache leant forward, his hand hovering near the execute icon on his console and waited until the last gunship was inside.

'Move now,' he called to Riccs, and waited a few seconds as the huge behemoth of *K2* backed away, before he hit execute.

Everyone in the room shielded their eyes as the screens lit up with multiple detonations. Bache felt the *K2* shudder as the first shock waves enveloped them. It went on for a while, but the further away the ship got from the fleet the lesser the impact on the shields.

The twelve pilots, their jobs done, left grinning and slapping each other on the back, leaving Bache alone in the cabin. He tried making some sense out of the wreckage swirling around outside on his screen, but the orientation was confusing without a holomap.

Suddenly and without warning he found himself dazed and on the floor. His ears were ringing but he could hear sirens blaring, there was dust everywhere, or was it smoke? Then, just as he got his head together and decided to stand up, he went on the float.

'Shit, we've been hit by something,' he mumbled to himself, as he grabbed the edge of the desk to right himself.

There was a load of crashing from outside the cabin. He glanced over his shoulder and out the door, quickly realising everything in the hangar was on the float too. Looking back at the consoles, they were all dead and then it struck him—if the atmosphere shield on the main hangar entrance also failed, he'd be ejected out into space along with the contents of the hangar.

Pushing his legs against the console behind him, he sailed across the cabin and grabbed hold of the door frame. The cabin was up near the hangar roof, and he prayed the artificial gravity field didn't suddenly come back online while he was forty metres above the deck.

Peering around, he noticed a small matt black ship, a design he wasn't familiar with. From just its underside he could see it was designed for planetary insertions and had two missile-laden hard points sticking out from its flanks.

'Oh, shit,' muttered Bache, as he watched debris, some large, some small, clattering off the hull of the ship and its explosive payload as it ricochetted around the inside of the hangar. Looking down at the hangar airlock where he'd entered, for some unknown reason the inner door was open and a freight cart was crashing around inside. So that ruled that direction out for an escape.

The black ship was slightly closer now and had flipped over so he could see its upper side. Its outer airlock sat enticingly open.

Not wasting any time, he climbed up onto the side of the cabin then, timing his jump to coincide with the gentle rotation of the cabin and ship, he launched out across the void.

He soon realised he'd pushed a little hard, as he closed the gap surprisingly quickly and hit the little ship's hull just above the airlock. Grabbing out frantically as he slid over the ship's hull he snatched out at an antenna. Gripping it firmly, he swung around it one hundred and eighty degrees using his momentum and slid back towards the airlock. Managing to hook a foot around the airlock frame, he pulled with his leg, grabbed the edge and pulled himself inside. Crashing into the inner door, Bache turned and looked left and right to find which side the door controls were. They were on his left so he scrabbled against the ceiling with his hands. Luckily the ship was also turning in that direction, so he was able to punch the door close panel as it went by.

The door whined closed and he breathed a sigh of relief only seconds before the inner door hit him like an out-of-control skouter, rendering him instantly unconscious.

40

Unfamiliar marine ship, unknown location

BACHE WOKE WITH A START. He had no idea
where he was for a moment or two, before his
blurred vision revealed he was in a small airlock.

'Ah, shit, my head hurts,' he shouted, instantly wishing he hadn't as that made it throb
all the more.

He wiped his eyes to try and clear his vision
and noticed he had blood all over his hands. Remembering what had occurred, he pushed his

way over to the airlock inner door control and slapped it when he floated near enough.

The stink of unwashed marines assaulted him as the door slid to one side which did nothing to improve his mood.

'Fucking smelly bastards,' he moaned, as he pushed against the outer door and floated inside the vessel.

The cabin was tiny and had room for only two personnel, so he grabbed at one of the seats, swung around it and pulled himself down into the co-pilot's seat. It was at this point he realised from the view out the front screen, the ship was in open space and no longer in the hangar.

That was the reason he'd been knocked unconscious, the atmosphere shield had finally failed and ejected the ship out into space at considerable velocity.

A loud clattering of something hitting the hull woke him up to the fact there were eight missiles only a few metres away, all getting peppered with debris. As he swept around the controls for the master switch, movement outside caught his attention as a whole area of stars disappeared. Something big was nearby. He leant forward, believing it to be the *K2* and as his ship rotated, his eyes widened as he recognised it to be one of the Gata battleships.

'Oh, crap,' he moaned, realising one of the nukes must have failed to detonate. 'One of the bastards survived and that was what attacked the *K2*,' he said to himself.

He also realised, if he sparked his ship up, they'd notice the power signature coming online. At the present moment he was just another lump of debris and invisible.

One thing he had to do was try and stabilise the ship without using the main drive. Every time he looked outside it just made him feel queasy and he needed to make plans of how to combat that battleship. It looked like Whipper and Riccs had been caught unawares and with just the two of them against a fully complemented warship of that size, it was obvious it wasn't going well.

On most GDA vessels, although not being a pilot, Bache knew they normally had an emergency manual control system for the attitude thrusters. Moving over to the pilot's seat, he searched around before realising there was a small joystick under a cover on the end of the right-hand arm rest. Flipping back the cover, he toggled the stick. Nothing happened. He swore and began looking for something that might initiate the stick. He pushed and prodded everything to no avail until finally he sat back and glared at the thing.

'Come on,' he shouted. 'Give me a clue.'

Suddenly, it motored upwards out of the arm and glowed red. He had no idea what he'd done, but this looked positive and this time when he moved the stick there was an audible hiss from outside. The attitude of the ship changed slightly too.

'Fuck, yes,' he shouted and set about trying to curtail both the vessel's spin and slight tumble. Gradually, using the battleship as a point of reference and doing it slowly to avoid being noticed, he righted the ship in relation to the large Gata vessel.

Judging by the way the big ship was sitting pretty much stationary and only occasionally firing over the top of him, gave Bache the impression the *K2* was not returning fire. He couldn't see the battleship's shields flaring at all, so nothing was coming in the other direction.

Slowly, while slowing his ship's trajectory, he also turned it again to look back at the *K2*. He sighed and wished he hadn't. The main array was completely missing, sections of the main drive had also gone and he could see the glow of fires burning internally in countless locations.

'Shit,' he mumbled and began racking his brain for some clue as to what to do.

His trajectory was going to take him past and behind the Gata ship, so he let off on the slowing to let this happen. He reasoned all eyes would be on the *K2* and if he was behind the battleship, being spotted would be a lot less likely.

A small shuttle exited the Gata ship and headed fast towards the *K2*, disappearing out of sight as it entered the bridge hangar.

'Desulet wants to get off—and when he does, he'll need to eradicate any evidence he was involved,' Bache reasoned to an empty cockpit, realising with horror the *K2* had only minutes to live.

Almost everyone he knew was on that ship. He had eight small missiles against a battleship a thousand times bigger and with shields that would brush them aside like a dust mote. He couldn't remember ever feeling so helpless and an awful sick feeling in his stomach began to deepen.

He was behind the battleship now and had lost sight of the *K2* some fifty kilometres away. The shuttle appeared again, traversing around the bigger ship so they could open a gap in the shields for it to enter out of sight of the *K2*, and he suddenly had an idea.

Waiting for the shuttle to turn and pass him, he hit the master on switch, grabbed the POK off the console, slipped it over his head and waited for the drive to come online. He wasn't an experienced pilot by any means, but he knew the basics and in something so small, how hard could it be?

It was a huge risk, as his enemy signature

would suddenly flash up on the screens of every weapons officer on the battleship.

The shuttle went by, seemingly oblivious to him coming online. The drive and shields came online, Bache launched the ship in behind the shuttle. He'd overdone the acceleration somewhat, as his shield hit the shuttle's shield and almost tipped him forward out of his seat. But he kept the power on and the ship close behind the shuttle, giving any attentive gunners on the battleship no target.

The shuttle pilot must have been informed of him being there or already knew from the shunt from behind, because as soon as he was inside the shield he veered sharp right, giving the gunners a target.

Bache had expected this and swerved too, only he went down and under the huge ship, slowed right down and, hugging the hull, he toggled the master arm for the missiles.

The Gata battleships had three major nacelles protruding from their underside. Bache reasoned at least one, if not all three, would be the main arrays and they were an absolute must if he was to have any chance of disabling the monster.

As soon as the weapon system came online, cross hairs appeared in his omniscient vision and a trigger motored out from the left-hand controller. The little ship juddered and his shields flared as one of the smaller laser cannons got a bead on him for the first time. At least if he stayed this close to the hull the huge ship-killer lasers couldn't traverse low enough to target him.

Lining up the middle nacelle he squeezed the trigger, and the missile streaked away, only taking two seconds to reach its target.

'YES,' he shouted as the weapon hit the nacelle dead centre. His excitement quickly turned to puzzlement as nothing happened, apart from a big red stain on the nacelle's outer surface. The realisation hit him instantly—the missiles were dud rounds, this was a training vessel.

'No—no,' he shouted. 'That's just not fair.'

His shields flared again as someone else got in a lucky shot. Looking over his shoulder, he eyed the two new marine armoured suits squeezed into their alcoves against the bulkhead. They were the latest version and he knew from the fact they were bright white, they were training versions. He'd seen some of the grunts trotting around the *K2*, learning their operational limits and systems. He also knew their weapon systems definitely weren't duds though, they would be fully operational. From the arm-mounted lasers to the shoulder-mounted mini-missile and grenade launchers, they were a walking ship disrupter. They were a much lighter design to the older duradium shelled versions too, as they encompassed a personal shielding, similar to a small vessel so you could be a lot more nimble.

The more he thought about them, the more a plan formed in his head.

41

*Unfamiliar marine ship, attacking Gata
battleship*

BACHE ZIGZAGGED the ship to avoid the fire from the few smaller laser hard points dotted around the battleship. Luckily there weren't many as designers hadn't reckoned on attacking vessels ever penetrating the shields.

He flashed the little ship across its belly almost scraping the paint off the hull with his shields, turning upwards sharply to scale the port side and find a convenient hangar. It didn't take long as there were plenty to choose from and keeping his speed up and his fingers crossed, the little ship buzzed noisily through the atmosphere shield of a hangar amidships.

He breathed a sigh of relief seeing a row of what looked like troop carriers down the left hand side and a similar number of single-seat fighters down the right. The antigrav had automatically taken over now he was inside. He flew to the far end and landed quite hard in what looked like a servicing area. Breathing a sigh of relief, he was quite surprised the ship had got this far in one piece and especially glad Clunk hadn't seen that dreadful landing.

He saw a few personnel outside watching him quizzically, but they didn't seem overly concerned, and a lot of them turned away again and went about their business. He'd arrived so quickly, the news about an enemy ship inside the shields hadn't reached this hangar yet.

A banging on the airlock door signalled his anonymity had ended—not everyone was unconcerned about his sudden arrival. Drawing his side arm and concealing it behind him, he removed the safeties and opened both airlock doors to be confronted by a rather irate-looking Gata.

'There's a fucking speed limit coming into my hangar,' he raged, glaring at Bache. 'What's a human doing here anyway? And why have you got blood all over your face?' he added, his tone getting more and more suspicious as he stepped inside.

Bache smiled and quickly glancing out the front screen to check no one was watching, he pulled the laser pistol into view and shot the Gata in the chest.

The short-tempered hangar supervisor slumped to the floor unconscious, a look of shock having replaced the sneer. Bache checked outside again, dragged the Gata out the way and pressed the power up button on the bulkhead for the armoured suit nearest the airlock.

He knew these things came in several sizes, but he was in no position to be fussy. It was a little small for him and he grimaced as the pain in his head gnawed at him again as he squeezed himself inside the suit. He waited a few seconds as it automatically sealed him in and a profusion of displays lit up around his peripheral vision. He wasn't a trained operator, so it took him a while to orientate around the various menus, initiating the shields, arming weapons and so forth.

Once satisfied and with a row of green lights, he picked up the unconscious Gata surprisingly easily, stepped through the airlock and dropped down to the hangar floor. As he had parked at the far end, his ship shielded him from everyone's view and he was able to secrete the body under a pile of canopy covers stacked against the wall. He revelled in how strong the suit made him and warned himself against a dangerous sense of invulnerability. These suits were experimental and hadn't been fully tested in theatre. They also didn't have any GDA insignia, so those on board this ship hopefully wouldn't know he didn't belong. He code-locked the ship and made for the airlock.

These suits didn't clunk along like their predecessors and Bache found he was able to walk fast, silently and seemingly with a sense of purpose. A few looked him up and down, but more in the sense of curiosity than apprehension, and as he cycled himself through the airlock at the rear of the hangar, he brought up the battleship's schematics.

If these ships were designed using GDA guidelines, then there would be confluence nodes at regular intervals, that allowed maintenance engineers to service the vessel's electronics. There were only three apparently, which he thought was a little short-sighted, but it made his job easier.

Connecting into the ship's diagnostic systems was remarkably easy and again it all looked reasonably familiar. On his way to the nearest confluence node, he rooted out the data bank controlling the cameras, shut them down and code-locked the system.

Arriving at a nondescript service hatch a few minutes later, he realised the suit was too big to fit through. Luckily it was situated in a side corridor and he waited until he was alone, then flipped the hatch open just enough to fire a couple of fragmentation grenades inside.

Quickly closing the hatch again, he trotted away smartly. He didn't look back as they detonated with a double crack, followed by a load of debris bouncing off the rear of his suit's shields. The lights flickered and he adopted a wry smile as the service hatch spun over his head and impaled itself in the wall at the next junction.

Sirens began wailing, which he knew was a good thing as it enabled him to run in the direction of the second node without looking out of place.

Repeating the same thing twenty minutes later as he arrived at the second node, he noticed on his schematics this time after the explosion the arrays had been taken out of commission. Everything went black all of a sudden, followed by a red glow as the emergency lighting sparked up. He had quite a way to go to the third node and cursed the Gatas for not installing some sort of transportation system.

Twenty minutes later as he rounded a corner, he came face to face with two of the older style armoured suits. Moving to one side in order to let them pass, he was disappointed when they stopped. Their faceless and expressionless helmet visors regarded him silently and unnervingly for a moment.

'Identify yourself,' one of the suits ordered in its disconcerting electronic voice.

'Lieutenant Loftt en route to engineering,' Bache said, hopefully.

The suits stood rock still for a moment before speaking again.

'That name is not on the crew manifest,' the same one said. 'Shut your systems down and extricate yourself from the suit.'

They both clunked a step back and raised their weapons. Bache had to think fast. His suit was experimental and untested, while he knew their suit-powered energy weapons would be powerful and he had no idea how his shield would cope against them, especially at point-blank range.

He'd noticed something in the menu of offensive measures earlier and he selected and armed it.

'I just need to get permission from my commanding officer to go offline for a while,' he said, playing for time as the weapon charged. 'Ah, there he is now,' he added, pointing behind them.

As he hoped, the suit that hadn't spoken turned to follow his pointed finger. A green light flickered on in his left-hand peripheral vision and taking a quick step forward and to the side of the other armoured suit's weapon, he placed a hand on its shoulder and activated the weapon.

A huge flash of light lit up the corridor, and sparks flew in all directions that reminded Bache of an engineering welding bay. The suit slumped and puffs of smoke emanated from all the joint servos as they immediately burned out. Bache put himself behind the dead suit as the other one turned back and tried to engage him with its arm-mounted cannon.

Standing on tiptoe, Bache was able to get a lock on his assailant's helmet with his shoulder-mounted launcher. The miniature high explosive dart blew the suit back into the corridor wall, blinding it for a moment and giving Bache the chance to step around the dead suit, touch it similarly on the shoulder and give it the good news.

Again, a fire work display lit up the corridor and the second suit slumped, all its electrical systems overwhelmed and burnt out.

He knew his cover was well and truly blown now as several crew members had witnessed the altercation and would have reported it up the line of command. He had to get to the third confluence node as soon as possible to with luck completely disable the ship and give the *K2* a chance to survive.

42

____

Gata battleship, Berge system

HE SPRINTED NOW and if anyone got in his way, he just barged through them. The sirens throughout the ship continued to blare, most of the time to endless empty passageways.

Bache knew these ships weren't anywhere near fully crewed, so it didn't surprise him the further aft he went the quieter it became. Forty minutes later he finally got within a hundred metres of the node. It was a junction where he had to turn left and sensibly, he pulled up short and peeked around the corner. He was glad he did. Six armoured suits stood guard over the node hatch. His tactics for crippling the ship had been recognised.

'Ah crap,' he said to himself, as he trolled through the offensive measures menu again. Finding what he thought would help, he leant out into the corridor and fired two smoke canisters from his other shoulder this time, ducking back just in time as a blizzard of cannon fire came past in reply, filling the corridor in front of him with destroyed wall panels and light fittings.

'No polite dialogue this time then,' he said to no one in particular.

The firing lessened and he peeked out again and found the reason. The thick white smoke had completely filled the passage and made it impossible to see a hand in front of your face. He could hear the whirring of suit servos and the clunk of the suits advancing towards him. He knew this time if he waited here, he wouldn't be able to get so close as to use the same tactic as before.

Noticing a door to his right, he melted the lock mechanism, entered and left the door open as an enticer. Switching his boots to a magnetic setting, he walked up the wall and onto the ceiling. Crouching up, he waited.

The doorway soon darkened as a suit loomed outside and a blaze of cannon fire ripped into the room. Bache hadn't had time to check what was in this particular room in his haste to enter. It turned out to be some sort of store, the contents of which exploded and caught fire. He thought it might have been bedding for the crew on this deck, but whatever it was, it burnt extremely well.

The suit clunked into the doorway, a blue laser light scanned the room, piercing the smoke and flame. It only took the suit operator a couple of seconds to realise his target was above him, but it was still too late, as Bache reached down and touched the top of his helmet.

With the armoured suit disabled, Bache dropped back down and peered around it. A second suit stood outside and seeing Bache behind his decommissioned colleague, he tried unsuccessfully to get a target lock.

Bache used his suit's huge strength, lifted the dead suit, plunged through the door and barged straight into the other one. He heard its servos whining as it attempted to keep itself upright, eventually crashing into the wall behind, where Bache was able to reach around and zap that one too.

His world suddenly became a sea of lightning flashing around his shield and he found himself hurled back down the corridor.

A third armoured suit had been loitering back at the junction five metres away. Bache chastised himself for not checking. Just because the GDA armoured marines operated in pairs, wouldn't mean these guys would too.

The suit clumped towards him and he remained exactly where he was, allowing the operator to think he was down permanently. When he considered the suit to be close enough, he sat up suddenly and fired a missile at the armoured faceplate of his adversary. Only, it wasn't a missile. He'd forgotten to change back from smoke grenades and the canister clattered against the armour and dropped to the ground belching smoke.

He could hear the operator laughing as he brought his cannon back up. The smoke became Bache's saviour, because as it obscured him, it enabled him to leap up and left, avoiding the cannon fire that hit the ground where he'd been a split second before.

Following the wall, he soon found one of the other dead suits. Again he heaved it up and flung it in the direction of the operational one. His foot hit something and reaching down, he retrieved a dropped laser cannon, turned it round and blazed away blindly into the smoke.

He must have hit something, because a bunch of expletives emanated from within. Bache quickly made use of the doorway for cover again and waited for the smoke to clear a little. When it did, the operational suit had seemingly fallen over his colleague and was in the throes of righting itself. Its laser cannon was lying beside it and Bache targeted that, sending it clattering and spinning further down the passageway. The armoured suit had two things to do now, stand up and reselect another weapon. Unfortunately for him he tried to do both at the same time, which is where his inexperience with the unit became apparent as he only succeeded in falling over again.

Bache shook his head in disbelief, which he instantly regretted as pain speared his skull again and he felt the drip of fresh blood down his face. He wasted no more time and stepped quickly over to the struggling suit, similarly zapping it and leaving the operator helpless inside until someone eventually came to their rescue.

'Three down, three to go,' Bache said to himself, as he glanced back up the corridor just to check none of the other three had entered the fray.

The ship juddered then lurched savagely under his feet nearly causing him to fall. He hoped that was the *K2* fighting back. Meanwhile, the fire in the storeroom had worsened, filling the corridor with even more smoke.

He checked his suit inventory, and found he had three smoke grenades left and seven missiles. He knew if he didn't crack on, reinforcements could arrive and he'd be well screwed. Peering around the corner again, he found the other three armoured suits had bunched in close to the hatch and were all facing his direction. Counting to three, he leant right out again and unleashed the last three smoke grenades. As before, the cannon fire storm blitzed the walls around the junction, causing more burnt alloys and composites to rain down around him.

One thing he had noticed, was their fire was always down his side of the corridor. So he waited for the smoke to completely enshroud the passageway before squeezing off a few quick rounds with the cannon he'd picked up and dived across the corridor to put his back flat against the wall. As expected the return fire went down the opposite side. He dropped down onto his hands and knees and crawled towards the enemy as fast as he could, hoping they didn't think to use their laser imaging through the smoke.

He reckoned he'd got about halfway when one of them did. He stood and began zigzagging, before unleashing all seven missiles. Cannon fire immediately began flashing by and for the first time he was glad of the width of the corridor. One finally grazed his shield, sending him sprawling, but he was up again and sprinting and swerving. He barrelled on knowing he should be getting close, when his shield suddenly lit up again. It slowed him, but such was his speed he hit the first suit full in the face at enough velocity to topple it into the one behind. The third one tried to turn and zero in on their assailant, but he was too slow and his suit got zapped as Bache dived over and touched its boot.

The other two were still in a tangle and he was able to dispatch their suits quickly and easily. He breathed a sigh of relief, stepped over to the node hatch and opened it. He'd dropped the cannon when he'd run into them, so he stooped down and picked up another and walked over to the other side of the passageway as he didn't want to get caught in the explosion when he fired into the node.

He didn't get the chance. His suit unexpectantly shut down and suddenly became very heavy around him.

'What the fuck,' he said, struggling to move.

'That's exactly what I said,' said Desulet, striding into view with a smile on his face and clutching a tablet in his hand.

'Oh, that's just bloody marvellous,' mumbled Bache, as six Gata soldiers surrounded his dead suit with laser rifles in the shoulder.

43

Gata battleship, Berge system

'You've done well,' said Desulet. 'Ten out of ten for initiative. I can see why you're the President's blue-eyed boy. Only thing is, you didn't realise these new experimental shielded suits are a project I initiated.' He held up his tablet. 'Which also means I have the full schematics and the access codes to the two prototypes. Which to be honest, I thought I'd lost. That's until you so kindly brought them to me.'

'Why didn't you shut down the suit earlier?' Bache said, having to raise his voice to be heard now the suit was dead.

'You cleverly shut down the cameras. We had no idea what or who was attacking us and I'm the only one with the codes for the suits,' he said, grinning.

'Why so happy? If you don't mind me asking,' said Bache. 'Your plans are in tatters, along with the fleet you spent years building.'

'It's a big deal for my boss, but not so much for me,' he said. 'Whatever the outcome, I've made sure I come out of it smelling of corallin blooms.'

'Your boss?' Bache questioned. 'This hasn't been your operation then?'

Desulet grinned again and nodded at his men. They dragged Bache in his dead suit through the ship and out to a hangar on the starboard side. Desulet had been conversing with someone on his tablet and as they arrived, a sleek black private yacht swept into the hangar at speed. It slowed, turned and settled with barely a jolt. Bache raised his eyebrows at the skill of the pilot and thought whoever it was should give Clunk a few landing lessons.

A side airlock hissed and sank inwards before sweeping upwards, revealing an elderly lady wearing a gold lamé dress and leaning on an intricate silver walking stick. Bache had a sudden and uncontrolled sharp intake of breath as he recognised who it was.

'Oh, you've gotta be fucking kidding me,' he moaned, as Ystolion Flast stepped carefully down from the airlock, the gold thread in her dress shimmering in the bright hangar lights.

'Good morning, Mr Loftt,' she mocked, in a cold and mirthless tone. 'I've looked forward to this day for some time.'

'So, this has been you all along then?' he said.

'Well, originally it was my husband's project,' she said, curling her top lip. 'You remember my husband? The one you helped murder, along with my darling son?'

They all staggered as the ship shook again. Flast turned and glared at Desulet.

'You're supposed to be disposing of that

fucking GDA ship and make sure there's no survivors.'

'You're actually going to obey that order are you?' Bache's muted voice called from inside the dead suit.

'You see, young man, I have to remain in my position until the operation has come to fruition,' said Desulet, as he turned to leave.

'Forty-seven thousand crew,' shouted Bache. 'What about their fruition?'

'Stop moaning, Loftt,' growled Flast. 'The mining rights for two systems outweigh a few casualties.'

Bache realised he had to try and do something. He gritted his teeth and surged forward in the suit as Desulet walked past. It toppled over, taking the two soldiers holding him down too. They all clattered into Desulet, who also fell, his tablet crashing onto the deck heavily, the screen breaking and going dark.

Icons suddenly lit up inside Bache's helmet, he felt a surge of adrenaline as the suit began to power up again. The moment he found he had movement, he rolled over and smashed the tablet to pieces with his fist.

'Shoot him,' Desulet screamed, pushing himself away and glaring at his destroyed tablet.

Bache hadn't wasted a second of his new-found agility and had his shield up as a first priority. The timing was optimal, because as the soldiers' laser rifles pulsed, the bolts dissipated around the suit in a spectacular lightning display, catching the two soldiers who'd fallen with him and rendering them unconscious.

Flast shook her head and scowled at Desulet, all the while backing slowly towards her ship. Bache on the other hand was able to stand again and using his arm-mounted laser weapon, he downed the remaining soldiers.

Desulet, meanwhile, had stood and sprinted for the hangar airlock. Bache turned and got one shot off towards him before his shield was hit by a cannon bolt that knocked him off his feet again. Desulet hurled himself through the airlock door and disappeared as it closed behind him.

Bache swore, turned back and fired a volley of shots at Flast. She by this time was inside her ship's shields and the bolts dissipated up and around the hull. He cursed again as she too vanished behind an airlock door.

Bache had only just got himself off the floor once again when Flast's ship jumped from inside the hangar, the vacuum snap sending him sprawling in the other direction this time.

He didn't need the suit's guidance to find his way back to the aft confluence node as he'd memorised it. He also didn't walk there, as he guessed Desulet would have that guarded again and this time with a lot more personnel. He grinned as he drove a heavy loader at its maximum speed, sliding around on the corridor floors. He hit the walls at nearly every junction. The machine was only designed to operate on the rough-textured hangar floors and its composite wheels had barely any traction along the super-smooth passageways.

Reaching what he knew to be the last corner before the node, he gunned the machine, ducked down and threw it at the bend. Wall panels crashed around him as he all but removed the apex of the corner and slewed sideways into the outside wall. Peering through the loading forks he could see around twenty personnel surrounding the hatch and all training their weapons on him.

The blaze of fire came a split second later and lumps of loader and corridor panelling rained down and around his shield. His speed didn't falter though, if anything he was able to squeeze a little more from the electric loader now he was travelling in a straight line.

Realising they weren't able to stop the thing, the soldiers began slowly backing up, then running in the opposite direction as he closed on them. Three of them were in armoured suits and unable to get out of the way. They continued firing while clumping backwards until the loader ploughed into them at thirty kilometres per hour.

Bache kept his head down, punched the brakes and swerved into the wall as he reached the hatch, ripping it off its hinges. Two of the armoured suits weren't moving, but one of them, the one that had been at the rear, was trying to get up. He dived off the loader, grabbed one of their dropped laser cannons and with his back to the opposite wall, fired into the node four times.

He lowered his head and closed his eyes as the inevitable explosion blew out a whole section of the wall right in front of him. The shield took the brunt of it, but he still felt some of the force against his chest, knocking the wind out of him. Now the loader had stopped, the soldiers had about-faced and begun to get brave again, sending random fire back towards him. Bache pulled himself together and as he began to return fire, he suddenly found himself on the float and a whirring noise all around as emergency hand holds motored out from the walls and ceiling. The hit on the node must have disrupted the artificial gravity generator.

He had a dilemma, as he needed both hands to hold the big cannon and also to move around. The loader floated over and he was able to kick against it to push himself back the way he had come. When he was in the right position, he fired the cannon several times at the loader. This did two things that benefitted him. Firstly, the recoil pushed him off down the corridor in the direction he wanted to go and secondly, the loader was sent spiralling in the opposite direction and towards the enemy.

A warning alarm sounded that he was sure he hadn't heard before and checking the readout in his peripheral vision, he realised why not. 'Hull breach' flashed in red and checking his surroundings, he realised with horror he was accelerating. Wherever the breach was, he was going there at an ever-increasing rate and in a short space of time, he would be outside the ship and in considerable trouble.

44

Gata battleship, Berge system

ALTHOUGH HIS SUIT was designed to operate outside in the cold environs of space, he didn't want to be floating around aimlessly in between two huge duelling warships. His shields wouldn't save him from the ordnance they'd be hurling at each other.

He activated the magnets in his boots, counting that if he got near enough to a bulkhead he might be able to attach, but the speed he'd attained worried him.

The corner he'd rounded at speed on the loader came up and he braced himself as he was slammed into the outside wall. He grabbed at a couple of the handholds, but they just ripped out of the wall, such was his weight and momentum.

Bache thought he was hallucinating as the corridor suddenly became narrow and seemed to bend around to the right. He hurtled into it, his shield alarm shrilling a warning of overburden. A handhold appeared right in front of his face. He snatched at it and this time, because the collision had dramatically slowed him, he held on.

Breathing a sigh of relief, he turned to check there wasn't anything following and about to crash into him from behind. His moment of euphoria was short-lived, as all he saw was a sea of stars.

'Oh, shit,' he shouted at no one, as he realised with a deep foreboding, the ship was no longer around him. The wall he was clinging to was just that—a twenty-metre section of internal wall floating all on its own in deep space.

He ducked as a soldier slammed into the wall just above and to his left, his dead limbs stiff with cold, and as he rebounded the body turned. Bache recoiled as grotesque lifeless eye sockets, where the fluid-filled eyeballs had expanded and exploded, regarded him coldly and accusingly.

'Fucking outrageous,' he mouthed, glancing around fearfully. He couldn't see either ship, although the fact that they were both matt black probably didn't help. A lump of something spewing fluids and gas zipped past and he was really glad that hadn't hit his wall. Something bright flicked through his peripheral vision, causing him to let go with one hand so he could follow it.

'The planet,' he whispered, realising with growing dread that he had forgotten the ships had been close to Berge and its gravitational field would eventually pull him in to his certain death.

Zaphir popped into his mind, along with his father, and he felt a deep wretchedness at not being able to say goodbye. Then he castigated himself for being so defeatist. He was still alive, there were always options.

It was at this moment, as he swung around with one hand clinging onto the wall panel, he noticed a faint glow below him. It was a large section of the planet's broken moon, the one they'd hidden beside earlier, and it was close. The system's binary star was glowing off its ochre-coloured regolith and as he watched, he realised he was getting slowly closer and seemed to be curving down towards its surface.

That's interesting, he thought. *It's still got a degree of gravitational pull.*

He quickly discerned that if he was going to hit that, he didn't want a large section of wall crushing him into the surface. It didn't have an atmosphere either so he wouldn't burn up or anything, but he'd have to make sure he wasn't travelling faster than his shield could cope with. It was almost impossible at this altitude to gauge his speed over the surface.

After what seemed like an age, but was actually only twelve minutes, he could discern individual rocks on the approaching section of moon. Although still fast, he thought his speed was manageable. The moon section was actually travelling around the planet in the same direction as him, it was just he was the faster of the two. Thinking about what he had to hand to slow him down, he did have his arm-mounted laser. It did have a certain amount of recoil and would certainly slow him, but the downside was it would use up the suit's power supply quickly if he used it a lot.

Glancing at his remaining energy and oxygen levels, it indicated seven hours and thirty-nine minutes if all he did was hang around and breathe.

'Crap,' he mumbled softly, looking at the wall section again with renewed interest. He realised, with the acute angle he was coming in at, if he could turn that to be underneath him, it could take some of the impact of the landing, so long as it didn't dig in too much.

He conducted a test and fired the weapon on a high stun setting at the left-hand side of the wall. It worked, the large piece of reinforced composite began rotating very slowly.

Over the next few minutes he repositioned the wall so it was underneath him, using the least amount of energy he could get away with. The surface was close now, although being on top of the wall, he couldn't see how close. Pulling himself in tight with the handhold he braced for the inevitable crash. He knew it would hurt, he just hoped it wouldn't damage his suit.

WHUMP. The impact took him completely by surprise. He didn't hear it, but he certainly felt it. Even with his shield, he was sure he just broke at least one rib. It went all smooth again and he realised with the tiny amount of gravity, he'd rebounded and would be coming in again.

Looking up, he was face to face with the ochre regolith. The wall had hit and was rotating, so his nightmare of it coming down on top of him was now an almost dead cert. He let go and kicked it away as hard as he could, forgetting this would send him into a spin. His left arm hit first on the second bounce and he certainly heard this one, as his helmet crunched onto the surface a split second later. Pain shot up his arm and across his chest as he took a deep breath. He thankfully took the third hit on his back, which flipped him over onto his front. Shutting his eyes, he held his breath and waited for the fourth impact and after what seemed like way too long, he took a breath and opened one eye.

Four identical rocks lay just in front of his visor and it wasn't until he moved his head, did he realise he was stationary and there was only one rock. His visor was badly cracked.

Painfully, he stumbled to his feet. His chest was agony now and he could feel his wrist swelling up inside the suit. Looking around through the slowly settling dust, he saw the section of wall about a hundred metres away surrounded by its own cloud of regolith.

He was also surprised to see a collection of petrified flora sitting blackened and stiff as far as the eye could see.

'There must have been an atmosphere here at some point,' he said to himself.

WHUMP.

He ducked as something large impacted a

few hundred metres away. He didn't so much as hear it, but felt it through his feet.

'Shit,' he shouted, glancing up nervously and trying to walk normally. This he quickly realised was impossible, as one meaningful step had him floating for a moment before gradually coming down again. It was like trying to walk along the bottom of a swimming pool, only worse.

'Fuck,' he said, swearing again. 'Even if I see it coming, I can't get out of the way.'

He began very slowly, strolling towards the big lump of something that had hit a moment ago with the idea that if he sheltered next to that, the odds of something hitting in exactly the same spot would be less. Then again, the more he thought about it, he realised that was probably crap.

An alarm in his suit made him jump. He stared at it for moment, not quite believing what it said. Oxygen level was getting critical. His suit must have a leak.

'Ah—just perfect,' he mumbled and on reaching the unrecognisable lump of spacecraft half buried in the surface, he sat down, tilted his helmet back and stared up at the planet. A constant stream of shooting stars flashed across its surface as more battle debris burnt up in its atmosphere.

'That's actually quite pretty,' he said, before thinking about Zaphir and his father again. Only this time, there were no options. No ships, no lifeboats and no oxygen.

Before long, he found no matter how hard he tried, he couldn't get enough air in and he began feeling light-headed. He closed his eyes, when in the distance he felt another WHUMP.

'Missed me,' he chuckled before falling into unconsciousness.

45

GDA gunship, Berge system

'FUCKING WAKE UP, you lazy bastard—d'you know how bloody heavy you are in that stupid suit?' shouted a voice Bache thought he recognised from somewhere close, although his mind was a little confused as to where he was and what was going on.

Bache struggled open one eye to see a blurry helmet, cracks all across the visor, lying a few centimetres from his face. He tried to reply, but there was something over his mouth. Pain ripped up his arm as he tried to lift his hand to see what it was and then his chest joined in as he took a deep breath before the floor pressed against him and the deck beneath surged upwards.

'Boss, you're going to have to look after yourself for a while,' said the voice. 'I'm going to be a bit busy. There's a lot of shit flying around out here.'

Bache suddenly remembered who it was and wanted to laugh, but he knew that would hurt, so he just concentrated on breathing the oxygen in small shallow breaths. He was cold, he couldn't remember ever being so cold, and as his memories came flooding back in a rush, he wondered how long he'd been sat on that moon in a dead suit. Glancing down, he noticed Clunk had wrapped him in a thermal blanket.

The journey didn't take long. He soon recognised the buzz of passing through an atmosphere shield, then having to scrunch up his one open eye from the sudden brightness in the cockpit, emitted by the harsh white hangar lights.

He moaned from the pain searing across his ribs as Clunk lived up to his name. The almost immediate whine of the airlock doors caught his attention, the sound of boots squeaking on the floor and a cacophony of barked orders as several pairs of hands lifted him. He gritted his teeth and moaned again. There was a sharp sting on his neck and everything faded into a land of echoes and softness.

Clunk watched as the medical team whisked Bache away. He slumped down on the edge of the airlock and released an audible sigh. It made him shiver at how close it had been. Spotting Bache on the moon's surface had been down to blind luck. Quite how Bache had got there without a ship, Clunk couldn't hazard a guess. He sat there for a while, trying to make sense of everything that had gone down in the last couple of weeks but failed miserably, until the hangar airlock cycling caught his attention.

He jumped up and stood sharply to attention

as the captain swept into the hangar and made a beeline towards him.

'Is he alive?' Captain Whipper asked, peering inside the gunship.

'They've already taken him to the medical centre, sir,' said Clunk. 'He was moaning a lot, so I think he was.'

'Moaning, eh?' said Whipper. 'Sounds like he was fine.'

They both turned as one of the GDA's most lethal and latest heavy gunships screamed into the hangar, closely followed by an unmarked passenger yacht and a second similar gunship.

'Who the fuck is this?' Whipper shouted above the racket of the antigravs.

Clunk was surprised the captain didn't know.

'The bridge must've given them clearance, sir,' Clunk replied.

The yacht landed, its single airlock facing them beginning to open almost before it was down. The two gunships put down either side of the yacht, disgorging a dozen marines who quickly formed a protective ring around the smaller ship.

Both Clunk and Whipper straightened up in unison as an older man, dressed in long white and gold robes of office, climbed down from the yacht and strode purposefully towards them.

The captain took a quick glance at his tablet as it chimed to inform him the GDA President, Jamill Xutan, had just been given permission to board.

'No shit,' he mumbled. 'Could've given me a bit more notice.'

Xutan's customary smile was noticeably absent. He looked pale, and Clunk couldn't remember the President ever looking so harried.

'Are we here in time, Captain?' Xutan asked. 'It appears my communications have been compromised as of late.'

'If you're asking if the ship is out of danger, then, yes it is, Mr President,' said Whipper. 'But it seems only due to the heroics of one man.'

Xutan tilted his head to one side and stared at Whipper.

'Don't tell me—Lieutenant Loftt?' he said, his demeanour brightening as he said the name.

Whipper nodded.

'Is he here?' the President asked.

'Central medical centre, sir,' said Clunk.

'How bad?'

Clunk and Whipper glanced at each other.

'We don't know yet,' said the captain. 'I'm told he was semi-conscious when he arrived about half an hour ago.'

Xutan nodded.

'Is Desulet here?' he asked. 'He seems to have gone missing, along with the admiral of the fleet and his overbearing wife.'

'Desulet disappeared back to the enemy battleship shortly before we destroyed it,' said Whipper.

'What? So, he was here?'

'Yes, he was orchestrating the attack,' said Whipper.

Xutan balked slightly, his eyes wide.

'I authorised no attack on anyone,' he said.

'No, Mr President,' said Whipper. 'He was orchestrating an attack against us, because we thwarted his long-planned attack on the planet below with a secretly constructed Gata fleet using leaked GDA military technology.'

Xutan's mouth hung open for a moment while he digested that information. He slumped slightly and dropped his gaze to the floor.

'That explains a lot,' he said finally. 'The only reason I'm here is because young Loftt sent me a message to my old personal tab address. It was just by pure chance I saw it and they didn't. From that, it came to light just before I left that all my correspondence over the last few weeks or so has been intercepted and sometimes altered.'

The captain turned and nodded at the two gunships and the marines covering every corner of the hangar.

'That explains all this then?' he said.

'Actually, no,' said Xutan. 'After reading Loftt's message, I instructed my new personal assistant to liaise with the admiral and get a fleet over here as soon as possible.'

'But I guess the admiral wasn't anywhere to be found?' questioned Whipper.

'Well, I did discover that. But that was after my aforesaid assistant attempted to assassinate me.'

'Fuck the ancients,' blurted Clunk. 'Oh, sorry, sirs,' he added quickly, realising he'd actually sworn in front of the President.

The President almost smiled, while Whipper glowered at him.

'No apology needed young man,' said Xutan, holding his hands up. 'I believe those were my exact words at the time.'

'Thankfully, it seems he failed,' said Whipper.

'Indeed,' said Xutan. 'The virtues of having a personal shield.'

'I seem to remember your assistant had been with you for decades,' said Whipper.

'She was,' he said, as a look of sadness washed across his face. 'Massive heart attack a few weeks ago. Although, now with the current turn of events, I'm beginning to wonder if it was of truly natural origins.'

'Where did your new assistant come from?' Clunk asked.

'Desulet,' said Xutan, almost spitting the name. 'Came with glowing references.'

'Hmm,' grunted Whipper, appearing philosophical for a moment. 'A lot of time and planning went into this, I'm so thankful it's been thwarted. Not just for us, but for the population of Berge down there,' he said, pointing to the blue planet turning slowly and visible below through the atmosphere shield.

'So, you believe Desulet is dead now?' Xutan asked.

'That hasn't been confirmed,' said Whipper. 'But we do know he's no longer on this vessel. Unfortunately, we detected two small jump signatures from inside the Gata battleship just after its shields went down.'

'So, he could still be a threat?'

'Not so much now I'm reckoning,' said Whipper. 'They'd built fourteen of those battleships.'

'How many are still out there?' Xutan asked, concern evident in his tone.

'None, sir,' blurted Clunk with a grin. 'We fucked 'em all up.'

Whipper rolled his eyes, exhaled and shook his head before speaking.

'What he said, Mr President,' giving Clunk a glare.

Xutan stared for a moment.

'You're telling me you've defeated fourteen battleships of that size with one Katadromiko cruiser?'

'One Katadromiko cruiser and one Lieutenant Loftt,' said Clunk, grinning even more.

'Well—fuck the ancients,' blurted Xutan, returning Clunk's smile. 'That feat will certainly warrant some recognition, and talking of young Loftt, can you escort me to the medical centre? I really want to see if that boy's all right.'

'Absolutely,' said Whipper. 'I want to see how that crazy idiot is too.'

'Permission to tag along, Captain?' Clunk asked.

'Of course, pilot,' said Whipper. 'You did save his life after all.'

'You did?' questioned Xutan, turning to Clunk.

'Uh huh,' he replied.

'It's yes, Mr President,' growled Whipper.

'Sorry, sir—yes, Mr President,' he said, correcting his earlier faux pas.

Xutan nodded and grinned.

'Well it seems to me, young man, you might just have saved one of the navy's most valuable assets.'

'Please don't tell Loftt that, Mr President,' said Whipper, ushering them towards the personnel airlock at the back of the hangar. 'He'd never let us hear the end of it.'

46

Central Medical Centre, Katadromiko 2,
orbiting Berge, Berge system

THE NOISES WERE QUIET, rhythmic and emphatically soothing. Like waves gently lapping outside your beach hut during an afternoon siesta. He felt cocooned in warmth, safe, without a care and wanted this tranquil sensation to last forever. Then a sudden sharp sound irked him and he tried to ignore it.

'Lieutenant.'

It came again.

'Lieutenant, wake up.'

'Go away—I'm busy,' he mumbled.

'LIEUTENANT.'

He snapped his eyes open and wished he hadn't as bright lights assaulted his retinas. Squinting, he could make out a blurry face above him and a white ceiling beyond.

'Lieutenant Loftt, you have visitors,' the indistinct face insisted.

After a moment of confusion about recognising that was indeed his name and what in the ancients was going on, he croaked a reply.

'Where am I?'

'The *K2* medical centre, sir—you've been knocked about a bit.'

He focused his vision to discover a pair of rather attractive eyes above a medical mask blinking back at him.

'Hello,' he said, attempting to sit up, that did nothing but send a mountain of pain through his entire body.

'No, no,' she said, resting her hands on his

shoulders. 'The doctor wants you to stay still for a few hours to let the bones fuse.'

Bache glanced down to find beams of red light encompassing his body and realised why he felt so warm.

'You have an important visitor,' she continued, nodding and glancing towards the private room's door.

Bache turned his head to the left to find three concerned faces staring back from outside the room.

'Mr President, Captain, Clunk,' he said, beckoning them into the room with his right hand as his left seemed to be strapped to his side.

Xutan led the way and smiled as he approached.

'Glad to see you're on the mend, Lieutenant,' he said. 'I'm led to understand you've had a busy day.'

'So it seems, sir,' Bache replied, racking his brains to remember what had happened. He opened his eyes wide at one particular recollection as the events of the last few hours came back.

'FLAST,' he blurted loudly, then wincing with a sudden pain across his chest.

'Beg your pardon?' said Whipper.

'It was Ystolion Flast,' he continued, a little less enthusiastically this time.

'What was?' asked Xutan.

'Everything.'

'Have you had a knock to the head as well, Loftt?' said Whipper.

'No, sir—she was there on the battleship—her husband bankrolled the whole thing from the beginning and she continued it after his death. It was all for mining rights on Dresse and the Gata worlds once the grey Nkris had Berge and then ruled the region with the fleet of battleships.'

'That fucking woman again,' said Xutan. 'Is she dead now?'

'I don't think so, sir,' said Bache. 'She jumped away from inside the hangar shortly before the battleship was hit.'

Xutan gave the captain a glance, remembering their earlier conversation about jump signatures.

'I always had my doubts about Desulet,' he said. 'He always said the greyness in his coat was just down to age and stress from the job.'

'What about the admiral, Candor Henns?' Whipper asked.

'You'll be shocked to hear, Henns was sponsored for the job by Desulet and unsurprisingly his wife too,' said Xutan.

'Is he going to be prosecuted for his part in this?' asked Bache. 'He was attempting to have the captain and me locked up.'

'If we can find him,' said the President.

'It seems he's gone missing too, Lieutenant,' said Whipper.

'So, we're off the hook then?' said Bache, hopefully.

'Absolutely, young Loftt,' said Xutan. 'Which reminds me, the admiral of the fleet position is currently vacant.' He turned, raising his eyebrows at Whipper.

'Ah—don't look at me, Mr President,' said

the captain, putting his hands up in surrender. 'I'm a ship's captain, not a politician.'

'That's disappointing,' said Xutan. 'Personally, I think you'd be very good. Never say never, perhaps one day.'

Whipper smiled and turned back to the patient.

'Talking of positions vacant,' he said, staring at Bache. 'When this ship's repaired, I'm going to need a new chief engineer.'

'You want me to recommend someone?' Bache asked, seemingly surprised.

'No, Chief Engineer Loftt, I want you to accept the position.'

Bache's eyes widened.

'Really?'

'I'd be honoured,' said the captain.

'So would I,' said the President. 'And well-earned too.'

'Oh, shit,' mumbled Bache, pulling a face of horror.

'Something wrong with that?' Whipper asked.

'My father'll kill me,' he said. 'It took him twenty years to reach that position.'

'Knowing Tirexion, he'll be as proud as punch,' said Xutan.

'You know my father?' Bache asked, seemingly surprised.

'I make it my business to know who the smart and trusted people are within our organisation, Bache— your father is certainly one of them.'

Bache smiled at the President and turned to face his captain, his expression becoming a little more serious.

'I accept the position, Captain, thank you,' he said. 'I won't let you down.'

'Bloody right you won't,' Whipper said, nodding towards the President. 'You've made that vow in front of a very substantial witness.'

'Good, right,' said the President, chuckling. 'I think I have some politicking to take care of on Dasos.' He turned for the door, stopped and turned to Whipper. 'Look after that young man and if you change your mind about the job in the big chair over the next couple of cycles, let me know.'

'Yes, sir,' said Whipper, watching the President as he left the room to rejoin his security detail for the trip back to the hangar. Turning back to face Bache he spoke again.

'Have you had a falling out with Mye?' he asked.

'I'm not sure,' said Bache. 'She wasn't very happy about Clunk coming with me to Dresse, I know that much.'

'Hmm,' grunted Whipper. 'She's asked for a transfer to another ship.'

'Oh,' was all Bache could think of to say, as a sick feeling washed through his stomach.'

'You know I can't really stop her if she's bent on going?'

'Yes, sir, I know that.'

The conversation stalled for a second or two before the captain spoke again.

'You do realise the chief position is a lot more hands-off, Loftt? No more fun crashing around the galaxy in gunships.'

'After the last few days, sir, I'm kinda glad,' Bache replied.

'What about me, Captain?' asked Clunk, looking hopeful.

'Well, I'm sure the engineering department will need a duty pilot,' said Whipper, raising his eyebrows at Bache.

'So long as you practise your landings,' Bache said, with a smirk. 'I don't want to be repairing bent struts every day.'

'Deal,' said Clunk, grinning from ear to ear.

EPILOGUE

Hangar 213, Katadromiko 6, *orbiting Dresse,*
Dresse system

BACHE LIMPED over to the small freighter as it shut down its antigravs. It had been discovered he also had a fractured leg from the hard landing on Berge's moon, adding to the collection of broken ribs, collarbone and wrist. Even now after nineteen days of bone fusing treatment, the limp was still evident and probably would be for a week or two.

He waited as the airlock cycled and smiled warmly as a very wide-eyed Kolde and Geerten stepped tentatively down onto the hangar deck.

'Welcome,' said Bache, stepping forward and giving both of them a hug.

'This thing's enormous,' said Kolde. 'The pilot flew us up and down the length of the ship before coming inside.'

'You haven't seen the half of it,' said Bache.

'So this is the ship you told us about then?' Geerten said, turning and nervously staring out through the invisible atmosphere shield.

'No, the *K2* is in for extensive repairs in the Jagnorite System. It got pretty banged up dealing with those battleships. This is the *Katadromiko Six*.'

'I take it from that you know where they went then?' said Kolde.

'They were an invasion fleet for a planet called Berge, one of the purrers' home worlds.'

'Where are they now?' Kolde asked.

'Destroyed.'

They both stared at Bache in amazement.

'What, all of them?' Geeten asked eventually.

Bache nodded.

'How many of your ships did that take?'

'Just the one ship and a bit of luck on our part and a bit of stupidity on theirs,' admitted Bache.

'Shit, really?' said Geerten, his face a picture of awe as he glanced around the hangar again.

'So, our world is no longer off limits then?' Kolde asked, changing the subject.

'No,' admitted Bache. 'After everything that's gone on in the last few years, it's a bit late for that. This ship is here to aid your world with the integration into a spacefaring race. Which, by the way, you don't have to have if you don't want it. You're also formally invited to join the GDA. Again, not something you have to do. But, of course, I do recommend it.'

They both smiled.

'Well, you would wouldn't you?' laughed Kolde.

'It's the least we can do to make up for the treatment you've had over the last few years, especially as it seems it was some of ours that instigated and financed the whole sorry affair.'

'Hmm,' grunted Kolde. 'That was the problem some of the elders had. Could we ever trust you going forward?'

'That's the reason for the ship being here,' said Bache. 'You've been harshly treated to say the least. So this vessel is at your disposal for as long as it takes and I am too, as it's going to be quite a while before my ship is fully operational again. Another thing you're going to have to consider if you join the GDA, is your race is going to need a planetary ambassador. Personally I would like it to be one of you two if you think you're up to it?'

'The elders might have something to say about that,' said Geerten. 'Perhaps you could have a conversation with some of them. There are a lot of communities to bring together.'

'Our society has been hugely fragmented since the purrers came,' said Kolde.

'You do know I'm not a trained negotiator?' said Bache.

'No, but you're a friend to our people—you

put your life on the line for us,' said Geerten. 'Something the elders respect.'

'To be honest, we wish we could do something for you to repay the debt,' said Kolde.

'Don't worry about that,' said Bache, lifting up his arm to display the new triple gold bands around his cuffs.'

'You've been promoted?' Geerten asked.

Bache nodded and grinned.

'Do you know what happened to Welt?' Kolde asked.

'We never saw him again after you left in the purrers' flyer,' said Geerten.

'No idea,' said Bache, deciding not to tell them. 'Come on,' he said. 'There's a fabulous bar overlooking the atrium on deck one ninety. I feel the need to buy you two a drink.'

'A drink sounds great, but what's an atrium?' Kolde asked, as they followed Bache towards the airlock.

The small island on Panemorfi was one of the more remote on the ocean planet. Owned by a distant construction corporation, it had absolutely no connection to the old Flast empire and Ystolion felt safe here.

She watched from inside the palatial villa partially built out over the water, as her private yacht overflew the building. It flared and landed gently on the sand in the circular clearing of indigenous blue-tinged palm trees only a short walk away. Her security detail searched and escorted the two passengers across to the building.

Both Henns and Desulet had spent several weeks hiding out on a remote ship construction platform in the Jagnorite system and were obviously pleased to be somewhere a great deal more comfortable. They both grinned widely as Ystolion met them in a broad marble-lined reception hall.

'Good afternoon, gentlemen,' she said, returning the smile and ushering them off towards a pair of double doors to the right. They opened automatically as she approached before leading them into a room with a panoramic view of the ocean through floor-to-ceiling windows. She stepped behind a huge wooden desk and pointed at the vista. 'Not a bad view is it?'

They both agreed and as Henns watched a small boat zipping along on the horizon, Desulet glanced down at the floor.

'What's with the plastic on the floor?' he said. 'You having some decorating done?'

'Ah, no,' chuckled Ystolion. 'It's to stop your blood staining my expensive flooring.'

The laser pistol appeared from under the desk in a split second and before Desulet could react, a hole the size of a fist was punched through his chest. He slumped to his knees, his mouth moving but nothing coming out, before finally falling backwards and a huge pool of blood growing around the body.

'See what I mean?' said Ystolion. 'Stupid Gata's bleed way too much.'

Henns had frozen to the spot. He was unarmed and with the doors now closed behind him, he had nowhere to go.

'Don't look so terrified, Candor,' she said. 'My cleaning schedule doesn't include you. It was his incompetence that got us where we are,' she added, nodding at the body on the floor. 'In fact I have a little job for you. Pull it off and my faith in your abilities will be dutifully restored.'

'What job?' he asked, sceptically, his eyes never leaving the laser pistol hanging by her side.

'There's a certain piece of technology I want you to acquire for me,' she said, placing the pistol back where it had been concealed, much to Henns' obvious relief.

'GDA and military I presume?' he said, swallowing nervously.

'Actually, no,' she said. It's something new the Theos have invented and as you may know, they're not GDA members and they keep themselves very much to themselves.'

'They're on Paradeisos aren't they? In a bunch of empty cities under impenetrable dome shields. Is it a weapon?'

'Again, no,' she said, turning her back to him and staring out at the view. 'It's a piece of medical equipment. Rumour has it, they've called it an autonurse and I want one.'

'That's it? That's all you want? Some fancy medical scanner?'

'There's a ship containing a hand-picked private military team on standby. You get me that autonurse and our previous deal will be honoured.'

'The private surgeon, the money, everything for me and my wife?'

'Everything for both of you,' she said, turning to give Henns a matronly but at the same time disquieting smile.

FROM THE AUTHOR

I wanted to say a huge thank you for choosing to read *The Lieutenant*. I sincerely hope you enjoyed the third adventure in the *Bache Loftt* series.

If you did enjoy this novel, it'd be fantastic if you could write a review. It doesn't have to be long, just a few words, but it is the best way for me to help new readers discover my writing for the first time. I use the best and most imaginative reviews in my marketing too.

If you'd like to stay up to date with what's going on, you're welcome to join my reader group at my website www.nickadamsbooks.com

and receive a bi-monthly newsletter, advance notice of new releases and cover reveals. I will never share your email address and you can un-subscribe at any time.

You can also contact me via Facebook, Insta-gram, X, or by email. I love hearing from readers – I read every message and try to reply to everyone personally.

Thanks again for your support.
Nick Adams